I0597966

GRILL!

THE MISADVENTURES OF
AN RV PARK FAST-FRY COOK

DIANE STEGMAN

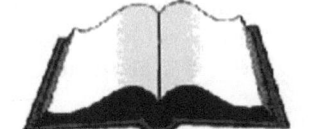

CCB Publishing
British Columbia, Canada

GRILL! The Misadventures of an RV Park Fast-Fry Cook

Library and Archives Canada Cataloguing in Publication

Stegman, Diane, 1948-
GRILL! The misadventures of an RV park fast-fry cook / written by Diane Stegman.
ISBN 978-0-9809995-8-7
I. Title.
PS3619.T4485G75 2008   813'.6   C2008-903413-9

United States Copyright Office Registration # TXu1-344-538

Cover design by Jen Hansard: www.jenhansard.com

Publisher: CCB Publishing
             British Columbia, Canada
             www.ccbpublishing.com

This book is lovingly dedicated to Bonita and Bandito,
my dearest companions.

ACKNOWLEDGMENTS

I would like to thank Jennifer Groman Hansard for her kind and gentle patience in effectively helping me to dig deeper, be more precise, and for her wonderful cover design and map. I would also like to thank her for her constant corrections on my use of commas, a problem I've yet to overcome. She has changed my writing life forever.

I would also like to thank my dearly departed friend Sherrain, who was there for me from the very beginning wanting to read "More! More! More!" I think she would be proud.

And then I have my sisters to thank for reading through the book during its conception and have not mentioned once that they think I'm nuts!

Thank you Bonnie Kaye, you are my hero and friend forever.
Thank you Chris and Dennis Calaba—for everything!
Thank you Dr. K.

I love you Mom and Dad. Within the frailty of aging and caring that we experience together on a daily basis, we have touched the very core of love and all that life truly means. I am blessed to be sharing this precious time with you. The past is just a story—the future will always be unknown—the present is our only reality.

INTRODUCTION

"I own my life, and only mine.
And so I shall appreciate my person.
And so I shall make proper use of myself."
- Lakota Sioux mantra

Can we cut clean, swift, and painless the cords that bind us to our unhappiness? Yes, some can—I did. Some don't need to go any place other than where they are—how nice. This particular experience was more painful than I had anticipated. After all, this wasn't my first, nor was it my second or third time to have run off to greener pastures. I was also surprised at how life-threatening this one escape that bears the title of *GRILL!* turned out to be, but I think I am wiser for experiencing it, at least I think I'm wiser. I'd like to believe so anyway. In the end of my great escape I was left with a story to tell.

We are all on an endless search to find our proper place in this crazy world that we are living in, a place where we are true to ourselves, our planet, and our environment. As for myself, I want to have more life stories to tell and I want to always feel passion for the creative process, which is my most favorite thing of all.

So, yes, this is a story based on one of my true life experiences. Not every sentence or paragraph is *exactly* how or when events occurred. I have embellished the truth in several instances—that is my prerogative as an artist and writer. I have changed the names and places, so if you recognize any of the characters in this story, just keep it to yourself and no one will ever know.

GRILL!

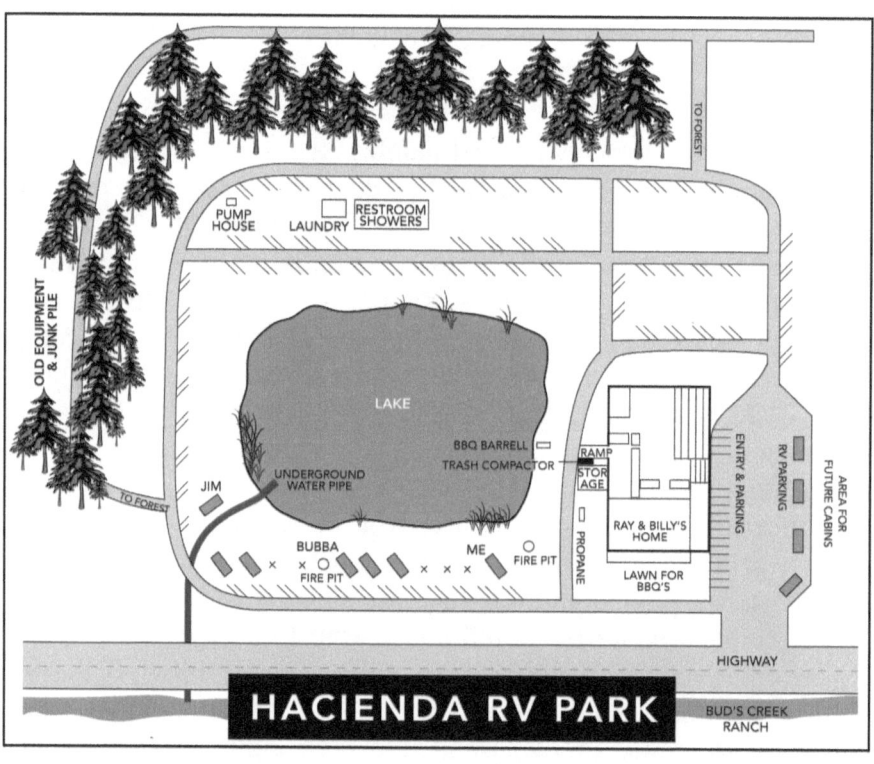

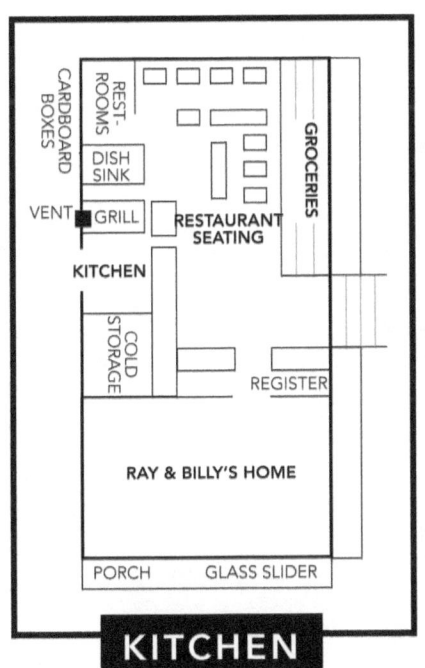

KITCHEN

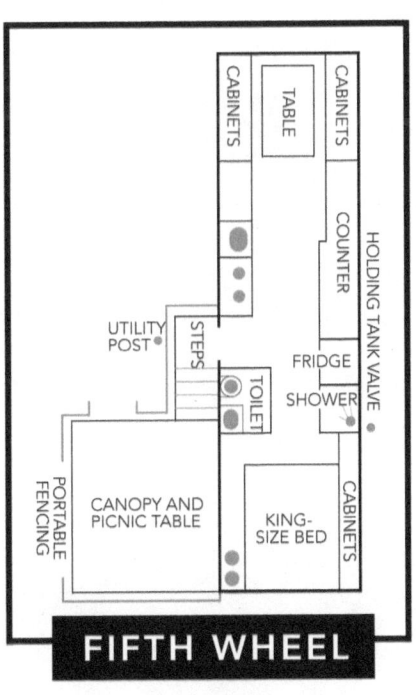

FIFTH WHEEL

GRILL!

CHAPTER ONE

Question: How do you make God laugh? **Answer:** Make a plan.

That is exactly why I have given up on life plans.

Not that I have lived by this joke question for the entire length of my fifty-one years. It's just that I heard this joke the other day and it seemed to justify my current vagabond lifestyle. Someday, perhaps, I will attempt to figure out yet one more plan, but for now I am behind the wheel of my car loaded with everything I own including my two Chihuahua mix friends. They are staring at me with big ears silhouetted by sunlight as they sit atop a pile of blankets in the passenger seat. "Are we home yet?" seems to be pleading from Bonita's anxious and concerned little barks. She wants to get the hell out of this car! Her partner in crime, Bandito, tends to keep his concerns internal, yet I know they are there.

"No, my little darlings. We are homeless for the moment." I mutter, unsure of how long this "moment" will last.

We had a very difficult night last night. It was our first night on the road leaving Ashland, Oregon, my sister, my rented mobile home, and my second shitty underpaid job in a two-year span. I had no plan; but I did have a tent and my first day and night went something like this:

I had driven most of the day heading south in search of a working summer vacation. By late afternoon, I was ready for a break so I found an RV park in Jamesburg. The space cost me $20. I felt pretty proud of myself. I had never camped alone before. The first thing I had to do was retrieve the portable dog fences from the bottom of the trunk. I had brought three of them. They extend to sixteen feet each, giving my dogs forty-eight feet of freedom. My plan was to surround the tent so I could have my own space and my dogs could be relatively free. The fences were more of a problem than I had wanted. They consumed too much trunk space and were very heavy, but folded up quite nicely.

It was a beautiful June day and I had picked a spot near a thick wall of blackberry brush. It wasn't until I had completely set up my tent, fences, and Coleman stove, that I had the thought that bears like blackberries! Suddenly, my protective fencing seemed like it was made of toothpicks. I pushed the horrible thoughts out of my mind and continued setting up camp. I had to remind myself that this was going to be a great adventure and fears were not welcome.

I fed the dogs and made myself something to eat from my provisions. The coffee was out and ready for morning. My padding and blankets were ready for a warm comfortable night's sleep. I had decided that I would leave the tent's skylight open for the night to watch the stars. After a nice evening walk with my dogs, I settled in for the night with my fluorescent lantern and a book.

Off in the far distance I could hear the low drum of thunder. It was a very dark moonless night when I turned off the lantern for lack of interest in my book. Reading felt a bit too casual under the circumstances, since my concentration was bouncing all over the place. Bonita and Bandito were nervous and I could feel them staring at me like I was crazy even in the pitch black of the tent. They were waiting to go to bed someplace other than right here.

It was hard to get comfortable. My down comforter, folded in half, was not as soft as I had hoped. I could still feel the chilly, hard ground beneath me. Wait just a minute! I began to recall the last time I had slept in a tent. That was about ten years ago on a stupid cut-short trip to Alaska with my once dear friend Jodi. We were going to hike and camp. She started her period on the plane, which made me nervous, since we had just read a notice about bears in Alaska. We read together that it was not a good idea to hike when a woman is menstruating due to the fact that the bear would follow the scent. On our first night of sleepless, bearless camping, I woke with my neck bound as tight as cement and as painful as if it were broken. I also caught pneumonia. Both events caused by, what I later learned, *perma-frost*. This happens when you sleep on the ground in a tent, the ground being frozen twelve inches below the surface. Needless to say, we caught the first flight home and never spoke to each other again. It took me two months to regain my strength.

The sky suddenly burst with light followed by thunder that was slightly louder than before. I crawled out of the tent to search for an approaching storm. Weird, I saw no clouds. As I crawled back into my tent I had to remind myself that this was not Alaska. I was in the sunny state of California.

I lay in the dark with the dogs. It wasn't too long after that when a burst of light lit up the entire tent. I could see the dogs in that split second. They were on both sides of my head staring down at me, eyes wide, and ears high like stone statues. I had to laugh. I was laughing quite loud when the bolt of lightening hit very near to us like a bomb, followed by the heavy slow plops of rain hitting the tent, the plops increasing like microwave popcorn. I had to hurry and put the skylight cover back on the tent. By this time the wind had kicked up and it was dark, so I turned on my car lights facing the tent so I could see. It was now pouring, and I was wet and the dogs were panicked. I put them in the car, grabbed all my wet blankets, wet clothes, wet stove, wet tent, and stuffed everything into any and all extra space in the trunk and back seat. Once in the car, I turned on the heater, saw the time (1:30AM), and we watched and ducked the passing thunder and lightening storm until dawn, which was quite beautiful in spite of the circumstances.

I had not counted on storms. The inside of my car smelled like wet dog and down feathers. All that the storm left in its wake were wonderful puffy pink clouds. I had not removed the fencing, so I put the dogs in their yard and made coffee on my Coleman stove. It was around 5:00AM at this point. I was still wet. I told myself that I could not do this again, that today—no, this morning, I would find a job and a house!

I began to unload the wet tent and blankets from the trunk to make room for the wet heavy fencing, put the dogs in the car atop the pile of wet blankets in the passenger seat, drove to the restroom and shower area, dried my hair and changed my clothes. By 6:30AM I was back on the road headed south through the national park. After an hour on the road I saw a small café. The day was warming up quite nicely. I parked, got the dogs out for a short walk, and then went in to see if they were looking for any help. I also needed a good breakfast.

There was no newspaper, so after my wonderful breakfast I approached my waitress with my inquiry. "No honey, this here is a family run place," the plain looking, middle-aged waitress said as she looked me over suspiciously as if I was being evaluated. I had noticed that the other lady working there was probably her daughter and was about eight months pregnant. "But I do believe that Billy at Hacienda RV Park down the road apiece needs some help," she continued. As she spoke, I detected a hint of mischievousness that quickly replaced any suspicion that she had about me.

I bid my thanks and as soon as I was outside I looked down to see if I had egg on my shirt or something that might have looked out of place when the woman gave me the once-over. I wonder what someone must think of me.

There was not much tourist traffic, but I found myself caught in a line of many heavy-loaded logging trucks driving way too fast. I began to be concerned about the insurance on my car that my son was supposed to get for me.

At about 8:15 I cruised by the Hacienda, but did not pull in. What in heaven's name would I do at an RV park? I could see that they had a restaurant, store, and a pond. If I worked there where would I live? This is not a town; this is in the middle of nowhere. I had driven about 20 miles on a deathtrap highway to get here, but decided it was worth the risk to drive on and look for greener pastures. Half hour later, I approached a small town, perhaps not a town, but a motel, café, Post Office, and some scattering of homes. I went into the motel and spoke to the owner. He could see my loaded up car out in the parking lot with what looked like from this vantage point, two rat-like oversized cats sitting in the front seat. "Damn, I just hired someone, but I do believe Billy, down at Hacienda RV Park needs some help. Let me give them a call for you." I could not hear the conversation that took place in his office, but he returned to confirm that this was so. I began to understand that everyone knew everyone within fifty miles of each other.

A little while later, I found myself back at Hacienda, dragging my feet up the stone steps to the restaurant. At the entry I noticed a large ashtray overloaded with butts and many had tumbled to the ground below. A large trashcan overflowing with foul trash complimented the scene. A fat trail of ants was thriving to and from the can. Once inside, I realized the spacious log building was actually quite impressive with a bustling crowd of hungry vacationers. I could see that they needed help.

Inside I could smell bacon and pancakes. The counter for registration was immediately to my left. I saw a person at the counter that could possibly be Billy finishing up with a traveler about his RV space. Suddenly I heard a bellowing male voice coming from somewhere in the kitchen beyond the restaurant seating area. "HEY HENRY, YOU OLD GOAT! YOU EAT ALL THEM PANCAKES AND I'LL LET YA HAVE YUR BREAKFAST FREE!"

Looking in the direction of the roaring voice, I saw the chalkboard menu with the day's special. 'BUBBA'S SPECIAL: BISCUITS AND ROADKILL SKUNK. MADE WITH RATTLESNAKE GRAVY.' I was pretty sure this was just a local joke of some sort.

"Kun I help ya?" Said a warm voice from behind me.

"Yes, my name is Denise and the....."

"Oh, you must be the lady looking fur work! I'm Billy." Now at this point I was not sure of the sex of Billy. It appeared to be in its early seventies with very short salt and pepper hair, wearing a western shirt, and a cigarette hanging out of its mouth. Its kind eyes settled me down, but I remained puzzled. I also noticed at this point the tall gentleman dressed in pajamas who was peeking from behind a doorway. He, too, was in his seventies and looked like an old handsome rancher who had seen better days. Oxygen hoses clung to his nose as he puffed on his cigarette. I think he winked at me.

Billy saw the direction of my eyes. "That's Ray, my husband." Mystery solved. What an odd-looking couple.

"Yur gonna be my cook." Billy announced with pride.

"Pardon me?" I felt my eyebrows rise in shock.

"I said yur gonna be my cook!" Billy really meant this. The cigarette bounced as she spoke.

I fumbled for a way out. "But I'm not really a cook per se. I was hoping you might need a waitress or counter help." I added in a fragile smile for first impression's sake.

"Nope, I need a cook." Billy was staring into my eyes as if I had no choice.

"Well, that's very kind of you, but I have to think about it. I guess I need to know if there are any places to rent near here."

"No need fur that. Gotta home fur you right here."

"Pardon?" Did I really hear that?

"Right out back. There's a fifth wheel sittin' empty. You can live right there." She is now pointing towards the kitchen area and, I presume, beyond the interior walls to the outside.

"I have two little dogs." I warned her.

"All right with me. We love animals. Have a dog myself." Sounded too good to be true.

I got right to the point. "How much?" It better be really cheap for me not to turn around and get back on the highway.

"How much fur what?" She took a deep drag from her cigarette.

"I'm sorry. How much to rent the trailer?"

"Nuthin'! It comes with the job, which, by the way, we pay $6.75 an hour. You split the tips with the waitress." Billy snubbed out her cigarette in the over-loaded ashtray.

I told Billy I needed to check out the fifth wheel first and then sleep on it. We walked outside and she pointed out the fifth wheel to me. It looked quite roomy and fairly new. It was parked behind the restaurant and next to the pond on the edge of the park twenty yards from the highway. I inquired about a motel for the night. She suggested a small town off another highway about thirty miles in another direction. I said I'd call her later tonight with my answer about the job, even though I had already made up my mind.

So that puts me in the current moment at Hacienda RV Park in Bud's Creek, California. Before I head off to the motel, I need to call my sister and family to tell them about my new job and place to live. I need to put their worries to rest, but right now I'm a little fearful of my quick decision to leave my life in Ashland and settle into an RV park as a cook. When I left yesterday I was full of confidence and exploding with a sense of adventure. Now I am beginning to wonder if I am just plain nuts. If I were a normal, stable, well-grounded, middle-aged woman, a crazy scheme like this would never enter my mind. I suppose I've chosen the unknown obstacles that life will throw at me in exchange for the predictable, daily nuances of routine and servitude.

I can still see and hear my sister when I was preparing to leave for this road trip. My mobile home was empty except for the large pile of items in the center of the living room ready to go into the car. I drove to her mobile home, four spaces down, with some yard tools and assorted house wares that I no longer needed in the large trunk of my new Suzuki Aerio, a gift from my two well-grounded real estate broker sons. "Denise, you can't do this! What are you thinking? Do you really think someone's going to just hire you on the spot? Where are you going? How will we reach you? You're fifty-one years old for God's sake!" Lori was crying hysterically at this point and threw the rake back into the trunk scratching the paint on my new car. Perhaps I was being a bit too casual about my decision to travel the national parks of northern California with a tent, $400, and two Chihuahuas in search of a fun summer job.

"I promise I'll call you every day." I lied in all sincerity. My hope was to calm her down a notch. In truth I could never call every day. I have no cell phone and I might not be near a phone booth at all times. Maybe this is a major part of her concern, but

Lori did not have to work for pompous pricks. Lori was a retired postal worker, who is now on disability for all the surgeries and damage done to her body from carrying around fifty pounds of junk mail for seventeen years. I guess I'm trying to avoid physical and mental damage to myself at this late stage of the game.

Lori and I have always been very close. We have so much in common, our likes and dislikes in things to do, places to be or see, same tastes in food. I will miss our friendship, but I can't expect her to take me on as a dependent.

I want to call Lori and tell her that I have a job and a place to live. I also need to call mom and dad and my two sons. I now understand their fear for me. I want to gleefully brag that I knew all would be well and put their doubts to rest. I look back at my car that seems too low to the ground. I hope all the weight inside is not going to hurt the suspension. Bonita and Bandito are watching my every move. It's already getting hot and I'm very tired from last night's ordeal.

Since I was truly stuck between a rock and an RV park, I knew that I would take the job. I really had no choice. I picked up the phone before I could talk myself out of it.

"Hi Lori! This is Denise! I got a job and a place to live!"

"You're lying! It's only 9:30." She still sounds pissed off at me.

"I swear! I'm at Bud's Creek at an RV park and this wonderful lady named Billy was so excited to meet me. She couldn't believe her good fortune that I came in when I did. She wants me to be her chef here at her restaurant. Well, maybe not a chef as we know it, but her cook. Then, you won't believe this; she said I could live in this empty fifth wheel behind the restaurant!" I've always over-dramatized things in my favor.

"Oh my gawd!" Lori screamed.

"Lori, it's so beautiful here! They have a lake with ducks and the fifth wheel is practically new!"

"I'm so relieved! How did all this happen? I'm sorry I didn't have any faith in you." She sounds genuinely sincere, so I open up as well.

"I know. I'm sorry that I made you so nervous. You know me after all these years. I guess I follow a different path that even I don't understand."

I call my sons and mom and dad, making it brief, and finish the chore of comforting the family fears.

As I hang up the phone, I feel a tingling sensation on the back of my neck. Reaching back to rub the spot, I feel moisture on my fingers. I turn my hand to look at my fingers and am startled to see a few drops of blood. What in the hell? At closer inspection of my fingers I notice the teeny tiny body parts of a mosquito. I do hope this is not an indication of a mosquito problem. Mosquitoes absolutely love me! I don't just get an irritation from them, I get a violent reaction. I'm sure the pond has a lot to do with that.

My need to use a restroom at the moment leads me to explore my new surroundings for a few minutes before I leave to the motel. As I drive slowly toward the bathroom building, I notice a tan chunky gal with a bit of a biker look to her, moving sprinklers around the park. She sets one with a spray of at least fifty feet right in the direction of a family's beautiful recreational vehicle parked and set up for their visit. I watch it blast the RV's outer patio wall, spraying the table set-up, chairs, and ice chests. She hops in her golf cart and rides away, chugging the last few sips of a beer. The only remains of her is the thump, thump, thump of the sprinklers against the RV, breaking the silence of the morning.

I park next to the restroom and walk toward the door. There is a table next to the entry that has an ashtray with a cigarette burning, two open beers, and an empty one lying on its side about to roll off the table that is piled with various cleaning supplies. I hear two female voices from inside a doorway marked supplies. I proceed to enter the restroom door and find it locked. A sign on the door reads, "Please keep restroom door shut. For guests of Hacienda ONLY!" At this point, one of the voices startles me.

"You furget yur key?" She has the cigarette now and is holding the beer. She looks to be in her early thirties and has the worn out look of one who has been drunk all her life. "No. I actually don't have a key just yet. I was just talking to Billy about a job for the

9

summer." I answer.

"Cool! Doin' what?" She seems to be a harmless, happy drunk.

"She said she needs a cook."

At this point the other gal comes out of the supply room. She seems more normal, but is not interested in who I might be.

"What's yur name?" The gal with the beer asks.

"Denise."

"I'm Ruby and this is Brenda. Sit down. Ya want a beer?" Ruby is so excited that she accidentally bangs her shin on the bench, but did not seem to notice or feel any pain.

"No thanks, it's kind of early for me."

"It's twenty-four seven for me. Billy could really use a new cook. She's getting pretty tired. Been doin' this fur far too long. She's got Bubba but he can't keep doin' all three shifts. He's still got all the trash to haul and mowin' the grass. Terry, his girlfriend, has been doin' all the watering even though she doesn't really work here. And Ray isn't too well. Here, let me open the door fur ya. We have to keep it locked cause so many travelers and campers think they can just pull in here and use our restrooms then leave."

Brenda doesn't say anything, and seems like she just wants to finish up her job and get going.

Ruby opens the door and follows me in. The restroom has five large shower stalls and four toilet areas. They must have just finished cleaning because it smells like Pine-Sol. I decide on the first stall.

"So ya gonna take the job?" Ruby's voice echoes loudly against the walls.

"I think so. I'm going to stay in Brandon tonight to think about it."

"God, I hope ya take the job. You seem like a really cool person. Ya gonna stay in the fifth wheel?"

"Billy offered it to me."

"Cool! Billy is really a neat lady. She offered this job to me. I've been here on and off for a couple of years. Billy has really saved my butt many times."

"Well, I better get on the road. Hopefully I'll see you later." I say as I exit the stall.

Ruby follows me to my car. Bonita and Bandito start barking at the approaching stranger.

"Cool! You got puppies!" Ruby is at the car window rubbing Bonita's head. Bandito has jumped into the back and is barking angrily, as if he was insulted.

"They're not really puppies. They're actually about ten years old, just Chihuahua mixes."

"I love dogs! Have a new one-year old Shepherd mix. Maybe after you start working here you can come out to my place and we'll let the dogs play together. I'm just down the road 'bout ten miles. My cabin sits right next to Bud's Creek."

"That sounds fun. We'll see how it goes. By the way, where is Bud's Creek?" I ask.

"What do ya mean? This is Bud's creek. Oh, I get it. Ya mean where is the creek itself."

"Yeh, the creek itself. How do I get to it?"

"Any side dirt road ya see off the highway. It runs 'long side it for miles."

"Great! I'll have to stop and check it out on my way to Brandon. Thanks and nice meeting you. Bye Ruby. Bye Brenda!" I had to shout to Brenda. She was standing by the restroom wall watching us. She waves back lazily. As I get in the car the musty odor makes me aware of all the damp camping items that need to be air-dried. Perhaps I can do this on the picnic tables when I return tomorrow.

It's about 10:30 and the dogs need to get out for a while, so I decide to find a dirt road off the highway on my way to a motel in Brandon and check out Bud's Creek. I hadn't really noticed all the campsite turnoffs before on my way to and from Hacienda. I guess I had a lot on my mind. I pick a turn off after about five miles and pull into the dirt entry. I see one car in the dirt lot, but no one is around. The dogs are excited and know they are about to get out of the car. I leash them up with their extending leashes that give them sixteen feet to explore and feel like wild animals. I can hear the creek roaring beyond the tree line and we walk towards it.

The water is running strong and clear from the winter snow melt off. As I stare at it, it washes away my stress and worries. It is quite beautiful and peaceful. I see a man some hundred yards down the creek fishing. Two empty 'Bud' cans float near the shore. An empty pack of Marlboro cigarettes and a worm container sit near a rock a few feet away. I laugh to myself thinking about the true meaning of Bud's Creek. I pick up the trash and put it in the plastic poop bags I always carry on walks. We wander the creek's edge for about half an hour. I fill up a second poop bag.

"You must be fishing for mountain lion," a deep voice says. The man I had seen fishing was now approaching us. The sudden sound of his voice startles me.

"Oh, fishing for mountain lion?" I question.

"That's a good idea using Chihuahuas as bait. I really like your fishing reels." Bonita and Bandito were currently deep under a bush looking for a lizard. All that was visible were the two thin black lines from their retractable leashes. We both start laughing and end up chatting for a few minutes until he wanders up the creek in search of a better fishing spot.

Suddenly I become aware of a burning pain on the back of my neck. I reach back to feel the tender hard lump of the mosquito bite. I remember I have some tea tree oil somewhere in the car and am happy to know my favorite 'cure-all' will come in handy.

We hop in the car to head for Brandon to find a place to stay and replenish the supplies—ice, juice, fruit, and a can of chicken for the dogs. I just ran out of the boiled chicken and brown rice mixture I have prepared for them for ten years.

All routines that I have created for at least the past ten years have been broken the moment I got in the car and left Ashland.

CHAPTER TWO

The town of Brandon is more substantial in size than anything I have seen since leaving Ashland. I drive the entire length of it just to see what would be available to me thirty miles away from my new job. The mile-long strip of commercial buildings seems to have all the regular places to fulfill my needs—Safeway, Rite Aid, hardware store, motels, restaurants, thrift store, and drive-through coffee. I run into Safeway to get the few things I need at the moment, then head back to the motel called White Fences that I had spotted at the beginning of town, with a sign below that said, "Small pets welcome".

It took me awhile to get to, and unload the few things I would want for the night. I find my tea tree oil and dab it on my neck, which really hurts. I feed the dogs and take them for a long walk through town. The sun is setting as I put the dogs back into the room and walk across the street to a restaurant for a nice dinner.

Upon returning to my room, I sit and count the money I have left from my original $400, which is $180. This is only my second night on the road! I'd never last! Let me think: gas—$80, campsite—$20, breakfast—$10, this room—$65, dinner—$20, Safeway—$25.

I pick up the phone to call Billy.

"Hi Billy, this is Denise. I've decided to take you up on the job offer."

"Of course you have! I never thought that ya wouldn't." Billy replied matter-of-factly.

"Listen, Billy, I'm really just on a working vacation, so to speak. I can only promise you that I'll stay for the summer. I'm headed south after that to be near my parents and family."

"I understand and that's fine. You just stay long enough so that Ray and I can take a vacation for the first time in seven years and we'll all be happy."

"Billy? There are only two things that could make me leave, because I am a woman of my word and a darn good hard worker. First, if my parents, who are in their eighties, get ill and need my help; and secondly, if I am no longer happy there. You see Billy; I really need to be happy right now." I'm surprised at how easy the truth comes out of me when speaking to Billy.

"Oh you'll be happy, I'll see to it! You just come on by in the morning. I'll give ya the keys—one to the fifth wheel, and one to the restroom. Even though the fifth wheel has a bathroom, we need to straighten out a few things in there first; it's been sittin' empty for a spell, so ya might need to use the facilities in the park for a day or so. You just get yourself settled in for the day and we'll start to work day after tomorrow." We each hang up the phone relieved.

By this time, Bonita and Bandito are both cozy under the covers. I think I've stressed them out a bit. I climb into bed myself and fall sound asleep.

After a nice long hot shower in the morning I pack up, walk the dogs, and head straight to the drive-thru coffee place to prepare for my drive back to Hacienda. With the pressure of being homeless lifted and the caffeine pumping through my veins, my eyes are opened and I am able to take in the beauty of the national park. "We're going to have lots and lots of fun walks, you guys." Bonita and Bandito are listening to every word. Bonita lets loose with a series of her loud piercing yelps that say, "We better, or I'll make your life miserable!" She can be such a pushy little bitch at times. Bandito is ducking his head as if to say, "Please shut her up!"

Along the way to Hacienda we stop at yet another day use area and breathe in the wonders of nature. I feel so in my element. How often I have wanted to live in a serene and peaceful environment, letting my dogs run free without something around their neck to hold them back, working in my garden, collecting wood for my fire, and living where I could catch glimpses of wildlife. I realize that at fifty-one years of age, it is rather late in my life, and I can't regret the choices or mistakes that have made me a hostage to myself. For now, here I am, and I'm going to make the most of the moment. Whatever happens after this day, this place in time, is not a concern. I can always worry later. For today, maybe just for this hour, I have no past. I have no future. I am ageless and free.

I carry this tranquil state of being as I get back on the highway towards Hacienda. The parking lot has several cars in front and three RVs have engines rumbling. Two are pulling out. I notice for the first time the billboard below the Hacienda sign, 'Annual TRI-TIP dinner Friday 4PM.' That's tomorrow! Well, that blows my theory about an easy-going casual job. Am I cooking? Billy couldn't really expect me to do that! There's no way. I take a deep breath to stop my anxiety from ruining my morning of joy.

I park and walk up the stone steps. It's a warm cloudless morning and feels as if it could even turn hot. The RV spaces look half full of guests. I hear the golf cart off in the distance somewhere. The trashcan is worse than yesterday, and now has a bad odor. If that doesn't get emptied soon, I will do it myself. It makes the place look so trashy. I can smell the pancakes and bacon from out here. There are five people in line at the cash register, which is also the RV registration counter. Someone other than Billy is working behind the register. She is showing someone a map of the premises and handing them a key. That same roaring male voice I heard yesterday is now laughing loudly at something. The restaurant is full, and a few people are shopping in the aisles for supplies. A small lady about my age scurries from the restaurant to the register with a worried look on her face. I have never seen anyone walk that fast. She rings up a breakfast customer while the other lady checks-in a guest and then scurries back to the restaurant. It's almost as if she has roller skates on, but she doesn't. She better slow down.

I look over toward the kitchen and read Bubba's special for the day: 'DON'T KNOW WHAT IT IS. BUT IT'S ALL GRILLED UP WITH MUSKRAT GRAVY.' As I gag in disgust, I hear that booming male voice yelling, "BETTY! ORDER UP!" I see the very top of the head of the lady with roller skate feet, zoom behind the glass-fronted meat counter that separates the kitchen from the restaurant, and pick up the order.

"Can I help you?" says the lady who was checking in the guest.

"Oh yes, hello. My name is Denise. I spoke with Billy about a job, and she had told me to come and pick up the key to the fifth wheel and a key to the restroom today. Is she here?" I gaze toward the doorway where Ray was standing yesterday, but no one appears.

"Yes, hello Denise. My name is Vi, and Billy told me all about you. Welcome! I'm kind of busy, but the keys are right here."

Vi hands me the keys and at that moment I hear and feel the heavy steps of someone on the wood plank floor approaching the counter. I assume its Bubba. I turn around and see a large man in his late thirties with short dark cropped hair. He looks really strong and has a large beer belly that looks as tight as his muscles seem to be. His navy blue shirt is splattered with grease. He also looks mean and intimidating. He pretends to ignore me, but I can tell he's checking me out. He must have heard the conversation with Vi and myself, since the building is so large and every noise seems to echo.

Vi does not introduce me and he fiddles with something behind the counter before he stomps back to the kitchen, stopping along the way to bang the back of an old rancher eating breakfast. "DID YA GET THAT CRAPPY OLD TRACTOR RUNNIN' YET HENRY?" he bellows out as he puts one of his heavy logging boots up on the redwood bench. Henry must be a regular customer since I had heard his name yesterday. Betty scurries past them on her way to the register and almost slips on a wet spot rounding the corner of the table where Bubba is talking. "BETTY! DAMN IT! SLOW THE HELL DOWN! HOW MANY TIMES I GOTTA TELL YA THAT!" She ignores Bubba's comment but I notice her cowering body language as she passes him, like a frightened puppy. She quickly continues her fast pace to the register. Bubba sounds like a big bully to me. Hopefully I don't have to deal much with him. I'm not sure if we'd get along very well.

From what I can see, Bubba is everything I am running from. If he were my boss, I'd never have considered this job in a million years. He reminds me a lot of my father, my ex-husband, my boss in Ashland, and a few of my last and final relationships. Bubba is the type of man who is self-focused, inconsiderate, loud, and completely unaware of how his actions distress those around him.

I leave the chaos and drive over to the restroom to relieve myself before I get to work on the fifth wheel and unpack my car. My toilet stall has no toilet paper. Maybe Ruby is around and I can tell her about that. Someone is taking a shower and I can smell fruity shampoo.

As I slowly approach the fifth wheel my stomach tingles with anticipation. I'm not sure if it is excitement or fear. Bonita and Bandito have been observing all that is going on from their vantage point on the pile of blankets, and recognize that we are at some final destination. I need to set up the fences before I can do anything else. A redwood picnic table is about fifteen yards away. I go over and grab one heavy edge and walk it, one side at a time, closer to the trailer. I need to lay out the damp tent and blankets that are on top of the fencing. Bonita's demanding bark is driving me nuts; so making the dogs comfortable is my number one priority at the moment.

With everything drying in the warm sunshine, I get the fencing set up around the table, and give the dogs food and water. Next, I dab some tea tree oil on my itching neck and get the keys out of the car. As I walk toward the steps of the trailer, I can hear the golf cart whizzing by on the dirt drive that is on the highway-side of the trailer. The entry faces the lake so I do not get a good look at Terry, but I am aware of how fast she is going, and get a good taste of the dust she's stirring up.

The trailer steps go straight out from the doorway. One side has a railing, and the other side is open and dangerous. It would be easy to fall off if one weren't careful and it seems to me that the fifth wheel could have been parked two or three feet up from this point to avoid the utility post that is located dead center at the bottom of the stairway. It will be awkward avoiding that post while hauling my belongings to the inside, and hopefully, not breaking my neck by falling off the unprotected side. I suppose at some point I could turn the steps so that the open side is against the wall of the trailer and away from the utility post, but not right now, and not alone because they are made of heavy steel.

At the top of the steps, I turn to look at my view of the park. Hacienda is shaped like a football arena. The lake, or pond, depending on how you see it, is not quite as big as a football field, but close to it in size. The surrounding parking spaces, laundry, showers, main building, would be the stadium area around the field. At about two o'clock and thirty yards from the fifth wheel is a giant propane tank where the guests probably buy their propane. Across from the dirt drive behind the restaurant, and sitting next to the lake, is a big oil drum looking thing, cut in half, hinged open, and set on steel legs. Perhaps it is a homemade barbeque of some sort. The rest of the view is of the lake, which is only a stones throw away, and the beautiful mountain range behind. The lake has lots of cattail grass and small brush growing around the perimeter. Billy calls it a lake, but it is just a large pond. I see a group of mature ducks, possibly twenty of them, quacking toward the rear of the kitchen, so do the dogs. They love to hunt and would love to be let loose right now. "Hush! I said hush!"

Terry has driven to the rear entry of the restaurant, which is at about one o'clock and fifty yards away from the fifth wheel. She is drinking a beer in the idling golf cart. Bubba comes out, gets himself a beer from the ice chest in the back of the cart, and they drive off turning their heads to look back at me. Breakfast must be over.

I turn around and notice that the door to my new residence seems pretty abused. The plastic window has slipped halfway down inside the core of the door. Most of the aluminum sheeting is loose and not connected to anything. I put the key in the door and feel it unlock. As soon as I open the door it falls on my foot, and pain shoots up my leg. I see that the top hinge is broken off and the bent hinge on the bottom holds the door from coming completely off. It's as if the door has been slammed a million times and finally broke apart. Aggression on a door could only mean one thing; unhappy aggressive tenants. This is not good, and makes me feel uneasy about the bad vibes that float out like vapor as I lean the broken door against the outer wall.

The inside is a completely different story. It stinks! I mean it really stinks! I step over several objects on the floor to get to the windows. I pull back the curtains to reveal a thick film of dirt and fly specks. Dead flies are collected between the screen and the windows. I open every available window and also the two sky lights, which crank open for air. The horrid aroma overpowers my mind and I don't know where to begin so I go to the car to find my snacks and pull myself together. I eat a banana and drink some juice at the picnic table to refuel for the long day ahead of me. As I sit at the table, Bubba and Terry drive by with a load of full trash bags in the back of the cart. They skid to a stop at the back entry of the restaurant, dump the trash next to a huge pile of empty cardboard boxes, pop open another beer, and take off again. I guess it's not their job to be the welcoming committee.

I head back into the fifth wheel and plan my attack. Dishes are piled all over the sink area; most of them are still coated with old dried food. The small refrigerator is full of moldy food and the inside walls are coated with specks of mold. There are blankets, clothes, papers, and empty bags of fast food scattered everywhere. On top of all the debris there is a thick layer of road dust. I begin to open the cabinets and find more leftover food. An open bottle of ketchup has completely turned dark and hard inside. I look in all the cabinets now to confirm my belief that they are all packed with crap! I venture into the tiny cramped space of the toilet and unexpectedly feel the burn of tears brimming over my eyelids as I realize the source of the pungent odor. I feel distressed and disgusted all at once. Is it possible that the holding tank has not been emptied since whomever the hell, crazy-ass, slime bag, grub lived here? I wipe away the tears and try the water pump to the toilet and realize that I need to plug in the electricity, hook up the water, and light the water heater. The contents in the holding tank are probably as dried up as the bottle of ketchup. Okay, I need some trash bags, duct tape, bleach, rubber gloves, sponges, paper towels, and that blue holding tank chemical. It's time for battle.

I find all the items inside the store area of the restaurant at inflated prices. The trash in front has been emptied. Vi told me that Billy had said not to turn on the water to the inside just yet, because there's a broken pipe somewhere. She said to use the water straight from the outside. There was a hose somewhere under the trailer. If I needed a bucket she had one. She also told Vi to tell me that Ray would be by later to check out where the water leak is before he fills up the propane tanks, and to be ready to go to work at 7:00AM, because we all had to pitch in for the busy day ahead with the barbeque in the evening. Vi said that Billy and Ray had gone shopping for the barbeque in Redding and would not be back until pretty late. Isn't Redding a hundred miles or so away? I thought to myself.

After plugging in the electricity, which seems to be in working order, I begin filling trash bags with everything inside the fifth wheel that is not bolted, glued, hammered down, or part of the trailer. There is not one single item in the stuffed drawers and cabinets that is worth a dime except a large kettle that I decide to keep for cleaning purposes. I don't mess around taking my time on this current cleansing excavation. When I clean, I show no mercy. I pile the rancid trash bags by the bottom of the stairs. Mid-way through this task, I decide to look for the hose under the trailer. While under there I notice the thick, gray pleated plastic tubing coming out from the holding tank. I find the opening for sewage over by the electrical post and stuff the pleated hose into it. The hose makes a dry crackling noise. I probably need a new one of those too! I put the water hose into the toilet, turn on the water and begin to fill the tank. The water hose has several leaks along its length, so I quickly turn off the water, dry the hose off, and use the duct tape to seal up the many drips. After repairing the hose and filling the toilet tank with water, I add the thick blue chemical, probably more than recommended and continue filling up trash bags. I use the entire box of twenty heavy-duty trash bags; five of the trash bags contain ripped, dirty blankets and discolored pillows. The other fifteen contain clothes, towels, dishes, old food, and hard-core trash! Next, I retrieve my Coleman stove and fill the large kettle with water from the hose. I put the stove and kettle on the picnic table to heat for cleaning. I hear a lawn mower off in the distance and notice the park is getting full of RVs. People are wandering about the premises, fishing and walking their dogs. My dogs bark like crazy every time someone with a dog walks by. I need to get this done to the point that I can bring them inside the trailer.

My loaded car has most of the practical items needed for living fairly comfortably—a small vacuum, a small microwave, an ice chest, a boom box with my CD's and cassettes, a few dishes, silverware, tea kettle, drip filter for coffee, a couple of small pots and pans, bedding, toilet paper, and a small assortment of packaged and canned food. I have a habit of keeping my chaos fairly organized.

By now my car has all four doors open and boxes and bags of my provisions are spread around. I get the toilet paper and vacuum and head back inside the trailer to take a quick, creepy, crawly-feeling pee in the toilet. I will drain the holding tank after it soaks for a few hours and hope that its contents have broken down enough to flush down into the sewer. While pulling up my pants, I hear an approaching diesel truck coming down the highway going extremely fast, shaking the trailer like an earthquake. At the same moment I hear pounding on the exterior wall of the trailer. In my panic to escape the confines of the tiny cubicle, I slip on a small area of water that had leaked from the duct taped hose and ram my hip on the door knob of the tiny bathroom. The pounding gets louder. I limp over to the door, which I have bungee-corded open and connected to the side of the trailer, rubbing my new bruise. It's Ruby. She has a beer in her hand and has tears in her red eyes.

"I'm sorry to bother you Denise, but I'm so upset! My dog, the one I told you about yesterday? Well, he got bit by a rattlesnake this morning and I just know he's going to die! Billy's gone and I need to take him to the vet, but I don't have any money. I don't mean to be a pain in the ass or anything, but could you lend me a twenty? I promise I'll pay you back!" I don't see a car or a dog and wonder how she got here and where the dog is. She continues talking. "I'll bet this place is a mess! Last guy to live here was the last cook Billy hired over a year ago. He was a druggy, and ripped Billy off for hundreds of dollars. He's even suing Billy and Ray over something that never happened." Ruby's nose scrunches up in disgust. "What stinks?" Ruby is no longer crying and I'm appalled to think that I will be sleeping in the bed of a "druggy."

"I think it's the holding tank. I'm trying to clear that out. Listen Ruby, I'm pretty busy and don't have much time. I'll loan you the twenty, but I'll need to get it back as soon as you can repay me. I'm kind of short on cash myself these days."

"Cool! Thanks Denise! I promise." After the supplies at the store and this twenty, which I might not ever see again, I am now down to $110. Ruby walks away and heads toward the restaurant, tossing her empty beer can on the ground.

Steam is rising from the pot on the Coleman stove. I get a couple of towels to carry the hot kettle with, go pick up the empty beer can, drop it into the trash bin ten feet away, and carry the heated water into the trailer. I put on the new rubber cleaning gloves and pour bleach into the hot water. I start a smaller pot of water to heat up in case I need more, and I can't help but think that I will certainly need more. The water turns a mustard tan as soon as I dip my wet rag back into it. Nicotine! It's coated everything! I wipe like a mad woman. No nook or cranny escapes my feverish cleaning— inside cabinets, outside cabinets, walls, counters, and bathroom. There are now several flies that have entered uninvited. I hear the dogs barking and need to stop cleaning to bring them in and feed them. First, I bring in the second pot of water, empty the first, and refill it to heat up again. I get the dogs and shut the screen door that is attached to the broken front door. To my amazement it works just fine. It even snaps shut. I hope this will keep those darn flies out now.

Bonita and Bandito are very happy to have joined me. They explore the small confined area they are in. Bandito runs and jumps up the two steps that go to the double bed in the far rear of the trailer and acts like he's ready to play. Bonita looks concerned and apprehensive. I feed them, and then go to the car to find my Bug Zapper; a tennis racket-shaped tool that has a battery operated electrical current to zap flies and mosquitoes. I zap until I feel I have conquered the majority of them.

After another hour of cleaning with bleach, I feel satisfied that I will be living in a slightly more sterile environment. I know I have only touched the surface of all the details that need to be done to get the trailer up to my standards, but I have all summer, so I begin carting in all my belongings. I have no idea what time it is, so I check the clock in my car and see it is 4:00PM. I go back inside and set my travel alarm, so I can at least know the time.

The sun is approaching the edge of the mountain range. There is a slight breeze coming up, and the drying tent has blown onto the ground. I roll up the dry tent and put it in the trunk of the car and bring in the dry blankets and down comforter. I lay the comforter on the bed first to separate me from the old, well-used, discolored surface of the "druggy" mattress, and then place the fitted sheet over the comforter. I make a mental note to purchase some Lysol. After that, I make my way back outside to find the valve to empty the holding tank. It was easy to find over on the highway side of the trailer where a large red arrow was pointing down to it reading: 'To empty holding tank turn valve to the left.' As I do this, I hear and see the rumbling, heavy, discolored water gushing through the fragile pleated hose on its way to the sewer. When I no longer hear water in the hose, I shut the valve off. I go get the water hose and refill the tank through the toilet and add more blue chemical. Now that the trailer seems to smell better, I make a tuna sandwich and drink a small glass of wine. I finish eating and go outside to drag all the plastic trash bags over to the pile that Bubba and Terry have going.

"Okay kids! We're going for a walk!" I announce to Bonita and Bandito upon my return. They are out of their minds with excitement.

I decide to walk the dirt drive outside the fifth wheel that leads away from the main building parallel to the highway and wind around the entire oval-shaped park. I had noticed earlier that the small row of trailers next to the highway, like mine, seem more permanent, while the temporary RVs are on the one end and the other side of the lake. The dogs are very happy with their sixteen feet of mobile freedom they are allowed with the leashes.

The sun has just dipped behind the mountains highest peak. There is still plenty of daylight left. It didn't get too hot today. Thank heavens for that.

About six spaces from my trailer, I approach a trailer that has the golf cart parked in front. So this is where our charming couple live! The area has the look of a full-time tenant. I see the lawn mower, a few attempts with potted flowers, an older, red, beat up Jeep, a huge fire pit with a huge pile of logs next to it, and various bent up cardboard boxes filled with empty beer cans.

Bonita and Bandito see the tiny kittens darting from under the trailer at the same time that I do. They shoot out like bullets from the extending leashes, barking like idiots, springing to a halt and flipping their little bodies around when the line runs out. I have learned through time to keep a firm grip on the handles. They want, need, and desire to rip the heads off the cute little kitties. I hang on tight and slowly reel them in.

With my presence made known, I feel embarrassed. I get a chill down my spine when I realize that Bubba and Terry are probably observing me from somewhere inside their trailer. "Bad dogs! You stop that! Do you hear me? That's not nice!" As we pass the golf cart parked on the side of the road, I see the ice chest tilted in a sea of empty beer cans in the cargo space of the cart.

We continue walking around the park. About five spaces down from Bubba's, I see a large cement drainpipe extending into the lake. Water is flowing at a steady stream from its opening. I presume that the flowing water is the continuous source and supply of the lake. A group of mud hens honk and float near the rippling water. Bits of trash float near the waters' edge.

As I round the farthest curve at the far end of the park, I see the forest of pine trees that borders the park. There is a dirt road that curves off the main circular drive and disappears into the forest.

Good road for a private walk, I think to myself. On closer inspection of the pine trees, I can see fragments of color beyond the tree line, like large tractors, or equipment of some sort. They are barely noticeable, but it's evident that there's a back area in there for storage of some kind.

I hear the golf cart start up and come my way around the park. Are Bubba and Terry after me for scaring the kittens? Instead, they zoom past me laughing loudly about something, each holding a beer, leaving in their wake, thick, floating dust. How could anyone drink that much beer all day long and still function? I don't get it! I see them disappear down yet another side dirt road further down, possibly another entry into the forest storage area.

At about mid-way on my walk, I hear the grinding of a truck trying to get started. The sound is coming from deep within the cover of the pine trees; back there, in the forest. What in the hell is back there? I will explore this soon.

Guests are enjoying their spaces, grilling up hot dogs and hamburgers, swatting flies, and most of them have satellite dishes set up or in the process of getting set up. So I guess the deal is to eat and watch TV in the presence of nature. I do not see many of them walking around. "Ouch!" I feel the sting of a mosquito bite on my ankle. "Gosh darn it anyway!" I hurry up our walk so I can go cover my legs and feet. Mosquitoes love this time of the evening. I am only wearing my flip-flops, a short-sleeved t-shirt, and capri pants. I look at the lake and see the thin layer of mosquitoes floating above and around the water's surface. We pass the group of ducks resting beneath the cattail grass. I am very happy that the dogs did not notice them.

As I round the front of the main building, bypassing the straight path to my trailer which is behind the main building, I hear the rumbling engine of a large and really old looking dump truck. It looks beat to shit! It shakes and rattles its way to the rear of the restaurant. There is a pile of trash bags about halfway up the teetering side wood panels. Oh, I get it. That's where they put all the trash. Then what? Whatever, I'm sure I will find out later. Bubba is behind the wheel and Terry is following him in the golf cart. They disappear out of view behind the restaurant.

The front parking lot is full of restaurant customers. The majority of the cars being Jeeps, well-used trucks, a couple of all-terrain scooters, and cars with license plates from many different states. Two logging trucks, empty of driver and logs, are parked with engines running on the other side of the highway. Three RVs are in line by the edge of the lot and some kids are climbing the small fence that borders the park. Someone is obviously registering for a space inside while the family waits. Billy must have quite a crew working for her! I suddenly feel very insecure and apprehensive about my new job as cook. This must be the only place to eat for miles!

I walk the final curve toward my trailer and climb the inconvenient, awkward stairs. Once inside I unleash the dogs and peek out the window next to the dining table. I see Bubba standing with his back to me, looking at the pile of trash bags. He is standing in front of my pile of additional trash bags. His heavy stumps of legs are spread apart and his fists are planted on his hips. He lifts his baseball cap with one hand and scratches his head violently, the hat flapping back and forth. Terry rattles on dramatically about something, pointing in my direction. He turns around, looks toward my trailer, and pulls on some thick work gloves with a scowl on his face. Wow! Those two make me very nervous!

Smoke is pouring out of a vent that is next to the back door of the kitchen. I smell the grilling hamburgers and steaks, my stomach growls. I open a can of organic vegetarian chili, not because I am a vegetarian, but because even though I enjoy meat, I try to not eat it from a processed source, such as a can. I heat it in my microwave and pour myself another glass of wine. I eat in the silence and watch the shadows fade while night approaches on my first night at Hacienda.

"Darn it! I forgot about the front door!" There is still enough twilight outside to duct tape the hanging pieces of aluminum back on. As I begin, I hear the hum of a machine over by where Bubba is loading trash. He is placing the full bags of trash in some sort of large trash compactor. You can hear the snap from the contents of the bags as they slowly get crushed. He then tosses the flattened oozing bags into the dump truck. Glass explodes within the one he is currently crushing. I think it is one of the bags that I put over there because I had filled a few with old dishes and pans. The trash compactor makes a high-pitched screeching sound, and is then silent.

"GOD DAMN IT TO HELL! WHO THE HELL PUT THAT SHIT IN THE TRASH? DAMN SON OF A BITCH, STUPID ASSHOLE! TERRY GET ME THE BIG WRENCH NOW! AND THE FLATHEAD SCREWDRIVER! HURRY UP DAMN IT I HAVEN'T GOT ALL NIGHT!"

If Bubba is aware that the bag was from me, I cannot tell because he does not look in my direction. It was his yelling that seemed directed at me. Geez! Couldn't he tell that the bag had heavy glass and steel in it when he picked it up? If it were going to break the machine, wouldn't he have known not to put it in there?

Terry hands Bubba a tool. "I SAID THE FLATHEAD SCREWDRIVER DAMN IT!" Terry's panicky reaction, and Bubba's loud demand reminds me of my childhood when I tried to help my father with his tools while he worked on his car. I could never pick out the right screwdriver. It's interesting what makes the doors of memories open unannounced.

I hurry and finish duct-taping the door as best as possible without looking in Bubba's direction. I'm aware that the sound of the tape ripping off the roll is echoing across the entire park because all the noisy machines are silent at the moment. Duct tape is loud that way. The door looks horrible, like a badly wrapped, silver-gray, square mummy, but the small Plexiglas window is now covered up and held in with the tape and most of the hanging parts are covered with tape. I have to lift the door that is only connected by the bent bottom hinge and set it gently on the threshold. As it balances there I take the bungee cord and loop it through the broken door handle. I pull the hooked ends of the stretchy cord and hook them on the handle of the stove that is right next to the door. I'm proud of my ingenuity! It also serves as a door lock, which at this point, I think I need.

I sit in the dark trailer with another glass of wine on the seating area by the table that faces out to the dump truck and Bubba. I have the curtain open just enough to watch what is going on out there. Who needs a TV when you have this!? The dogs are curled up on each side of me. "Darn it! I need a shower! I have to get up tomorrow and go to work!" The dogs jump to attention.

It is more comfortable at this point to drive my car around the front of the main building and go to the showers. I don't want to walk by Bubba and Terry.

The showers are roomy and the water is hot. The warm water running down my legs makes my new mosquito bite burn. I lift my leg to see not one, but five new bites beginning to swell. There is a big bruise on the top of my foot from when the door fell on it and another tender purple area on my hip. I feel the bite on my neck and can't believe that it's more swollen than earlier today. Day one and I already have battle scars. I dry off and change into some sweats. As I walk out of the building I can hear the dogs barking through the screen door of the trailer, which I can see across the lake. A family is walking their dog by my trailer. I drive back to my trailer. I made the shower quick because I am exhausted and need to just sit down for a while.

The pile of trash is loaded by the time I get back. Bubba is trying to start the engine of the dump truck again. The air stinks like rotten food and I need to swat several flies out from my face as I enter the trailer.

I return to my spying spot at my dining table with my wine and tea tree oil, dabbing the oil on each bite. I wonder if Bubba ever got the trash compactor fixed.

The dump truck suddenly fires up and Bubba roars the engine alive several times, as if he were taking out some aggressive behavior in the form of noise.

As Bubba drives away, I am left in a space of time where I can feel my feelings again. My heart begins to beat a little faster as I become aware of the craziness of the stupid choice I made to take a working vacation. "Be accountable for your choices!" That's one of Dr. Phil's famous and favorite statements. I just love Dr. Phil! I'll try, Dr. Phil. I'll try.

A bright outdoor light pops on from the edge of the roof behind the kitchen. A female comes out to smoke a cigarette. I can't really see what she looks like. She looks nervously around and pauses as she looks in my direction. I don't hear the dump truck running anymore, but I hear the golf cart on the other side of the lake coming back around the other way. It stops when I presume they are back at their trailer. Someone else comes out the back door and throws several cardboard boxes into the cardboard box pile, which at this point, looks to be about ten feet high and fifteen feet wide. It's Betty! I can tell by the way she is moving! Roller-skating with boxes. Roller-skating back into the kitchen.

Car lights shine through my front curtain window and the sound of gravel crunching fills the quiet night as a vehicle slowly passes by on its way to the rear door of the kitchen. As soon as this occurs, I hear the golf cart fire up again and charge in my direction. Three people exit the back door of the kitchen. Bubba and Terry buzz by and halt at the van that is now parked. Everyone seems to be talking at once to the two passengers who are exiting the van. I hear Bubba belt out a loud laugh. It must be Billy and Ray returning from shopping in Redding. Bubba opens the rear door of the van and everyone starts hauling the tons of heavy boxes into the kitchen. I worry again about my new job. I have a feeling that working here and living here at the same time is going to require spontaneous involvement at odd hours. Am I expected to run out there and help right now?

Ray is rolling his oxygen tank behind him as he wanders over towards the big oil-drum-barbeque by the lake. He lights a cigarette. The van gets emptied and Billy drives it back around to the front. Terry walks by the fifth wheel on her way home, leaving the golf cart for Bubba. She is not very steady on her feet, and is mumbling as she passes my open window.

Bubba joins Ray over by the oil drum and starts wading up newspaper, and then stuffs it into the barbeque. They are talking, but I can't quite hear the words. Bubba lights the newspaper and flames light up the whole area. Ray says something and Bubba rolls Ray's oxygen tank over to the back door of the kitchen away from the flames. He goes inside the kitchen door and returns a few minutes later with a drink for Ray and a beer for himself. He gives Ray his drink and sets his beer on the redwood picnic table where Ray is sitting, then goes back over to the pile of cardboard boxes and grabs several. He brings them back to the fire and drops them on the ground. He starts ripping them apart and tossing them into the flaming barbeque barrel. Both men stare, as if in a trance, into the fire, their faces glowing orange. Bubba goes back for more boxes.

This talking, ripping, burning, and drinking goes on until I feel myself falling asleep at the dining table. I get up and set my alarm for 5:30, crawl up into my bed, and close my eyes to the flickering glow outside. I drift off to sleep with the sound of coyotes yipping somewhere close by.

CHAPTER THREE

There was no need to set my alarm. Bandito was tapping my back gently with his paw. He does this when he needs to go potty. I look out the window and admire the beautiful pre-dawn indigo colored sky. I see that it is 5:10, so I turn the alarm to off. Bandito is staring down at my face like he is in a hurry. His muzzle is turning gray now. He used to be pitch black from head to foot. Bonita, who is pumpkin in color, peeks her head out from under the covers. "Okay! Just a minute. Let me get some shoes on." I had slept in my sweats, so there was no need to change into clothes. They start bouncing around on the bed like excited children. The holding tank still has an unpleasant odor. I will need to empty and refill that one more time before I go to work. After leashing up the dogs, I carefully unhook the battered door and hook it open to the outer wall of the trailer with the bungee cord, then close the screen door.

No one is around yet. I see lights on in some of the visiting RVs. The oil drum barbeque has a thin trail of smoke coming up from it, and I notice that the pile of cardboard boxes are now gone. The golf cart is still parked where Terry had left it last night. Bubba must have walked home. There is a dog looking at us from the lawn area next to the main building. It looks like one of those cattle herding dogs and does not seem interested in us. The dog lies back down on the porch area by the lawn.

Bonita and Bandito have done their business, so I return to the trailer. They climb back into bed and lay down. They know my routine. They do not bother with me until I've had my coffee, and today I need it bad!

While my bottled water is boiling on the Coleman stove, I walk around the trailer to open the holding tank drain valve. I'm hoping that this will do it as far as cleansing goes. I put the water hose into the toilet to refill the tank. I heat up some soymilk in the microwave, and put coffee in my small, single cup, Melitta drip filter. The tea kettle outside is beginning to whistle.

With hot coffee in hand, I sit and watch the sky turn to day and enjoy the quiet. A man walks along the shoreline of the lake with a fishing pole. I assume that Billy must stock the lake with trout. I hear the approaching quacks of the ducks as they waddle towards me along the shoreline coming from the direction of Bubba's trailer. I can hear a logging truck coming down the highway. It barrels by, disturbing the peace and quiet of the morning, reminding me of what I got myself into—a working vacation. I turn off the hose and pull it back outside and take a second cup of coffee into the trailer to get ready for work.

My dogs begin to growl when they hear the heavy crunching of logging boots walking past my trailer. I look out to see Bubba passing by holding a cup of coffee. He hacks up a loogie and spits next to my trailer. What a gross man!

The group of quacking ducks is at the end of the ramp that leads to the kitchen. Bubba opens up a side storage unit and comes out with a pan full of feed. He carries the pan near to the lake. The ducks are quacking like crazy following him. They scramble to eat as fast as possible when he throws the seed on the ground. Bubba then disappears into the kitchen. Well, he can't be all that bad if he likes ducks and feeds them! They must live down by his trailer.

By 6:30 I am adding the blue chemical into the toilet. I take the dogs out one more time, and then settle them in the trailer for the day. I'm hoping I get a lunch break so I can let them out for awhile. I leave only the screen door shut thinking that the dogs would at least have something to look at, and hopefully, not bark at. If I were to leave them in the fenced area they would bark all day! Fifteen minutes later I walk past two RVs waiting for propane on my way to the front entry of the main building. Stopping at the doorway I read the restaurant hours: 6:30AM to 8:00PM. Two cars and one motorcycle are in the parking lot. Billy's van is off to the side near, what I think, is her connected home. I take several deep breaths and walk into the unknown.

A tall bulky woman wearing Bermuda shorts and a brilliant white T-shirt with the American flag imprinted on the front is standing behind the register. She looks to be my age and is admiring her long acrylic fingernails, which, even from ten feet away I can see, are also American flags. Because of her concentration on her nails at the moment, I have a few seconds to observe the restaurant area. There is no Bubba's special, instead the chalkboard reads: 'TRI-TIP BBQ TONIGHT! 4:00PM.' People are at the tables eating huge piles of pancakes and hash browns. At the same moment that I am looking in the direction of the kitchen, Bubba walks over to the chest high meat counter holding a large chopping knife.

"KAREN! HOW DO THEY WANT THAT STEAK COOKED?"

"Rare!" I hear a voice answer, but do not see her.

Bubba's eyes catch mine in a brief instant of recognition. He does not smile at me, but I smile at him. He turns around and lets loose with one single loud laugh. I exhale away my sudden irritation.

"I have the feeling you must be the new cook," she says.

"Yes, I guess I am. Hi, I'm Denise."

"Glad you're here. I'm Helen." Helen reaches out to shake my hand, but up high, with fingernails fluttering so I can take a better look I guess. We don't really shake hands, as one would normally do. Instead, I am forced to take her hand softly, up high, like you would with a queen. I do not comment on her nails, because I personally think they're horrid!

Helen starts taking charge of my day. "Billy and Ray are still sleeping, but she'll be up after a bit and get you going later at the grill, probably for the lunch shift when Bubba has to get the barbeque going. Come on back here and I'll show you our time sheets for the week. We have a lot of things to do today. It's always crazy when we have a barbeque."

I fill out my personal information and my time sheet for

7:00AM.

"Now I'll take you over and introduce you to Bubba and Karen."

I feel a knot clench up in my stomach at the thought of being face to face with Bubba.

Helen walks ahead of me. I now notice her red tennis shoes. She walks and dresses as if she does not realize that she is in her fifties. We walk past Karen who is taking an order from a family of five, probably RV guests, and Helen leads me behind the meat counter to the grill area. We pass the dishwashing area where many used plates, bowls, and cooking utensils are piled. Many of the plates have partially eaten pancakes on them. We then walk by a chopping table with a huge bowl filled with the makings of potato salad. Celery, onion, and black olives wait to be chopped next to the bowl. A vat of boiled potatoes are cooling and the skins are peeling and cracking. Bubba looks very serious as he turns the many piles of hash browns with one hand, and with the other hand he is rotating two fried eggs in a Teflon pan. A pile of bacon is being kept warm on the edge of the huge flat grill where the hash browns are cooking. The left over space on the flat grill is filled with three giant pancakes. There is a grated grill to the left of the flat grill that has two steaks sizzling with the smoke floating above in a thick layer. The microwave behind Bubba goes off with a high pitched buzz and Karen rushes past us on her way to some sort of cold storage unit located in-between the microwave and deep fryer.

"Bubba. This is Denise." Helen stands there with her arms crossed keeping her distance from the grill area.

Bubba keeps up with the constant motion of cooking, but turns to acknowledge me. His eyes are bloodshot. He smiles, almost flirtatiously, and says, "LET ME FIX YA UP WITH SOME BREAKFAST. YUR GONNA NEED THE ENERGY TO MAKE IT THROUGH THIS DAY. SINCE I'M THE COOK, YUR GONNA HAVE TO TASTE WHAT BREAKFAST SHOULD TASTE LIKE."

Bubba seems to be making it clear to me that he is the cook. Fine with me. He isn't a bad looking man with his rosy cheeks and manly stature, but you can feel his intensity and see his puffed up chest and intimidating gestures. His stomach and overall appearance is slightly bloated. He's a real 'man's man' in a backwoods sort of way.

"KAREN, ORDER UP!" Bubba yells, and then to me he loudly says, "GO SIT YURSELF DOWN AND I'LL BRING YA SOME BREAKFAST." It sounded like an order from a drill sergeant. I could use a large dose of comfort food anyway, so I go and find myself a seat. Helen prances off back to the register.

I chose an empty redwood picnic table to sit at and take in the surroundings. The décor is ranch style. Large photos of cattle and steer hang on the wall of each booth. An old horse drawn carriage hangs precariously from the high log ceiling.

"Hi. I'm Karen. Bubba says he's gonna make you some breakfast. You want some coffee?" Karen is also in her early fifties, thin with short-cropped hair. She seems nervous or high strung in some way. She's not too interested in me at the moment. I'm sure she has tons of things to do.

"Sure, coffee would be great! Thanks." I guess I don't get to decide what I will be eating, and what's the deal with all us fifty-year old women?

After a few minutes, my breakfast arrives on two giant platters. One platter is holding three pancakes the size of basketballs with two ice cream scoops of whipped butter. The second platter has three fried eggs, hash browns, four pieces of bacon, and two slices of sourdough toast. I look over towards the kitchen and see Bubba leaning on the meat counter watching me. He tips his baseball cap in my direction. I smile back in acknowledgment. Good gawd! If I ate all this, I'd blow up! I might as well eat what I can while I can. I'll bet this is some sort of rite of passage. If it means I can only pass if I eat the entire meal, then I will surely fail! I hear Bubba belt out with one of his loud laughs from over by the grill area. He is alone in there, so the laugh must be directed at me and his own private food joke.

I whittle away at an edge of the pancakes, eat two eggs and part of the hash browns. I wrap the bacon in my napkin and put in it my purse for the dogs when I get a break.

"We've got a lot of work to do. As soon as you're finished, bring your plates to the sink and I'll show ya what we need ya to do for now." Karen was standing next to me with her arms piled with dirty platters from the tables. Her tone sounds irritated with me for eating. Maybe I should have refused the free breakfast. Was that the test? If so, I was set up to fail either way.

The platters are as heavy as their size. I carry them over to the sink area and wait for Karen to finish ringing up a customer at the register. Bubba is at the grill on the other side of the wall, so I don't have to look at him.

"All righty! Here's an apron. Get goin' on these dishes. Then we have to make the potato salad for the barbeque. We also have corn to shuck, salad to make, beans to heat, fruit to slice, and sour cream containers to fill. I'm goin' out to have a smoke!" Karen spins around angrily and disappears around the corner of the wall, heading to the door to the outside next to the grill. I hear her say something to Bubba, and they both start laughing.

I turn to the sink and face my duty head on. The platters, bowls, silverware and pans are piled dangerously high. The dishwashing sink is filled with cold, dirty, sudless water and is also filled to capacity with dishes. Likewise, so is the rinse water. There is a large trashcan at the edge of the third and final sterilizing rinse sink packed with leftover food. I put on the gloves I find over on a rack, empty all three sinks, and then refill them with hot and sudsy, hot and clear, and hot with sanitizer. I scrape away all the wasted food into the trashcan. Karen who has finished her cigarette is clearing off more tables and bringing them to the pile. I do dishes for about two hours, changing the dirty water twice. I leave the pans for last. As I am about to dip a small Teflon fry pan into the sink, I am shaken to the core by Bubba's roaring angry voice. "DON'T PUT THAT IN THERE! DAMN IT! DON'T EVER PUT MY PAN IN SUDSY WATER!"

Was he watching me? And for how long had he been watching? Was he just waiting for me to get to his pan? I notice a few of the customers were looking in my direction to see what was going on.

"What? I don't understand." I'm confused at his anger about this seemingly simple problem about a small pan.

"IF YUR A COOK THEN YA KNOW NOT TO CLEAN THESE PANS IN DISH WATER, EVER! HERE, LET ME SHOW YA SINCE YA DON'T KNOW. YA TAKE A PAPER TOWEL AND WIPE IT LIKE THIS." Bubba begins violently wiping his pan with the paper towel. He takes it back over by the grill with me following him and hangs it above the grill.

"HERE! YA HANG IT HERE! NEVER WASH MY PANS!"

"Listen Bubba. You really don't need to be angry with me. I didn't know that was the deal with the pans. You could have told me that without yelling. Why was it over there in the pile? I'm really a reasonable person. You can tell me what I'm supposed to do and not do. I follow instructions very well."

Bubba seems surprised that I am not mad right back. I think he expected me to blow, but I just don't have confrontation in me. Never have. I've had to think about this a lot through the years and through the men that have had power over my life. I've pretty much come to the conclusion that some people thrive on debate and defense, that for them, this is a thrill, a blast, a passion. Personally, it shrinks me into a ball rolling away. I depart, leaving my debater to their personal agony and the emptiness of silence. I am happy, they are not. I save this kind of energy for more important issues or until I am pushed to the point of insanity, then they accidentally get from me the combative response they were looking for and I am left with shame. They are thrilled.

It seems that the breakfast rush is over. I am finishing up with the last of the dishes when Karen walks over to a large oversized coffee cup stuck under the counter. She dumps out a pile of folded dollar bills and begins counting. She and Bubba are exchanging small talk about the events of the morning crowd. They seem to be pretty buddy-buddy, and I am not included in the conversation. Karen divides the tips, and hands Bubba his half. They do not offer any to me.

"Good morning for us. Looks like fifty dollars a piece." Karen announces.

Wow, that sure will help when I start cooking! It pumps up the minimum wage thing to a more acceptable level.

There are no customers at this point in the restaurant. I hear Bubba go into the cold storage unit, when he comes out; I hear the pop of a beer can being opened. Karen approaches me. "I need ya to start peeling the skin off these cooked potatoes. I'll start getting the rest of the ingredients ready. When we're done with that, I'll need ya to get on the corn." I hear the back door next to the grill open and shut. I also hear the golf cart rumbling outside. Goodbye Bubba. Have a nice day! You're welcome you big jerk! What a bully! I feel my adrenalin flowing now. Why is it always a few hours late? I won't be sucked into his negative energy.

As soon as I have finished peeling the warm potatoes, Karen plops down a large bowl of boiled eggs. "Here, peel these too!" She is cutting up the potatoes and adding them to the giant bowl of potato salad. We are working side by side, yet so far away. I think I can warm Karen up to me at some future point. I feel that she could possibly need a friend; either that or she is having one hell of a menopause. Bubba has no excuse what-so-ever. He's just a big, stupid, uneducated jerk! Oh dear, I think I'm getting an attitude. It's too early for that!

The space between the meat counter and the table we are currently chopping at is only wide enough for one body. Helen squishes past Karen and me, our butts uncomfortably rubbing together. She opens the meat counter and gets herself a large handful of hamburger, using a sheet of wax paper.

"I guess I'll have to cook myself some lunch since Bubba is off duty." Helen says holding the mound of raw meat.

"Nothin's stopped you before. So what makes today any different?" responds Karen.

Helen is using the palms of her hands in order to protect her fingernails. She pats the wax paper covered hamburger into a patty then plops it on the hot grill. She then brushes a bun with melted grease from a stainless steel container and lays them gently on the grill, being careful not to let her fingernails make contact. She stands at the grill looking at her nails while the hamburger cooks. "Just want you to know. We have eighty-five confirmed tickets for the barbeque tonight." I'm not sure if Helen is speaking to both of us, or just to Karen. Is eighty-five a lot, or is that a low turnout? Karen does not respond, so I'm not sure how I'm supposed to respond. I say nothing. Helen continues. "And as we know, twenty or thirty extra guests usually just show up without tickets." Where have I landed? How could one small restaurant in the middle of nowhere be the center point of a major food source for some unknown hidden community? I really expected this job to be casual and easy going. Is it too late with too little money to run home to mom and dad? Would Lori take me in? My sons would love for mom to move in. Wouldn't they? No, I could never ever admit failure.

I need to get Bonita and Bandito out to pee as soon as possible. Is that bacon soaking grease into my purse? When will Ray fix my water leak? My mosquito bites are burning and itching again. That is one hell of a pile of corn to shuck! I think I'm having an anxiety attack, but no one notices, or even cares.

I stop ranting in my mind and take a deep breath. I close my eyes and chant to myself within the quiet place inside. 'I own my life, and only mine, and so I shall appreciate my person, and so I shall make proper use of myself.' I take another deep breath and begin again. 'I own my life, and only...'

"Billy I could never ever thank ya enough as long as I live!" My concealed chanting is silenced by the sound of Ruby who is over by the register hugging Billy, who is patting Ruby's back. Billy has a cigarette in her mouth and it bobbles up and down as she says something to Ruby in their embrace. Ruby has some cash in her hand and is crying. Billy starts heading in the direction of the kitchen with Ruby following behind.

As soon as Billy enters the kitchen area, an aura of control and reason seems to follow her. Karen smiles and Helen stands up straighter, no longer looking at her fingernails. I can feel Billy's powerful and reassuring presence; at least I am praying that she has some sort of power over these people. I need someone who is grounded in this whack joint, please!

Ruby leans on the meat counter and is looking in our direction with a sort of slobbery look on her face, a sort of sincere dreamy happiness with a slight bit of drunkenness.

"Hi Ruby." Both Karen and Helen acknowledge Ruby.

"Hi Ruby." I am the only one smiling at her.

"Denise! Hi! How the hell ya doin'?" I feel slightly more loved and appreciated at the moment, even under the circumstances. Billy taps my back in a reassuring way as she passes on her way to the cold storage unit. She knows that she has put me in hell! She's going to be my rock, my firm ground to depend on. She's glad I'm here. I just know she is! She knows everyone else is nuts! All is well.

Billy comes out with a dozen eggs and a twelve pack of beer. She puts it up on the meat counter and has Ruby sign a piece of paper.

"Thanks again Billy. Yur the best!" Ruby walks out of the building with her goods.

"First things first." Billy says calmly and directed at me. "Never, I repeat; never, loan that girl any money. You'll never get it back. Bless her heart. She means well, but she just can't get it together, always a crisis with her. The damn dog that I told her not to get in the first place, got bit by a rattlesnake yesterday and needs anti-venom. I can't let the brute die! Can't much afford to save it either. So Denise, how ya gettin' along?"

Karen and Helen are staring at me. "Great, Billy! Everything's just great!" I fib, while thinking about the twenty bucks I'll never see again.

"That fifth wheel gonna be okay for ya?" Billy asks.

"It's just fine. Thank you very much."

"Good. Now let's all get ourselves busy. People will be coming in for lunch, and we have a lot to do to get ready for the barbeque. Karen, get the slabs of tri-tip out of the cold storage and bring it here. I need to season it for Bubba to get on the barbeque pit. Denise, how's that potato salad comin'?"

"I believe it's about ready Billy." We have a leader! I'm so happy!

"Good. Good. Now we better get the corn shucked and get the beans in a kettle. It takes a few hours to heat up that amount of beans. Helen, get the lettuce and soak it in the sink." Billy has obviously been doing this routine for years.

"Uh, Billy? I'm sorry but could I go back to my trailer for just a few minutes and let my dogs out? It'll just take a minute."

"No problem! Just get yurself back here ASAP."

I walk out the back door next to the grill. My dogs are barking. There is a stench in the air, a mixture of smoky lighter fluid and something rotting. As I walk down the delivery ramp of the kitchen, I pass the large trash compactor. It has sticky ooze coming out from the bottom ledge. Flies are buzzing on and around the slime. There is a flytrap hanging above and near the trash compactor that is full to capacity with dead and trapped flies. I see the barbeque drum flaming, but do not see Bubba or Terry. Bonita and Bandito can now see me coming in view through the screen door and turn up the volume of their barking, in fact they even start howling like little wolves. I might have to shut the broken door from now on to keep them quiet.

Bubba and Terry are setting up picnic tables on the lawn area. I wave at them as I pass. They do not wave back since at the moment they are moving a heavy table, but I doubt if they'd wave anyway.

It's pretty warm inside the trailer. The dogs are panting, but do not seem overheated. I look up at the small air-conditioner in the ceiling and hope that it works when the time comes to need it.

"I've got a treat for you, but first let's go outside!" They are so excited to see me. I walk the dogs for a short distance from the fifth wheel, and then take them back inside. I feel so guilty, the same guilt I had for so many years raising my sons. Being single and working full time, would often necessitate that my sons be at home after school waiting for me for an hour or two. They were old enough to take care of themselves, and probably loved having the house free of a mom. By the time I'd get home they were usually playing with their cousins or friends and would happily tear into the chili dogs or pizza I'd bring home. Comfort food always helps erase any idea of abandonment or neglect, which was in my mind only, not theirs. It never felt right to not be at home waiting, wearing an apron, and holding a large plate of warm cookies. I couldn't help but worry, but again, I had made my choice to be single and self-sufficient. There are some prices to pay for freedom and survival.

"Look at this! Momma brings home the bacon!" I wave the crisp bacon in the air. Bonita and Bandito are very happy about this treat. I am forgiven once again.

I am not too hungry. That breakfast was enough to last me until dinner, but I grab an apple anyway, put it in my purse, and turn on my small fan. I lift up the broken door, set it on the threshold, and shut the duct-taped door.

When I return to the kitchen, Billy has three hamburgers cooking on the grated grill. There are a few customers sitting at the dining tables. The flat grill has two large kettles of beans in the back area and toward the front are the hamburger buns for the three hamburgers. Two of the six burners on the stove have two large kettles of water ready to boil for the corn when the time comes, and resting on the front four burners are pans with aluminum foil covering something very large. It could be the seasoned tri-tip. A small pan of chili is warming on the flat grill.

"I want ya to watch how we cook our hamburgers. Then we need the corn shucked." Billy is handling the pressure quite well under the circumstances. Karen and Helen are chopping lettuce and I can see that the energy level is getting intense. I guess they don't stop the restaurant business just because there's a barbeque.

Billy shows me how to prepare the platter for the hamburger and chiliburgers she is making. Some french fries are sizzling in the deep fryer that is behind the grill and next to the cold storage door. She makes a nice presentation with her food. The hamburgers are fat and juicy. The red onions and large slice of red tomato lying on a leaf of healthy green lettuce, looks colorful and appetizing. The french fries are crispy and seasoned. The chili poured over two of the hamburgers looks home-made. It is topped with grated cheddar and chopped red onions.

"Very nice Billy. That doesn't seem too hard to do. I think I can handle that quite well."

"Of course ya can! Just don't let this fool ya. There's usually a crown of thorns hanging above yur head." Billy points the spatula upwards above her head.

"A crown of thorns?" I ask.

Billy reaches up to touch the circular and rotating metal receipt holder for the orders from the waitresses. At this time she only has the one order, which she takes down and places under the platters next to the completed hamburgers. "Karen, order up!" she shouts. "You'll understand what a crown of thorns feels like when that thing up there is full." Billy gives me a very serious look from over her reading glasses.

By 3:00 things are percolating to a boil, and I don't mean just the kettles of corn. The kitchen area now has six bodies running around and into each other. Pots, pans, and bowls are either being used or sitting dirty over by the sink. There is Betty who is now back on duty, Billy, Helen, Karen, myself, and an older, gray-haired, sweet gal named Geneva, who popped in to make the fruit tray. We are all in constant motion, so I do not have time to get to know anyone beyond, "Excuse me. Sorry. Where's the dressing? Where do you want these? Oops! Excuse me." Billy has been cooking for the several restaurant customers in-between organizing for the barbeque.

At 3:30 we start putting tablecloths, salt and pepper shakers, and steak sauce on the tables outside. It's a beautiful afternoon. Some people have arrived early. Bubba is over by the smoking barbeque tending to the tri-tip. Ray is sitting on the redwood table next to Bubba having a cocktail of some sort. He smiles and waves to me as I pass by with loaded trays.

By event time we are in full swing. Billy has the juicy tri-tip sliced and ready to serve, which Helen carries out with Billy following. Billy will personally serve this to her friends and guests. The other gals will service the tables and clean up after the event. I have been told to start cleaning the kitchen, and to keep an eye on the remaining corn and beans on the stovetop. I am also to cook and serve any restaurant customers who wander in for something other than tri-tip. Vi, whom I had met when I first arrived at Hacienda, was manning the guests, groceries, and register. Billy had earlier apologized to me for the chaos of my first day, and was very glad I had come into her life at this time. She assured me that things would settle down, and to not let this scare me away. So I keep that thought in mind as I look at the unbelievable pile of dishes and large sticky vats and bowls that need to be cleaned. One of the large trays that held the cooked tri-tip is sitting by the stove with a few left over pieces screaming to be tasted. I am now hungry, so I eat one of the slices. It's so good! Wow! My taste buds plead for more. I also eat a chunk of french bread and a slice of watermelon.

I see as I am starting the dishes, that most of the customers can not eat the entire hamburger, so I wrap up some leftovers for the dogs when I return to my trailer. I scrub for two and a half hours. I can hear behind me the opening and closing of the back door as everyone comes in and out for various reasons. I had to cook one hot dog and one grilled cheese with fries. After all, I had been cooking most of my life anyway. I'm quite happy with my first stab at being a fast-fry cook.

Bubba enters the kitchen and goes to the cold storage and comes out with a twelve pack of Bud. He looks kind of looped. He leaves with a bang of the door.

When I have completed most of the dishes, and the crowd has left the premises, Billy tells me to take a break for a half hour or so, but she also wants me back to finish the kitchen duties for the night. It has already been twelve hours since I came to work. I can't believe I am not done yet! Everyone is allowed to take home whatever tri-tip is left, but to leave one uncut slab for tri-tip sandwiches to serve in the restaurant tomorrow. I walk back to the fifth wheel with my bag of leftovers.

Poor Bonita and Bandito, they are so confused! "Hi guys! I'm so sorry! Do you have to go potty? I've got a treat for you!" I had heard them barking a few times when I was hauling trays out to the tables. It wasn't real loud since they were inside with the door shut, but I'm sure all the noise and music was confusing for them. Thank God Hacienda doesn't have a barbeque every day.

I take them for a nice walk forgetting to put on long pants, shirt and socks. I get bit again on my ankles and on my lower arm. I feel my neck again and it is not any better. I put my tri-tip in the refrigerator, and slice up the hamburger for the dogs. I'll bet I never have to buy food for either of us all summer. Can I really do this all summer? I will certainly try. I should be able to save money. I don't have any expenses. I obviously get fed. If I can just stick this out then perhaps I will leave with a nice savings account and that could make it all worthwhile.

When I head back towards the kitchen, I pass the empty tables on the lawn. It is getting dark. That sheep dog is scrounging the ground for droppings of food. A short, stocky, male Indian with long hair is arguing with a plump female Indian on the dirt road between the barbeque and the rear entry to the kitchen. He is holding a six-pack of beer. She is screaming. "Who is she?! Ya dirty bastard! Who is she?!"

"Leave me alone ya dirty, ugly, bitch! I already told ya, It's no one!" He yells right back. They are both drunk. I must pass by this scene. It's unavoidable.

"Who are you? Are you the one?" She looks demonic as she addresses me.

"Excuse me? Are you talking to me?" I point to my chest, not sure if I am the accused.

"Are you the bitch he's been seeing?" She tromps angrily towards me.

"Excuse me? I never met this man before in my life. I'm new here. I'm the cook. I just started today." I'm a little nervous at this point. I keep walking toward the kitchen door. He starts walking away from her, weaving, almost falling. She turns from me and follows him, yelling at his back.

Oh no, drunk Indians! I find that extremely sad. I just finished reading a long book called Hanta Yo, meaning 'clear the way'. So this type of scene is fresh in my mind. It's a novel with a historical

45

story line about the history and beautiful spirituality of a small tribe of Lakota Sioux Indians. It is a love story that continues through three generations of a family and ends in the downfall of the American Indian through trade with the white man, most of the 'trade' being booze. Hanta Yo is also where I got my favorite mantra that I say to myself when I am stressed and need to center myself and thoughts. The one that begins with "I own my life and only mine."

Inside the kitchen I find Billy who is smoking a cigarette and having her evening cocktail. Ray is leaning on the meat counter with his own cocktail and cigarette. He is wearing his oxygen hose. They are chatting over the counter. "Well hello there pretty lady!" They both smile at me, so Ray's greeting is not a threat to Billy.

"Hello Ray. I guess we've not been formerly introduced yet." I reach to shake his hand. Ray gently squeezes my hand and does not release it right away. He holds it and tells me how happy he is to have me come to join the crew.

"By the way, I'll be by some time tomorrow to get yur water pipe fixed. May need some parts, so can't promise it'll be ready for a spell. I'll also get ya set up with some propane. Has anyone shown ya how to clean the grill?" he asks.

"Thanks very much, Ray. I'll look forward to having hot running water, and no, no one has shown me how to clean the grill yet." I look wearily at the warm slop pasted all over the flat grill.

"Okay, under the grated grill you'll find a big black pumice stone like brick. Now what I want ya to do is take that brick and hold it with both hands. Ya press it on the grill and grind away every bit of burnt grease and make it shiny like new. If ya can do this right ya got a job for life. Ya might need some of the fresh grease poured on while yur doin' this to make it a smoother ride across the grill. Then all the dirty grease runs down into this here trough and it flows into this hole and gets collected in a large grease trap below. Takes awhile, but has to be done every night."

Billy and Ray watch me do this task. The grill is still very warm so I have to keep my hands and fingers from touching it.

Exhaustion sets in and I just want to get in the fifth wheel.

"Okay, now the grease trap is right next to the grill. Reach down and pull that trap out and we got to empty that outside in the big barrel by the trash compactor. You'll see it when ya get out there." I pull the heavy dripping trap out and walk out the back door. I see the large, almost full to capacity, grease barrel. Yuck! There is a stick lying on top of the grease barrel to dig out the thick, black grease that won't come out of the trap. The goop in the bottom of the trap has the consistency of wet clay. It plops into the large barrel, making me think momentarily of an old outhouse. Grease splashes on my very dirty apron.

When I come back into the kitchen Ray tells me that he never saw anyone clean the grill as well as I did. Billy smiles and agrees. She also told me to come in at 11:30 tomorrow for more cook training. She'd meet me at the grill. She would also give me my schedule for the week at that time. She then shows me where the mop and chemicals were to mop the floor, gives me a hug, and tells me to get some rest after I finish. I was to lock the back door and exit out the front entry. Billy and Ray walk back to their own space.

By 9:30 I've turned out the kitchen lights and locked the back door. I go to clock out. I have worked for fourteen and a half hours. Outside it is pitch black. I can see giant flames lighting up the entire area by Bubba's trailer. I also can hear his much too loud country music. It isn't hard to see that Bubba believes in a fire as big as he is. It makes me wonder what the guests are thinking about the music and flames. I hope he keeps that fire under control!

I walk the dogs and then get out of my dirty cooking clothes. My wrists ache from all the chopping, lifting of dishes, and grill grinding. I will have time in the morning to relax, walk the dogs, and shower. I apply tea tree oil on all my old and new mosquito bites and fall fast asleep.

Chapter Four

The dogs wake me at sunrise when they hear someone walk by the trailer. I peek out the window next to my bed and see Bubba walking with coffee in hand to work. I have to be careful to remember that I cannot sit straight up in bed. This is the hitch end of the fifth wheel, and my bed is only two and a half feet from the ceiling. The ducks are quacking and headed along the shoreline running parallel with Bubba. I'm glad I'm awake early, so I can settle in a bit more before I go to work.

I take the dogs out for their quick and urgent need for relief, promising them a much longer walk later. On my way back into the trailer, I open up the valve to empty the holding tank one more time. As I do this, I look under my trailer at the dry pleated hose and see several small leaks puddle up the gravel beneath my trailer. I'll have Ray look at that when he comes to work on the pipes. I shut off the valve and get the hose to fill it up again.

While the tank is refilling, I drink my coffee outside on the picnic bench and let the dogs see the world from our surrounded fence area. The park looks quite full of RVs and a few people are wandering around fishing. A man straight across the lake is showing his small child how to cast his bobber into the water. I can hear them chatting softly about fishing. Sound travels in the quiet of the forest, except when cars or diesels pass on the highway. The back door to the kitchen bangs open.

"GET THAT DAMN BOBBER OUT OF MY LAKE! CAN'T YA READ? FLY FISHING ONLY!" Bubba stomps towards them raising the dust on the road. He spits to the side as he charges over to confront them. The man and child are frozen in place watching Bubba approach.

Bubba's voice echoes all across the area. Some guests come out of their trailers to see what is going on. Bubba reaches the frightened father and child. He grabs the fishing pole out of the child's hand and reels it in. "NO BOBBERS! IT SAID SO IN YUR FISHING RULES PACKET WE GAVE YA WHEN YA REGISTERED! I'M TIRED OF PULLING BOBBERS OUT OF THE WEEDS WHEN YA RULE BREAKERS LEAVE! FLY FISHING ONLY!"

I do not hear the man reply to Bubba. I only see him take his child by the hand and head back to his truck and trailer; both were parked twenty feet away from where they were fishing. I now notice the long pigtails coming out of the back of the baseball cap and realize it is a little girl. Bubba stalks off back to the kitchen. What a complete asshole! His lake? His Teflon pans? Bubba is just another employee. What the hell is his problem anyway? The little girl may never want to fish again for fear of making mistakes.

The man begins hooking his RV back onto his truck where the little girl sits waiting with her head looking down towards her feet in the passenger seat. She removes her baseball cap and throws it out the window of the truck. They leave within ten short minutes, driving a little too fast out of the park. If I had a nice nest egg sitting in a bank somewhere, and if I had half an ounce of sense, I'd be doing the same thing. I walk over to the empty space and pick up the cap which reads, 'Hacienda RV Park'. It has a trout embroidered above that. I throw it in the trash.

I take the dogs inside the fifth wheel just in time to find the toilet tank about to overflow. I run to turn off the hose, eat a bowl of instant oatmeal, gather my shampoo, tea tree oil, towel, a small amount of toilet paper (just in case) and clothes for the day. I decide to walk to the showers today. As I pass the kitchen, Bubba exits and seems surprised to see me. He is wearing a scowl on his face and one side of his cheek is puffed out. He spits out a stream of tar. Oh I get it. He chews tobacco!

"Good morning Bubba." You child abuser.

"MORNIN!"

I pursue a conversation. "That tri-tip was excellent!"

"I SERVE UP THE BEST IN THE COUNTY!" Gawd. It's his tri-tip too!

Running and quacking ducks heading in our direction disrupts any further conversation. This does not disappoint me in any way.

"GOTTA FEED MY DUCKS!" Of course they're his ducks. Who else could they belong too?

"Well, I'll see you later Bubba. I'm going to take a shower. Billy said to come in at 11:30 for training. So, have a nice day." Asshole.

Bubba is too involved with the ducks to say good-bye, but I am close enough to notice where Bubba is getting the feed. It's from a bag of dog food! These ducks have been raised on Billy's dog food! I suppose that's nutritious enough. The ducks look healthy anyway.

When I enter the showers, I hear two ladies conversing. They are washing their hands and complaining about the flies and mosquitoes. They agree to never come back to this park again and will talk to management about the lack of toilet paper. Thank goodness I brought my own. As I pass the toilet stalls I can see that one of the toilets is overflowing with poo and toilet paper, I gag in disgust.

The ladies have left and I am enjoying a good long hot shower. I am thankful that the showers are roomy and the water is hot. I dry my hair, which is now shorter than I've had it in years. It's so much easier than all those years when it was shoulder length. I guess we must all submit to the aging process at some point. I had cut it in Ashland when I was the head of housekeeping at a bed and breakfast inn. Too bad the owner was such a creep! I'll bet he misses me now. I was the only one who took pride in all the rooms. I had trained over twenty-five new maids who came and went. Most of them could not deal with the owner so they went off to greener pastures. I warned him I'd leave! He didn't believe me. Too bad Norman! You lose! If things go awry here I'll just pack up after I make enough money and split.

After drying my hair, I walk around to the front entry of the building. Vi is working the front register. There are several customers shopping and eating inside. Betty is zooming all around the place.

"Hi Vi."

"Good morning Denise. How was your first day?"

"It was very long, but I survived. Thanks for asking. Listen. Could you tell Billy that a toilet is overflowing in the restrooms, and that there is no toilet paper?"

"Oh Lord! Not again. Thanks. We'll have to send Bubba over there right away. Billy can watch the grill while he fixes that. Let's see, I don't know if Ruby is scheduled to come in today or not. Oh, I forgot, Little John is here today. He's up working on the motor of the pie cooler. He needs to get that fixed in the next hour, since Ginger is bringing in her week's supply of homemade pies. He can get on that new problem as soon as he finishes up with that. We'll take care of it. Thanks again. Oh, and Denise, I'm glad you're here to help Billy out with the cooking. She sure needs a break."

"Thanks Vi. I'll be in at 11:30. See you then." I sure like Vi. She seems educated, polite, and obviously takes pride in her job. She is also in her fifties. It makes me wonder why Helen, Karen, Betty, Vi, Geneva, Ginger, and myself have found ourselves working together in our later years at a remote RV park when we should be working in gardens and rocking grandbabies in our arms, or even finally fulfilling our life dreams, whatever that could be.

Walking back to my trailer, I realize that I had not heard the golf cart yet this morning. Maybe Terry is sleeping in. I see Ray leaning on the hood of his truck over by the propane tank drinking a cup of coffee. He is smoking and does not have his oxygen hose on.

"Good morning pretty lady," he says with a nice smile.

"Well, good morning to you too, Ray." Ray really does seem like a nice man. He's actually still quite handsome for his age. He's tall and well built, except for the beer belly. I can't tell if he is flirtatious or likes to be a father figure. I know I look slightly younger than I am, and most people are surprised when I tell them I am fifty-one. If I don't look in a mirror, I am not aware of my age either. I'm sure all the daily walks with Bonita and Bandito have helped to keep me fit, not to mention being a housekeeper for a year.

"So, can I come on over and take a look at yur pipes?" I don't know if he is making a sexual remark or not. Maybe it was just me thinking that.

"That would be great Ray. I need you to look at a couple of other things while you're there too." Oops! Was I really playing along?

"Let's get going then." Ray walks very slowly. I guess to conserve his oxygen, or his energy for looking at my 'pipes'. I can hear him taking deep breaths.

"Boy, what's with the front door?" Ray examines my duct tape job.

"Well, I had to tape it all together because pieces were falling off. I'm sorry it looks so ugly, but I did the best I could to make it work for now."

The dogs hear us and are barking inside.

"I'll have to measure that and order a new door for ya. I'll do that later. Let's see what's going on inside with the pipes." We work the door open.

"So these are yur little babies, huh?"

"Yes, they sure are. This black one is Bandito, and the brown one is Bonita."

"Welcome little guys! Ya could let them loose out here. They'd be fine. All the animals that live here are free to roam." I look towards the ducks.

"I don't think so, Ray. Not these guys. They'd kill a duck or chase the first coyote into the woods and I'd never see them again." I pat them on their heads.

"Little hunters, huh? Sounds like yur right on that one then. Okay, I think the problem is under here." Ray opens up the cabinet under the sink and gets on one knee to look inside.

"Yep! I see the problem. I'll need to get that valve at the hardware store. I might have time today. I have to take the garbage to Redding with Bubba around noon, so I can get it then." They take that beat up truck full of trash all the way to Redding?

"Great, Ray. That would be wonderful."

"Now, what else ya got to show me?" Gosh, why is all this sounding so dirty? Could it be the confined quarters we are in together or does Ray in fact have a sexual undertone that I am picking up on? It's probably just my repressed sexuality. Single at fifty-one can do that to you. "Oh, it's that pleated hose that comes out from the holding tank. It's old and cracked. It's also leaking in several spots."

We exit the trailer and Ray looks under to inspect the hose.

"Got one of those in the grocery area. Go in and ask Vi to get ya one. I'll help ya put the new one on. While you do that, I'll get ya a tank full of propane so you can cook inside. Can't use the water heater just yet until I fix that pipe." I leave to get the hose.

When I return from the main building, Ray is filling up my propane tank. He asks if I could carry it over to the trailer for him because he is running out of oxygen and can't quite find the strength. I can see as we walk back to the trailer that his breathing is getting strained.

He hooks up the propane and says he better get inside to his oxygen.

"Thanks Ray. I sure appreciate all your help." I give him a one-armed hug.

"No problem, pretty lady." Ray says, tapping my back. He walks slowly back to a side entry to his living area, which is over by the lawn.

Replacing the pleated hose was fairly simple. I always carry a few tools with me in the car. I'm pretty handy with tools. I've had to fix things for many years on my own. I take the cracked stinky hose over to the nearest trashcan and feel so much better about the progress on the trailer.

Inside I light the stove. It works! I can boil my water inside now. I can even heat water to wash in if I need to, which would be a good idea right now since I was handling that disgusting hose.

It is now 9:00AM. I am free for at least two more hours, so I decide to drive to the creek with the dogs and explore. While leashing up the dogs and putting them into the car, I notice an average height, extremely skinny man, exit the back kitchen door. He is carrying a toilet plunger and wearing a cowboy hat. He walks very fast and jerky, kind of like a person on speed. That man, I presume, is Little John. It's obvious that Billy and Ray do the best they can with what they've got. I knew I'd be appreciated somewhere in this world.

It's a warm beautiful June day. I am thankful for a few hours to myself. The dogs are alert and watchful sitting on top of the pile of blankets that I always have for them in the passenger seat. They are so small and love to look out at the passing world. We turn right at the exit of the park to explore more in that direction. I had only gone that way when I first saw and passed Hacienda and ended up at that motel where the man called Billy on the phone about the job.

Today is Saturday and there seems to be many vehicles on the road. Many of the turnouts have cars in them, probably fishermen. I chose a turnout about eight miles down the highway. There are enough parked cars and visible people to give me the security to hike further than I would if there were no cars or people, besides, I always carry pepper spray with me at all times when walking. Since I had adopted Bonita and Bandito from the shelter in Monterey nine years ago their social skills have always been lacking, to say the least. They bark and snarl at other approaching dogs, which makes the other dog, which might be loose, want to eat them! I haven't had to use the pepper spray yet, but have had some close encounters.

The creek is a beautiful, clear pale turquoise and running strong. We hike up the small pathway along the edge made from the many fishermen and hikers. All the trees are green and there is a cool breeze. The dogs are very happy exploring with me. I am happy to be in nature again.

We walk for about an hour and a half, and then head on back to Hacienda. The dogs will be tired and will relax better inside the fifth wheel while I am working. I will have had my dose of nature to get me through the day.

By the time I feed the dogs, and have some lunch, it is 11:15. I turn on the small fan inside the trailer, open the windows, and shut the door. Outside, I see and hear the large dump truck coughing its way to the rear of the kitchen. Ray is waiting there with his oxygen tank in hand. Bubba is driving. Ray climbs inside with Bubba and they drive past me. The stench is horrible! They leave a trail of drippy goop behind them. I pity the cars that will be behind them on the highway.

Billy is at the counter when I clock in. She says she'll meet me at the grill in a little while. I was to clean up from breakfast, chop tomatoes and red onion, peel potatoes for mashed potatoes and get them boiling, and think about a soup we could make for the day. She would show me how we put together a tri-tip sandwich for $5.95, which is today's special. Betty would help me with any questions I had, and Karen was coming on shift at 12:00. I was to train today to cook for lunch and dinner. Lunch and dinner! It never occurred to me until now that I'd be cooking both meals.

Betty is wiping off the special board out on one of the redwood tables. She starts to hang it back up with nothing written on it.

"Good morning Betty, or should I say afternoon yet? It's not quite noon, but hello anyway."

"Hello Denise! Are you ready to cook?" Betty moves so fast, she makes my head spin!

"As ready as I'll ever be. Are you going to write the day's special on that?"

"Oh, I never write anything on here. Bubba usually does this, but he was in a hurry to get out."

"Well, Billy tells me that today's special is a tri-tip sandwich. Don't you think we should write that on the board?"

"I won't, but you can if you want." Betty seems slightly frightened at the thought of doing this small project. Is that also Bubba's, and only Bubba's, special board?

"Here I'll do it." I take the large board from Betty's hands. I can't start harboring a bunch of fears on this job.

"Okay Denise, if you want. I need to finish with the ketchup bottles and dishes." Betty nervously looks around for Bubba.

I get the colored chalks I had seen by the counter and write the special with flowing letters and floral designs in the corner. It's time to get out of the road kill specials now that I am the cook. I hang the sign back up above the kitchen and walk back to the grill area.

The grill, the floor beneath the grill, the cutting boards, and every square inch of the cooking area is a mess! Globs of hash browns are stuck everywhere! The oil drip catcher pan is overflowing onto the floor. Fuck!

I start with the overflowing drip pan and am still cleaning Bubba's mess when Betty taps my shoulder and says that she has an order for two hamburgers. "Denise, I can cook these if you want. I've been here for six years and cook for Billy in a pinch when needed."

"Great Betty! That would be great! I need to get a handle on this mess. I can't cook in a dirty kitchen."

"I understand." Betty zooms over to the meat counter and grabs two fistfuls of meat and starts the hamburgers.

By 12:45 Billy enters the kitchen. I have begun to peel the potatoes and have water boiling for them. I had let Betty cook the few orders that came in so I could catch up on all I was told to do.

Billy jumps right in.

"Okay, let's get to training! Oh, and Betty, Karen had an emergency with one of her grandchildren, so she can't make it in until around 5:00. Ya could leave now. Denise and I will handle everything just fine until she gets here." How nice that Karen has grandchildren. I have not had that honor yet from my sons.

Betty has an order that she places on the crown of thorns. "This is an order for two tri-tip sandwiches."

"How'd they know we had 'em?" Billy asks.

"They read the special board. Denise wrote it on there." Billy smiles at me in a funny way.

"Good! Well, lets make a tri-tip sandwich then! The kitchen looks really clean. Good job! Have ya thought about a soup?"

"Actually I have, Billy. How about we make corn chowder from all the left over corn on the cob?"

"Excellent! Let me show ya how we make a tri-tip sandwich,

ya can serve it to the customers. I'm sure ya can wait tables? And then ya can scrape the cobs while I get the rest of the ingredients for the soup. We need to mash those potatoes as soon as they get cooked. We also need to bake some potatoes for dinner."

This is beginning to be fun. I've always enjoyed cooking and it's a career challenge I've yet to have. I like Billy and her gruff rancher ways. I know that she appreciates me. It is obvious that Billy and Ray are not in the best of health, especially Ray. It is also obvious that they respect the fact that someone with work ethics has come to them at a much-needed time. I give my best when I am needed and appreciated. What I've seen up to this point is an extreme lack of management. If Bubba is considered the manager in any way, shape, or form, they are in big trouble.

Karen comes on duty an hour early. I do not have much time to get to know her. She isn't a bad looking woman, but she has a pinched, angry mouth and she acts like she wants to go home the minute she gets here. The only time she smiles is when she serves the tables, and that is only to get the tips, which could make it better for me at the end of the day. So keep on smiling Karen or we won't get anything!

The soup gets made. I write corn chowder on the special board. The potatoes get mashed and baked. I learn how to use the meat slicer for the roast beef and turkey. I learn how Billy likes each dish prepared and displayed on the platter. There is a full menu from French dips, chicken fried steak, fresh fish, steaks, shrimp, artichokes, salads (three kinds), hot dogs, chili, Rueben's, ham, soup, gravies, sandwiches, and barbequed beef. Then for desserts, we offer fresh homemade pies from chocolate and banana cream, to apple, berry, and pumpkin which Ginger brings in at around 5:30. All made fresh today. It is a very busy restaurant and I had no idea that Billy took such great pride in what she had achieved all these years. The community depends on her for a good hearty meal, and travelers are pleased with the quality, especially for being out in the middle of nowhere.

We sell beer, sodas, ice cream, malts, milk, eggs, bread, bacon, coleslaw, fruit, RV supplies, propane, and worms for fishing. I see the many ways that I can be beneficial to Billy. I see my space and because she is so sincere, I plan to do the best job I can.

There is a small time gap in our busy evening for me to let the dogs out and feed them. Billy also lets me have a quick bite to eat off the menu.

At around 7:15 the back door opens and Bubba enters quite jovial and talkative to Billy. He seems a little more pleasant this evening. Ray follows him in and looks very tired and his breathing is strained. He does not say much and heads into his home area. Bubba tells Billy stories about their adventure with the dump truck. He walks over to talk to a customer he knows who is eating. On his way back to the kitchen he stops abruptly and looks up at the special board. His smile leaves his face. My heart sinks and I feel slightly intimidated by his reaction. I am also confused as to why that damn board could make him so pissed off! I am not going to have road kill written on there on my shift! He walks into the cold storage and grabs himself a twelve pack of beer and leaves without acknowledging my presence.

By 7:45 Karen is finishing up all the dishes and preparing the tables for morning. I am scrubbing the grill. Billy is smoking and having a drink talking to a friend by the meat counter. She comes into the kitchen and thanks me for all my hard work. I will be having Sundays and Mondays off since that is her slowest time in the restaurant. Yahoo! That's tomorrow!

"Billy? Could you do me a favor and look at this bite on my neck? It hurts like hell!" I bow my head and lift the small amount of hair to show her my bump. "Gawd! That there is one nasty bite! Let me go get ya some Campho-Phenique. Looks a bit infected. Better keep yur eye on that one." She returns with the ointment and invites me to have a drink at her place after I finish up the kitchen. She'd like to get to know me better and show me her place. I decline, but would love to do that at another time. I'm pretty pooped!

By 8:30, Karen and I have finished cleaning the kitchen and mopping the floors. She divides the tips up three ways, to include Billy, and hands me $75.00. I am very happy that I will be making some money.

I lock the kitchen door and clock out. As I walk through the front entry I notice again the overflowing trashcan and all the cigarette butts on the front porch. If I have time, I'll clean that up tomorrow. First impressions are the most important for the guests. That is so negative looking!

I see Bubba's flaming fire pit down the road. I just don't understand that! It's not even cold out. I can see his dark silhouette standing next to the flames that are three times his size. The shadows of the tall pine trees dance in the dark perimeter surrounding his area. I walk nearer to my fifth wheel and in the safety of darkness. What could he be thinking as he stares into his explosive flames? Is it thoughts of being a better man? Is it shame for ruining a father-daughter day of fishing? No, I doubt that is the case. I stay in hiding and watch this bully of a man who has awakened the wounds of my child within. He tilts his head back and finishes the last of his beer. His dark, heavy outline becomes the silhouette of my father, and I am suddenly seeing through the young innocent eyes of a different sort of spirit who stayed in the shadows and wondered if all men were angry.

CHAPTER FIVE

My aching wrists and itching mosquito bites wake me before Bubba and the quacking ducks. The dogs are sleeping in for the first time in quite awhile. I make my coffee and heat up a kettle of water to do the few dishes I have needed to clean. It's nice to be able to make my coffee inside. It gives me time to be alert and ready for any unforeseen obstacle that may await me once I open the door and step outside the fifth wheel. I am so happy I have two days off! I can get my bearings on my new lifestyle and finish cleaning and organizing the fifth wheel.

After setting up my boom box to listen to some music, the dogs are awake and ready to go outside. I walk them a short distance and then put them in the fenced area. It looks like another nice warm day. Inside, I turn on the air conditioner and it works! I turn it off and open the filter vent. The filter is clogged with dirt and nicotine, so I wash it in hot soapy water. Now the dogs will be cooler inside when I'm working. I'm sure it's going to get hot this summer.

Outside, the quacking and barking start up, and breaks the silence of morning. I look to see the ducks passing by. They are not as concerned about my dogs as much as my dogs are concerned about them. As I am quieting them, Bubba rounds the bend of the road walking towards us. He is drinking his coffee. I have no idea what to expect from him, so I wait to let him speak first.

"SO, WHO ARE THESE GUYS?"

"Good morning Bubba. This black one is Bandito, and the brown one is Bonita." Bonita loves everyone. She wags her tail a hundred miles an hour, and wants to lick anyone within reach. It's dogs she hates. Bandito could care less about other people. He sits and observes. Bonita loves up to Bubba.

As Bubba is petting Bonita, the sheep-herding dog walks up to the fence and Bubba. My dogs go off barking again.

"WELL HELLO, HARLEY!" Bubba pets the dog's head.

"Oh, his name is Harley. I was wondering about that dog. Does it belong to Billy and Ray?" I am trying to calm my dogs down. It is way too early for this ruckus!

"YEH, HARLEY'S A GOOD OLE BOY. WOULDN'T HURT A FLEA."

"So, are you on your way to work?"

"YEP!" Bubba takes a slug of his coffee.

"I'm thinking of coming in for breakfast, so maybe I'll see you later." I'm trying to find his soft spot somewhere in all that testosterone. I smile.

"THAT'D BE FINE." Bubba takes a final slug of coffee and shakes out the last remaining drops on the ground. I notice the brown stains inside of his coffee cup and cringe.

Harley walks over to the lake, jumps in, and walks chest high around in the water drinking. A group of honking mud hens clear away from the area that Harley has invaded. Bonita and Bandito are watching his every move in envy.

With the dogs back in the trailer, I go to take a shower walking past the rising RV guests. An elderly couple that recognizes me from their dinner last night greets me. "Good morning! Great dinner last night!

"Well, thank you! I'm new here so I need all the encouragement I can get. Did you enjoy your stay?" It appears that they are packed up and ready to leave.

"Sure did, but it would have been better if the trashcans were emptied. Makes a terrible fly problem," says the elderly man.

"Sorry about that. I'll speak to the owner. You have a nice day."

"You too." We all wave goodbye at each other.

As I continue to the showers, I notice all the trashcans are full to the brim. Some are even knocked over with trash sprayed about as if an animal had raided it. I don't understand why Billy wouldn't hire someone else to do that job. Bubba surely has too many things to be responsible for. How could he possibly do a good job on everything? Maybe I'm getting too concerned about details again, but I can't help myself, this is what I do. This is also why I kept the inn in Ashland so well maintained, because I care about details and appearances in homes and businesses. I care about the comfort of the guests. I'd like to have blinders on sometimes, but when you have been trained since birth to keep the trash empty and wash every dish as you cook or eat, and make your bed as soon as you step out of it, then it isn't easy to make a chiseled in stone habit disappear from your mind. My ex-husband thought I was the best thing to come along since slaves were chic. "Cinderelli, Cinderelli...La La La La La La La...," I sing as I walk to the showers, forgetting the lyrics to the Disney tune that I have always identified with, but conceding to the fact that my Prince never did show up, and that fairy tales were written by men.

After my shower I take the dogs for a walk around the park. I see Terry watering an area empty of any guests. I wave. She does not wave back. I put the dogs back in the fifth wheel and walk to the restaurant.

By now the restaurant is in full swing. Many of the guests have their trailers ready to take off and are having a full meal for the trip. I can see why I have Sunday and Monday off. The place will be relatively empty.

Bubba's special: DEEP FRIED RATTLESNAKE NUGGETS. I shouldn't let that get to me so much. It's just so annoying!

Helen is the waitress this morning. She is wearing white pants, red shirt with a flag pin, American flag tennis shoes, and her fingernails are still flags. Good heavens! What does she wear for the Fourth of July?

"Good morning Denise. Did ya come in for some breakfast?" Helen asks.

"Sure did, and I'm really hungry! I think I'll have bacon and eggs over easy with a side of sourdough toast. Oh, and make my hash browns extra crispy."

Helen has a hard time writing with those fingernails. I just can't get over the fact that she dresses this way at her age! "Okay. Sit tight. We're kind of busy, so it might be a few minutes."

"I'll be fine. Thanks."

Ray walks over to join me at my table. He wants to measure my door. He and Little John will be over later to do that and fix my pipe. They will also get my water heater lit. Ray is a very sweet worn out man. I can't help but like him, and worry about his health. Even so, it is not my business to ask him why he smokes when he needs oxygen. We are all hostages to ourselves!

My breakfast arrives and I inhale it. After paying for my meal, I walk outside. Terry is watering the front flowers. Most of them are newly planted small stubs of future flowers, not really flowers yet. I am able to get a better look at her. She is very tan! Too tan. She has a few tattoos on her strong looking legs and is wearing some beat up flip-flops. Her shoulder length dark blonde hair is healthy looking and her face is nice enough, but she has an overall bloated look of too much beer. When I say hello, she nods her head in acknowledgement. At least I got that much out of her!

A car pulls up and Ruby jumps out with a beer in her hand.

"Denise, hi!" Ruby says with a big smile.

"Hi Ruby." I once again think about the twenty bucks she owes me that I need to forget about.

"My dog is fine now. Billy saved her life. $500 for the anti-venom! Her muzzle is still the size of a basketball, but the vet says it will go down in a week or two." Ruby sucks down some beer with her head way back.

"Gosh, how wonderful of Billy to care like that! I'm very happy for you. Are you workin' today?"

"Yeah, gotta clean the restrooms. I owe Billy big time! How's the job comin'?"

"Just fine. This place is busier than I ever imagined!"

"No kiddin'. They sure do go through the toilet paper, that's for sure. Well, better get goin'. Let's get together later, okay?"

"Sure Ruby. You know where to find me."

Ruby finishes her beer and throws it in the overflowing trashcan. It balances for a second and falls off the pile.

I return to my trailer and get a trash bag. I walk back to the front of the building and empty the tall ashtray on top of the trash, stuff all the trash into the can, pull out the current trash liner, tie it up, and re-line the trash container with the bag I had brought. I feel better now.

"That's my job!" Terry has dropped the hose and is walking briskly in my direction. Her flip-flops are slapping at her feet as she tromps to face me.

"I'm sorry Terry. I just thought I'd help out. I had no idea it was anyone's job in particular. It just looked so bad. I thought I'd clean it up." Didn't someone tell me that Terry didn't really work here?

"Well, don't do that, it's my job!" Her hose was flooding where she had dropped it and mud was flowing into the parking lot.

"Sorry." Screw you.

I carry the trash to the back where the trash compactor is, where the smell is, where the full flytrap is, where the old cooking oil drum is. There's no doubt that this place has its few good points and its many bad points. I'm going to do what I can, when I can, while I'm here for Billy and Ray. Maybe no one here has ever heard of teamwork? Maybe they never met a team player? Maybe they're dangerous? I wonder what they think of me anyway. I don't believe I am doing anyone harm. Hopefully, Terry, Bubba, and Karen will eventually get the idea that I can make their jobs a little easier, maybe not. Who the hell cares anyway? Today's my day off.

I have a large load of laundry to do. I take the dogs with me in the car and drive over to the laundry room, located next to the shower building. We can take a walk during the wash cycle. Ruby and Brenda must be inside cleaning the showers and toilets since the supply room door is open and mops, cleaning solutions, cigarettes, ash tray, and open beer are once again on the table and scattered about. Hopefully all the trash cans get emptied after Bubba finishes in the kitchen. It would seem more efficient to keep up with the restrooms and trash while we have guests, instead of after they leave. At least they could appreciate the fact that we do keep things clean for them.

I'm really amazed at the amount of waste produced by travelers—paper plates, plastic forks, knives, spoons, cans, bottles, cups, charcoal bags, paper towels, uneaten food, broken toys, broken barbeque grills, and lots of broken RV parts that have been replaced or fixed while they were here.

Two of the three washing machines are being used. All I have is this one large load, so that's perfect. With the laundry started, I get the dogs out of the car to take a walk. The park is nearly empty of guests. I had noticed on earlier walks that there were a few trailers that seemed like they were just parked here, as if some guests leave a trailer here year round for future visits. Billy had told me that there are four guests that stay for the entire summer. That is probably who is using the other two washing machines.

We walk the dirt road for a while. Several of the cable wires coming from some spaces are pulled out and lying on the ground. I think they have been having trouble with the cable company. I had overheard a customer complaining about that yesterday. Obviously some of the guests don't bother with the cable since they are set up with satellite dishes.

Looking toward the forest, I am once again curious about what is back in there. I have my pepper spray with me, so I decide to venture down the path to see. It is so quiet today. Logging trucks must rest on Sundays from their pillaging, chopping, and hauling. I feel relief for the disappearing forests. It gets even more silent as we enter the area of thick pine trees. Bandito starts to get excited at the sight of all the junk ahead, he's a true junkyard junkie. I get a strange feeling in my gut as we walk along the dirt road of broken down and rusted vehicles, trucks, strange machines, broken farm equipment, trash, pans of old motor oil, a pile of barbed wire, motor home parts, a gutted motor home, another motor home that looks like it is stored back here, locked up, and possibly usable, pipes, fencing, an old flatbed truck full of trash bags, propane tanks, logs, hoses, sewer tanks, and various large unidentifiable rusted metal parts. I am horrified! The dogs are in heaven! Could this possibly be the 'Twilight Zone?' I see large paw prints by the dump truck full of trash and realize that these could be coyote or even possibly mountain lion, since some are so huge! I panic slightly, looking around me for signs of wildlife and prepare the pepper spray in my hand. The dogs smell the paw prints and Bandito starts to growl. Bonita is standing erect with her large pointy ears in the air. Her eyes are wide, her tail is sticking straight up and quivering, and she is sniffing the air. These animals are very near!

"Come on guys. Let's get going. Come on. Let's go now." I do not run. I know better than that, but I do take the shortest distance between this area and the road encircling the park, which is through the trees. I do not see anything on my way, but feel slightly light headed from the adrenalin rush. Back on the dirt road, the dogs look back toward the forest and pull on their leashes as if they would like to be let loose and set free to hunt for the target of the scent.

"Sorry guys. You don't get it, do you? Those are not lizards!"

They keep pulling in the opposite direction of my destination, which is the laundry room. I put them in the car with the windows open part way. They are still looking in the direction of the forest as I go to dry my laundry.

With clothes in dryer, I go to the restroom for a much needed pee that I came close to losing over by the junk pile. While in my stall, I hear Ruby and Brenda come in. They do not know I am in here and are in a conversation.

"He's just a fucking speed freak! Billy wants him out of here as soon as possible. He owes them over three thousand dollars! She said she was goin' to suggest to him that he just leave debt free, in trade for his motor home that he has stored in back. He's such a creep! Can't stand to look at him and his rotten teeth! Him and Bubba got in a fight last week. That's why he has the shiner. Bubba doesn't want him livin' in the trailer next to him anymore. He's supposed to be fixin' things around here, but he ain't worth shit!" It was Brenda talking.

I presume they are talking about Little John who was coming

over with Ray to fix the pipe. I flush the toilet and they become silent realizing that someone is in the restroom.

"Hi ladies! How's your day coming?" I say as I walk out of my stall.

"Denise! Hi! We didn't realize anyone was in here. How are you?" It was Ruby that spoke up. She is drinking a beer.

"Well, I'm fine now. I was walking the dogs and I think there were some coyotes or something out in the forest. Scared the holy pajesus out of me!" I wash my hands.

"Gotta be careful here. It's not a good idea to wander out too far without someone else with ya. We're havin' quite a problem this year with them coyotes and lions." Brenda responds.

"And them damn rattle snakes! Ya don't want them little babies to get bit like my dog. I don't think they'd survive!" Ruby adds.

"I'll be more careful now that I've had a good scare! I better go get my laundry, so I'll catch up with you later. Have a good day. Don't work too hard. Today's my day off, so I plan on getting things done. Bye."

"Bye, Denise." Ruby says as she begins spraying a mirror with Windex.

I stand in the laundry room gazing out the doorway at the forest while my laundry gets dry. The dogs in the car are still gazing in that direction too. I hear the golf cart over on the other side of the lake and look to see Bubba and Terry with trash in the back talking to Ray and Little John, who are near the fifth wheel. Breakfast must be over with. I suppose Billy is cooking lunch and dinner. Bubba's voice rises in some angry words I don't understand, but get the jest of. Little John responds in like manner. Ray speaks up to control the situation and Bubba drives off recklessly toward another trashcan. Ray and Little John walk to my trailer.

I throw the dry laundry into the car to fold later. They are at the trailer measuring the door when I get there.

"Hello pretty lady!" Ray greets me.

"Hello Ray. Sorry, I was doing laundry."

"No problem. I saw your car over there anyway. Figured ya be here soon. I think we got the measurements, so if ya don't mind; we'll just go inside to fix the pipe. It could take some time to get the door replaced. Don't know who makes this style anymore, or if they make it at all. We'll just have to wait and see. Sure do need to turn these steps around! How'd they get like this anyway? Is that hose working to the holding tank?"

"Works great Ray. Thanks!"

Ray does not introduce me to Little John. He is definitely skinny, and his teeth are certainly rotten. He has a black eye and a cut on his mouth. From the looks of him, he had no chance in hell against Bubba. He is jittery and obviously on some sort of speed. I leave the dogs in the car while they are working on the pipe, but go inside to watch. Little John is quite handy in that tiny space and fixes the leak in no time at all. They go outside to hook up the water to the trailer and light the water heater. I can hear it flaming up. Yahoo! My own shower! Ray has Little John fill up my second propane tank and hook it up.

"Now yur set, young lady! Ya let us know if ya have any problems with anything and we'll get ya fixed."

"Thank you so very much, Ray!" I give him a little hug. He seems to enjoy my gratitude and gives me a pat on the back. Ray is huffing for air at this point and I can see he needs to get going.

I feed the dogs some of the restaurant leftovers. I hope they don't get fat! It won't be that simple to boil the chicken and brown rice that I have fed them for all their lives. Maybe I just need to add some brown rice to some of this food.

Lori must be wondering what's going on. I need to call her. I should also call my parents and sons. I'll need a new calling card when I go to Brandon to get supplies. Where's my list? Yogurt, soy milk, eggs, juice, bananas, bread, coffee, brown rice, gin, frozen limeade, apron, duck feed, Lysol, calling card. I think there is enough time left to talk to Lori for now.

"You guys be good for a few minutes. I'm going to call Lori. I'll be right back. Maybe we'll go for a drive when I get back." I always forget I shouldn't tell Bonita these things. She understands too well, and goes off barking at me. "NOW! NOW! NOW! NOW! NOW! NOW!" Bandito looks at me from his bowed head.

"Quit hollering at me Bonita! I said in a few minutes. I'll be right back!"

Lori is not home, but I leave a message that I will call tomorrow. As I walk back to my trailer, I hear the commotion of many engines coming from several directions. Ray is approaching from the forest driving a tractor. He is wearing his oxygen and looks very proud of his tractor, like a little boy. He also has a cigarette hanging out of his mouth. Bubba has the dump truck and is driving to the rear of the kitchen. Terry is coming with more trash in the golf cart. When they all reach the back entry, Bubba gets out of the dump truck and starts up the trash compactor.

From the protection of my trailer, I watch the system they have together for the trash. Terry hands Bubba the trash. Bubba crushes it, and then throws the compacted goop into the front lift of the tractor. After the lift is full, Ray dumps it into the fragile dump truck. Bubba and Terry take a drink of their beer, while Ray dumps, and then the system repeats itself. The last time I saw this trash process, Bubba did not have the convenience of the tractor, because Ray and Billy were in Redding. Isn't there a local trash company? I close my windows. The breeze is coming straight in my direction, and it stinks! Good time for a drive. Maybe I'll go shopping now.

My pile of dry laundry is still in the back seat of my car, but due to the stink, I choose to bring it in after I go shopping. I bring the dogs with me. I won't be spending too much time in the store. It's not that hot, so I can leave them in the shade with windows partially open with a bowl of water. Anyway, they love to go for drives with me. I think I'll get an iced coffee drink for my ride home when I finish shopping. Lori and I would always get ourselves an iced coffee when we went shopping together in Ashland. I miss her.

Brandon is quiet today. I see full parking lots at two churches. The sky is getting kind of cloudy. I wonder if it is going to rain at some point. I pass a feed store and make a mental note to pick up duck feed. It is on the opposite side of the road, so I will go there after I shop. I head first to Safeway. I notice a small thrift store a block before I reach Safeway. My car automatically turns into such places. I just love thrift stores! Bandito is not the only junkyard junkie in this family. I have found some wonderful treasures through the years at thrift stores. Most of those treasures were sold at my garage sale when I left Carmel Valley. Even at garage sale prices I ended up doubling my money. It's easy to part with something that only cost five dollars or under. I go in and find an apron for work. It's handmade, and has ducks on it. This will be so much better than the beat-up, stained, blue ones they have at Hacienda. Geneva and Betty have their own aprons, so will I.

A shade tree on the far end of Safeway's parking lot is perfect for the dogs. I do my shopping in no time at all; sticking to my list, then head to the feed store for the duck seed. I sip on my iced café mocha as I leave Brandon and head back to the trailer. I can't seem to find it in me to call that fifth wheel trailer "home". I know it's just a temporary shelter.

I fight off a feeling of home sickness, not just for Carmel Valley, Ashland, or Lancaster where my parents live, because I really have no home. I miss family support. I miss family noise, laughter, and congregating in the kitchen being silly, or discussing each others current state of affairs, aches and pains, joys, and updates on nieces, nephews, and grandchildren. I miss hugging my big handsome sons and reveling in pride at how well they are handling their own life journey. I miss my mother. Her entire life has been only for us five children. She always wants to know our every move in life. She is sweet, tiny, and gentle. My father is another story all together. It's difficult to miss him. He's really a bulldog in a jumpsuit. Being a retired test pilot and Major in the Marines, he has tendencies toward a gruff and self focused attitude. Making his moves and decisions at the speed of the A-4 Skyhawk he flew. I love him in a fearful way. He and I seem to knock heads a lot. Dad has always been a heavy drinker. I feel the pangs of tears welling in my eyes. Everyone is so far away. Perhaps it's me that's far away.

While driving the last few blocks of Brandon, I see a big sale going on in the parking lot of Rite Aid. They have canopies set up and on sale for $29.99. I need one of those! I need it over the picnic bench to shade the dogs and myself. That would be perfect. My own patio! I buy one, sacrificing more of my depleted funds.

As I round the last bend before Hacienda, I realize it's still kind of cloudy, but there's no sign of rain yet. I see that it is 2:30PM; I still have lots of time left in my day. I think I'll unload the groceries, fold laundry, take another short walk with the dogs, and then just relax the rest of the day.

Back at Hacienda, things have quieted down. The stench is out of the air. Bubba and Terry are nowhere to be seen. I don't see anyone really, except ol' Harley. Perfect! I unload my goodies and laundry, walk the dogs, and then put them in the fenced area for a while. It is still not raining yet, and the temperature is wonderful! As I stand there watching the mud hens, a mosquito bites my ankle. Damn it anyway! I should have bought some insect repellant, even though I don't believe in putting chemicals on my body, perhaps this would be the time to drop that rule. I go inside to apply tea tree oil on the mounting itchy spots on my legs, arms and neck.

Tea tree oil has a very unique aroma. I am so used to the smell, but when someone else smells it, they are not quite sure what it is that they smell. It's tart and intense. I don't really care right now. I just need relief! Tea tree oil gives me relief. I put on socks, shoes, long comfortable pants, and long sleeved cotton shirt. I hate shoes! I'd much rather be in my sandals any day.

The iced coffee drink gave me enough of a buzz to want to go for another walk. I am dressed to avoid the mosquitoes, so I might as well get out for the last walk today. I get my pepper spray and put it in my pocket. This time, I take the dogs over on the other side of the lake. There are four new RVs parked in spaces but the majority of them are empty. Some kids are riding their bikes around the park. I decide to let the dogs dig for a while. They love that! We end up just off the dirt road about twenty to thirty yards, between the forest and the road. I am edgy about the coyotes, so I keep an open eye for any signs of them. Bonita and Bandito have chosen a fallen dead pine tree to walk on and dig under. They dig like little gophers. To my surprise, Bandito comes out of his current hole and has a mouse that he shakes and kills. I'm not real happy about this, but have submitted to the fact that this is what happens sometimes. He's very proud, and looks at me to see if I am watching. Bonita comes over to check it out, and then dives into the hole that Bandito had found the mouse in. She comes out with another mouse, and kills it. "Okay! That's enough! You two just better hope that you don't become part of the food chain yourselves!"

We walk back onto the road and round the park. Ray is sitting at a picnic table at the bend where the water pipe comes into the lake. He is sitting with a heavyset man by a trailer. They are having a cocktail together. The trailer is one of the more permanent looking ones.

"Well, good evening, pretty lady!"

"Hi Ray."

A dog that is chained up by the men jumps up from his spot under the table and lunges toward us. Thank God he is chained up! My dogs do likewise, and the chaos of barking ensues.

"Come on over and have a drink with us!" Ray yells out to me.

"I don't think that would work out right now, maybe next time. I better get these guys back to the trailer before they hurt your dog." They both laugh at that.

We pass Bubba's trailer. The golf cart is parked out in front. I hear a TV set inside. The kitties are over near a bush, so I walk the dogs on the furthest side of the road to make sure they do not see them. There is a truck parked to the side of the trailer next to Bubba's. That must be where Little John lives. Music is coming from inside the trailer. Everyone seems to be relaxing today.

At my own space again, I open a can of organic split pea soup and have an early dinner. By 5:30 I am having one of my favorite drinks, gin and limeade. I stay inside and fuss around with nesting details in the trailer while listening to my Native American Indian music and burn some sage to help purify the negative energy of the previous occupant. The gin is helping to take the edge off. I think about the power of music as the soothing sound of a flute vibrates the surrounding walls of my mind. It takes me to a place of silence and peacefulness I can seldom possess. I often want to remain in that place that music takes me to, but like a light switch, it evaporates in human routine and responsibility.

A few hours later, I turn the cassette to side B and take my first shower in the trailer. The space is claustrophobic, but the water is hot. I feel even better after the shower. I am soaking my feet and ankles in a bucket of warm water and Epsom salts at the dining area when I hear a knocking on the side of the trailer. It's Bubba! He's carrying a twelve pack and looks like he might be drunk!

"Bubba! What's going on?" I say as I open the door.

"YA NEED A FIRE PIT!" Sounds more like, "YANEEAFURPIT."

"A fire pit? Yeah, that would be nice." The Native American Indian music reaches the end of the cassette, clicks off, and vanishes.

"ALLBILLYAONEMORROW," when he really means, I'll build ya one tomorrow.

"Really? I'd love that!" What in the hell is he doing here? Where's his crazy ass girlfriend?

"WHERE YA FROM ANYWAY?"

"Me? You mean originally?"

"YEAH, ORIGINALLY." The word 'originally' is really difficult to understand.

"Well, I was born in Dodge City, Kansas, and my family is mostly German."

Bubba's out-of-focus eyes try to look me up and down. "I'M PORCACHEZ!"

I laugh, or should I say, I giggle. "Pork and cheese?" I say this because this is what I heard him say, and I can only believe that he is making some sort of a joke.

"NO! WHAT A YA TALKING 'BOUT! I SAID PORCACHEZ!"

"Bubba, I'm sorry, I don't understand. Pork and cheese? What is pork and cheese?" I start to laugh again. It isn't consciously. It's just that I don't get what he is saying, and he's drunk, and It's all coming out distorted in this stupid conversation!

"POR-CA-CHEZ!" he says as his hand grabs hold of my fragile door for support.

Suddenly, I get it. "Oh, Portuguese!" I say as I look near the stove for a knife, and wonder if I really had it in me to stab his hand if I needed to.

"YEAH DAMN IT! PORCACHEZ!"

"Sorry Bubba. I didn't mean to be rude, but it just sounded like pork and cheese." He's getting that look. The same look I remember from my younger days. That look that men get when they're horny, kind of a cross-eyed thing. Oh my gawd, he's interested in me!

"Well, Bubba, I sure do appreciate you dropping by. I need to get inside now. You know those damn mosquitoes and all. Have a good evening now."

"YOU TOO! I'LL BE BY TOMORROW AND BUILD YA A FIRE PIT. I'LL TURN THESE HERE STEPS IN THE RIGHT DIRECTION TOO!" he shakes the steel stairway checking its weight, looking something like an angry gorilla.

"Great, Bubba. Good night now." I say as I close the broken door leaving Bubba standing there. For heavens sake! Oh no! This is going to get weird! Terry would kill me for sure if she knew he was interested in me. At the same time, it is nice to be flirted with when you're fifty-one. Maybe I still have it in me. Good gawd, shut up! If I can't get someone other than a stupid jackass like Bubba attracted to me, then let me die an old spinster.

I pull the bungee cord as tight as possible, and hook it on the stove handle. I turn off the lights and crawl into bed, Bonita and Bandito following my lead. Before my head even hits the pillow, I jump back up out of the covers, climb down to find my pepper spray, check the bungee cord one more time, climb back into bed putting the pepper spray under my pillow.

I lie in the darkness of the fifth wheel waiting to hear one of the two drunk idiots creeping around outside my door. One to rape me and one to kill me, yet all I hear is the onset of a gentle rain shower.

CHAPTER SIX

I wake from a nightmare of a treeless world. A huge slobbering black bear is chasing me on an empty, dusty, planet. He must smell the blood, the blood from my period. The earth explodes! The trailer rattles. I instantly awake from hell. Three logging trucks speed by. I get out of bed and go to the toilet to check if I had started my period. Abruptly, I remember that I had a hysterectomy twenty years ago. Evidently I am not quite awake yet. I finish in the restroom and go to make some coffee. I open the windows to get some air. Outside it smells like wet earth from the rain shower in the night mixed with a hint of pancakes and maple syrup. Only here would you find this aroma. An RV is parked by the propane tank. I must have slept in.

It takes me a while to shake the nightmare from my mind. Bubba comes out to fill the guest's propane tank. He is talking in his loud, jovial manner, and laughs much too often. Who does he thinks he's impressing? Is his fake, friendly display for my benefit? The propane-purchasing guest seems to be ignoring him. After the RV leaves and Bubba returns to the kitchen, I unhook the door and take the dogs out to stretch and shake off my bloody nightmare.

Inside at my table, I once again count my money.

Let's see—canopy, $29.99+tax, around $35.00, $50.00 for groceries and calling card, $12.00 for duck seed, $5.00 for apron, $20.00 for gas, equals $122.00. I had $110.00 left, plus $75.00 in tips. That leaves me with $63.00. I believe payday is on Friday. Today is Monday. I better not spend any more money until then.

I cook myself some scrambled eggs with a slice of toast wondering what to do for the day. I could put up my canopy, take a drive to the creek and hike, call the family, empty holding tank, and, oh, watch Bubba build me a fire pit. That is, if he remembers that he said that last night.

I take the dogs out to the fenced area with my coffee in hand and think about where I would like my fire pit. It would be smart to keep it far enough away from the giant propane tank. Perhaps right there, in front of my picnic table. I walk around and turn the valve to empty the holding tank. I do not need to use the water hose anymore, since the water is now hooked up and I can fill it from a pump switch inside. With all this flushing, it should be squeaky clean by now.

Big puffy clouds fill the blue sky. I go inside to get the keys to my car. The large canopy box is in the back seat. After getting all the parts laid out, and reading the instructions, I begin to assemble my shaded patio.

I move the table and fencing closer to the side of the trailer, so that the canopy, table, and fence will be right outside, to the left of the steps, and connected to the trailer. I manage to construct the canopy, and use heavy rope to brace it to the trailer and picnic bench, just in case it gets windy. I am satisfied that it would take a tornado to blow this away. My trailer and picnic bench would go with it if that happens. I arrange the fencing so that I can just open the door for the dogs, they can walk down the steps without leashes, and be in the shaded, fenced area.

Breakfast must be over, because Bubba is leaving the kitchen and driving the golf cart in my direction. "WE GET SOME POWERFUL WINDS THAT BLOW THRU HERE!" Bubba is looking at my canopy.

"I've tied it down to the trailer and the picnic bench. I'm hoping it will withhold any wind."

Bubba gets out of his golf cart to check out the construction. "YEAH, THAT MIGHT WORK."

"That golf cart looks fun to drive." I am making small talk.

"SCOOTER! IT'S NOT A GOLF CART! IT'S A SCOOTER! CAN'T YA TELL THE DIFFERENCE?" You can see the blood rush to his cheeks when he's mad. It's not very flattering.

"Sorry." I say even though it's not true.

Bubba is now looking at the steps. Bonita and Bandito are looking at Bubba from the fenced area. He begins to open and move the fencing out of his way to make room to move the steps. I panic that the dogs will escape, and wrap the fence back together and out of Bubba's way. He lifts the steps like an elephant and slides it over to where it should be.

"Thank you Bubba! That will be so much better now. I sure appreciate that."

Bubba spits out a stream of tar. "NO PROBLEM! I'VE GOT STUFF TO DO, BUT I'LL BE BY LATER TO BUILD YA A FIRE PIT. TERRY AND I WILL BE BARBECUING TONIGHT. WE'D LIKE YA TO COME DOWN AND JOIN US."

"Uh, maybe Bubba. I'm not sure what I'll be up to then. That's very nice of you to think of me. Can I let you know later?" I already know my answer.

"YEAH, WHATEVER. I'M GOIN TO BE PLANTIN YA A LAWN HERE SOON."

"A lawn? Really? Right here? In front of my trailer?"

"YEAH, RAY AND I BEEN THINKIN ABOUT THAT FOR SOME TIME NOW. I GOT THE SEED IN THE COLD STORAGE ROOM IN THE KITCHEN. HAD IT FOR SEVERAL MONTHS NOW. WE'LL HAVE TO WORK THE SOIL WITH THE TRACTOR FIRST."

"Cool! A lawn would be extremely nice!"

"BETTER GO! " Bubba goes over to the rear of the scooter and gets himself a beer.

"Okay, see you later. I'm going for a drive after a bit, but I should be home later this afternoon," I tell Bubba.

"YEAH, THE FIRE PIT'S GOIN' RIGHT HERE." He walks over to a place some ten yards away from my trailer. I personally think it is too close to the propane tank, which has a warning on it (that I read on passing) that says, 'Do not smoke or have open flame within 40 yards of this tank'. According to my estimated calculations, that spot appears to be only about 20 yards away. I also think it would be too far away from my table to enjoy it properly. I say nothing to Bubba now, but will approach the subject later.

"Thanks for moving the steps Bubba." He drives towards his trailer.

As I stand there in a daze, I see the ducks playing at the water's edge, and it makes me remember the duck seed in the car. I put the dogs inside and get my car keys. The steps are so much easier to walk up now! I drive the car over to the rear of the kitchen. The bag is heavy, so I slide it out and over to the storage room. It is left unlocked during the day. I find the large bag of dog food with the pan inside for scooping, and lay the bag of duck seed upright next to it. I open the duck seed with a pair of scissors hanging from a nail on the wall. Outside I hear the ducks quacking. They are getting louder and approaching the storage room. Sounds like I'll get to see how they like the new feed!

"Well, hello there!" I say to the ducks. They are almost inside the storage room now, so I scoop a pan full and walk over to the lake's edge. I toss the seed onto the ground. They love it! I stand there watching, and look over in the direction of Bubba's trailer. My heart stops when I see his large frame far off in the distance, looking this way, with his hands on his hips. Why do Bubba and Terry make me feel so shitty when I try to do something nice? He goes back into his trailer and I drive to the front of the building to call Lori.

My radio is on in the car. At first I am not paying too much attention, since it is the news, and then I tune in when I hear about the fires in Oregon. It seems that there are several fires in the national forests of southern Oregon. More than 400,000 acres have burned! My God! That's nearly half a million acres! The fires are still out of control at this point!

I am glad that Lori answers.

"Lori! This is Denise. I just heard about the fires! My God! This is horrible!"

"Denise! I'm so glad you called! You should be glad you're not here. The smoke blowing in is horrible! It's so bad, that we have to stay inside with our air conditioners going! Cars are even breaking down, due to the ashes clogging up the filters. Ash is all over everything! This is devastating!"

I begin to cry. I feel the tears on my cheeks. I remember my nightmare of a treeless world.

"Denise? Are you still there?"

"Yes, Lori, I'm still here. It's just that this is so sad. Where will all the animals go? How much more will it burn? How did the fires start?"

"From what I've learned, they began during a heavy thunderstorm on Tuesday night. I think that's the day you left Ashland."

"Yeah, I remember that storm. I was camping." I cringe thinking back on that night.

"How are you anyway, Denise? How's the job coming?"

"Oh, it's just fine. This can be a really busy place at times. I'm learning how to be a fast-fry cook, that's for sure. There's a guy here named Bubba. He's a big ole' logging type of good ole' boy. I think he wants me, but I don't want him! He has a bitchy girlfriend and they kind of intimidate me, but besides that, Billy and Ray are wonderful people and I'm glad I'm here to help them out. I think I might be able to make some good money this summer."

"Cool! I'm glad everything is working out for you. You know you can come back here anytime you want. Maybe at some point, I can come see you with Tiki and the kids." Tiki is Lori's daughter. The kids are Lori's grandchildren, Jacy and Kiowa.

"I'd love that! Well, I'm using my calling card, and I still have to talk to mom and dad and my boys, so I love you, and I'll call you soon. I'll be thinking about you and I'm going to get a newspaper right now."

"I love you too. Take care."

I call my sons, but can only say 'I love you', because they are both in the middle of a large real estate sale. I call my parents, but only get an answering machine. Mom must be on the internet. Finally, I get a newspaper from a stand next to the phone booth.

Since I have to move my car, I decide to cruise the area. I drive down the dirt road into the forest, to see where the trash is, and also see if there are any coyotes in there, being the curious soul that I am.

That funny feeling I had in my stomach the first time I walked in here, returns. I am blown away by the amount of leftover forgotten junk! Skeletons of a lost life, place, and time; discarded in nature, a cancerous growth from humanity's carelessness. I am repulsed at the sight of it and have taken drastic measures to assure that I remain innocent of the crime of over-consumption. Practically everything I own can now fit into my car. The precious things, like photos of my sons when they were children, and the few things I treasure, are in half a dozen boxes in my parent's garage.

I have no desire to own things anymore. My motives for this type of behavior range from complex to clear-cut and can be summed up from the mental list I have stored carefully away, which in itself is a contradiction and burden, storing 'stuff' inside my brain. Someday I will discard those skeletons too. Primarily, it is an environmental issue. We are guilty of draining the earth of its natural resources to produce stuff, and then we need to build huge houses, houses far too large for our needs. Of course this is done so that we may have a quick profit in order to buy, build and store even better stuff in a better house. We need to have our favorite stuff near us so others can envy our stuff and want that stuff too, and then we need to build acres of asphalt, cement, and steel to store all the extra stuff we don't need, but can't throw away. Sometimes our stuff is no longer wanted or needed, so it is taken to a large hole in the earth that we have dug to bury our stuff. We need something to haul our stuff around in, so we buy three or four of these just in case one breaks down. We all have one of these, so we need more asphalt and cement so that we have pathways that spread from one side of the country to the next so that we have quick access to buying more stuff.

There I go again, being overly dramatic, but that is my complex reason in an over-simplified explanation, and I must remind myself, that I am currently taking advantage of those asphalt pathways, driving one of those things, hauling around my stuff, even as I think these things. The clear-cut reason I don't cling to stuff is this; I have moved too many times and stuff is a pain in the ass!

I guess I should add the third reason I just found inside my brain storage, which seems to be a psychological one. I found out far too young that money and things could have a far greater value than the living, breathing, child-bearing, human being that placed her trust in the hands of another human being. I learned far too late that I too, was replaceable and could be discarded as easily as the day's garbage. I've lived alone since I was twenty-nine when I left my empty eleven-year marriage and raised my sons alone. It's not that I want and miss having a partner in life, because I'm quite happy alone. How could I have adventures if I was all wrapped up in someone else's life?

I tried the marriage route. He loved money and things more than me. I was so young, hopeful, and believing. I wouldn't be young again for all the tea in China! Maybe everyone was right when they said I was nuts for waiving away my rights to the rich lifestyle that we had achieved together. It's been a struggle ever since that's for sure, but a struggle is better than the emptiness of a loveless marriage. Oh, I've had many friends and lovers since my marriage, but nothing of any value or depth. It was mostly that hormonal thing. Not now though. It's been seven years since I've even thought about dating. Inner contentment only grows stronger every day.

My sons and I had so much fun during their childhood. We were always busy, happy, hungry, playing, learning, and living a true, unspoiled lifestyle. I loved being a mom. I loved being needed. I loved teaching them right from wrong, even if I turned out to be wrong about what was right. Then they grew up. They moved away. They got married. I've been looking for the place where I belong ever since.

The search has not been depressing in any way to me. It's those who love me, who are dismayed by my apparent detachment to the things that society has labeled normal. Normal, like growing old in the same house, eating the same food, watching the same TV program. My life may not be normal, but it's not over! I have many adventures clawing at me to be discovered. 'I own my life, and only mine. And so, I shall appreciate my person. And so, I shall make proper use of myself.' I truly do appreciate my person, even though others have trouble doing the same. Others like Bubba and Terry. Ignorance, alcohol or drug abuse, addictions of any kind, are spirit killing and lethal to the soul. When these things control people, they walk through life with blinders on, never to see the good in others or themselves. When I am confronted with this type of person, it does not stop me from continuing on with my own journey. I may be frightened by callous behavior, but still, at the same time, I understand it. Some people are just damaged goods and have lost sight of their direction. Wallowing in their fear, they operate their lives in a sightless frenzy, their consciousness frozen shut. Understanding it makes it easier to forgive them.

It's the making proper use of myself that I am having trouble with. I have one thing going for me, and that is faith in myself. My day will come. On that day, I will know, from the depth of my soul, what my proper use will be. It probably isn't being a fast-fry cook at Hacienda RV Park. This is only another rough spot on my pathway to, hopefully learn and grow, and once again, move on.

The dump truck that I have been staring at, but not seeing, has several trash bags that have been pulled down, and torn open. The garbage is spread throughout the surrounding area, very similar to the baggage inside my brain. I begin to wonder why I had the need to torture myself by driving in here. I suppose I need confirmation on my wild, complex theory about human over-consumption. I've taken in the depressing site long enough. I've tried, convicted, and hung the guilty parties. Satisfied, I turn around and drive back to the fifth wheel.

Back at the trailer, I have some lunch, and feel a deep need to walk by the creek. The creek will be my sanctuary. My secret place to believe in unblemished, uncorrupted, silent, open space again. I guess I'm feeling melancholy, and a little lost. The trash pile overwhelmed me, bringing out too many bad memories. Right now it is difficult to see the good in the world. I scare those that love me with my vagabond life. I'm always running away from the ordinary and routine of regular life. I'll be fifty-two in a few months. I don't even think a twenty-year old would be here, doing this job, in this place right now.

I get the dog's leashes and head to the creek. We walk, and hike, and smell, and see, and sit, and snack, and then we do it again, until it is nearly dark. Repetition is therapy. I feel much better for it. The dogs are wet from playing in a pool of water by the creek's edge. They are also tired, and hungry. It will be a long five days for them and myself when I return to work tomorrow.

As soon as I turn into my parking space by the fifth wheel, I see the new fire pit. It is where Bubba had said he wanted to build it. Large stones surround the border of a deep hole. There is a pile of logs next to it ready to burn, and another picnic bench sits by the side of the fire pit. I can't help but to be heart-warmed by this kind gesture from Bubba. He may look like a big bully, but somewhere inside he has a spark of kindness. I suppose he knows if this is far enough from the propane tank, and I'm sure he has his reasons for putting it here.

By the time I feed the dogs, eat dinner, and make myself a drink, it is dark outside. With my newspaper in one hand, and a gin and limeade in the other, I head out to the fire pit where I build my first fire by burning the headlines of the burning forests, burning today's tragedies, and burning away my cares.

As I stare into the warm crackling flames, I hear crunching of footsteps on the gravel road.

"YA MISSED THE BARBEQUE!" It's Bubba and Terry is with him. They both have a beer in their hands, and they both have big smiles on their faces as they look into the flames of my fire.

"Oh, I forgot! I'm so sorry! I was having so much fun hiking with the dogs. Time escaped me. Thank you so very much for the fire pit Bubba! It's wonderful!" We all stare into the glow of the flames.

"ME AND TERRY BOTH BUILT IT."

"Well, thank you too Terry! I will certainly be enjoying this,

I'll tell you that right now! By the way, where can I get more firewood?"

"WHAT A YA TALKIN' BOUT? THERE'S A WHOLE FOREST OUT THERE FULL OF FALLIN LOGS. YA JUST GO DOWN ANY SIDE ROAD AND GET YURSELF SOME!" I wonder, as Bubba shouts his reply to me, why and how a simple, polite conversation can turn demeaning. How it makes my self-confidence crumble, how the little girl in me suddenly feels stupid and worthless. To avoid his eyes, I stare back into the fire and take a deep breath.

"Yeah, that's right, there is. Please have a seat and join me."

Bubba and Terry sit at the picnic bench with me. I'm a little nervous and would really prefer being left alone, but I'm quite sure that this is now Bubba's fire pit.

"Terry, I really haven't had the pleasure of meeting you yet. I'm Denise." I hold my hand out to shake hands with her. She shakes it.

"Nice to meet you, too." Her friendliness is so different than all the bad vibes I have been getting from her.

"WHAT IS THAT JAPANESE THING YA GOT PARKED OVER THERE? IT LOOKS LIKE A SEWING MACHINE BOX." Bubba and Terry laugh at that joke. I force a smile.

"It's a Suzuki Aerio. My sons bought it for me for Christmas."

"MUST HAVE NICE BOYS TO BUY THEIR MAMMA A CAR?"

"I sure do!"

Terry speaks up. "Hey, do you think that next time ya go to Brandon, we could tag along? Our Jeep is broken and we haven't been able to load up on groceries for a while." Terry's smile suddenly seems insincere, kind of like Ruby when she needed the twenty bucks.

"No problem! I have next Sunday off. Would that be a good time?"

"GREAT!" Bubba spits out tar, and then gulps the last of his beer.

"Uh, Bubba?" I need to get something said.

"YEAH!"

"I bought some duck feed today. I put it in the storage room for them. I hope you don't mind?"

"DON'T MATTER TO ME ONE WAY OR NOTHER! YA WANNA BUY DUCK FEED, THEN BUY DUCK FEED."

"Good. I wouldn't want to step out of my boundary."

"TERRY! WE BETTER GET GOIN! WE'RE OUT OF BEER!" They get up from the bench.

"Thanks again for the fire pit. I'll see you at work tomorrow."

"NITE!"

They walk to the rear of the kitchen, returning with a twelve pack from the cold storage room. They pass my trailer on their way back home.

"Good night!"

"NITE!" They say in unison.

I stare into the flames for another hour or so until they are red embers. From my peripheral vision I see a shadow moving by the bushes on the lakes edge. I watch the dark shadow creeping slowly, and then it is still. It is the size of a large dog. I am frozen with fear and hold very still. Then suddenly it lunges at something, and I hear the splashing of water, and the terrified quacking of ducks. I see the shadow walk back toward the forest with the light color of feathers hanging from its mouth. The rest of the ducks are in a frenzy! Bubba comes running down from his direction. By the time I can make out his figure in the dark, I see he is carrying a shotgun.

"GET INSIDE! THERE'S A COUGAR OUT HERE! I'M GONNA KILL THE SON OF A BITCH!" Bubba is too drunk to shoot anything in my opinion. He trips on a rock and skids on his belly as dust floats. He gets up and continues running. I go inside mostly out of fear of his gun and because I am holding my hand over my mouth to muffle an impending belly laugh. The sight of him landing in the dark like an elephant seal will stay with me for some time.

I climb into bed with the dogs. I must have fallen asleep

because at some point later, I am awakened by the sound of a shotgun way out in the forest somewhere.

CHAPTER SEVEN

It is so nice to be able to use the restroom, shower, and drink coffee inside my own space. We must be getting used to Bubba walking by, because Bonita and Bandito don't growl or bark and I do not peek out the window to see.

I leash them up and unhook the door to let them out. I really don't want them urinating in the fenced area, and besides, I don't have the fenced area enclosed all the way right now. To Bonita and Bandito's delight, all the ducks are settled happily in, under, and around the picnic bench, within the protection of our fencing! The dogs rush at them, full speed down the steps! I do not have enough time to press the brake button on their retractable leashes. The chaos explodes! Ducks are flapping and quacking! Feathers are flying! The leashes get tangled! All the ducks run, waddle and quack to the protection of the lake. My dogs are practically smiling with pride. I step in duck poop, which I can now see is everywhere within the fenced area and on the picnic bench. I suppose I better keep that closed at night from now on. I'll have to clean this up before I go to work. Maybe the ducks needed a safe place to sleep after one of the members of their family got eaten last night.

I walk the dogs over by the edge of the lake where I had seen the shadow and its duck dinner last night. Could it really have been a mountain lion? Bubba called it a cougar. I guess it's the same thing. Bonita and Bandito are very interested in this spot where all the feathers are scattered. On closer inspection, I see the wide paw prints imbedded in the mud on the lake's edge. Higher in the dry, dusty ground, I see the large, deep, wide spread, footprints made by Bubba running. A little beyond, about ten feet further, I see the indent of where he had fallen. I smile, enjoying the memory.

It isn't until we are walking back to the trailer, that I notice the smoky haze in the air from the fires in Oregon. The smoke has finally made it this far.

Once I get inside the trailer, I count my mosquito bites. There are nineteen! The one on my neck is finally getting better. Others are not so good. I got four new ones last night at some point. I now know that they can bite through clothes! I'm becoming more disillusioned about my working vacation every day!

After cleaning up the duck poop, I open the trunk of my car. I want to go collect firewood for tonight, since I had used up the pile Bubba had left for me. Somewhere in the trunk was a plastic tarp to line the inside of the trunk with. Once that was ready, I grab my gloves, an apple, leash up the dogs, and put them in the car. They love dirt roads!

There are many dirt roads to choose from. Some of them are private entrances to homes, some go to the creek, and some are logging roads. I pick one that is marked by the state for hikers and tent camping. I drive very slowly with the windows down half way. The dust on the road is so fine. It becomes a floating cloud behind us. I see an area off to the side of the road where there are several fallen branches, so I pull over to the side. The dogs are very excited! They want to go for a walk. I am not too comfortable about that. I haven't seen any other cars on this road since I turned onto it. I put my pepper spray in my hand, and leash them up anyway, just to let them out of the car for a minute or two, leaving my car door open for a quick re-entry. Once they have had their forest fix, I put them back into the car and go to collect wood.

My abrupt aloneness in the forest makes my tummy flutter. It's rare that I am not attached to Bonita and Bandito when out in nature. It's the same flutter I felt at the age of six or seven years old when I would make myself a peanut butter and jelly sandwich and walk alone into the adjoining canyon of our home in Palos Verdes Estates. We lived there for a short three years until my dad was transferred to Lancaster, California. I can still smell the eucalyptus trees as they swayed high above me. In the silence of the canyon I would unwrap my sandwich on a grassy patch and watch the clouds float by, the fluttering inside never ceasing. I have no idea why it made me so happy to be alone. I think I felt nurtured by the solidness of nature, by the tingling in my body, by the complete acceptance of my presence. I was too young to understand then what I know now—that nature is where you find truth.

These thoughts vanish when I hear crunching of twigs somewhere in the trees. I hold very still looking around, and see the large buck staring at me. He's so beautiful! This is the first buck I have seen since I began my journey from Ashland! Come to think of it, I haven't even seen any deer at all! Never occurred to me that they haven't been in the picture. When I lived in Carmel Valley three years ago, deer were everywhere! There was a dead one on Carmel Valley road on a daily basis. They ate all my roses! Groups of them walked the Pebble Beach Golf Course! Here I am in the national forest, and this is the first deer I see! My fear of a mountain lion fades away. He would not be standing here if there were danger around, so I enjoy watching him for a while.

I load my trunk with logs and branches and revel in the fact that I have fetched my own wood. I broke through my fears and did it! I even found a decorative piece of wood. It looks like a swan or a bird of some type. I will lean it by the pine tree next to my trailer. I've always enjoyed seeing things in wood. There is something very spiritual about the images that trees leave behind once they are gone or fallen.

A childhood memory floods my mind once again. When I was pre-teen, I would draw on the wood paneled walls of my room, bringing out the animals or faces that I saw hidden in there. My parents did not appreciate my creative outlet. On the beach of Carmel, I would find driftwood that had the form of something, and take it home to work on, bringing out the snake or animal that was already there. I even sold a few of them to some of my clients at my flower shop.

My flower shop. The stress of owning my own business was nearly the death of me. I sustained for ten years, until the damn landlords raised the rent so high that I folded. I don't miss it one single bit. I'm not really a florist at heart, even though I did have quite a talent with my unique displays. I just fell into that small shop by accident. I was working for another florist at that time, when a good friend came in to tell me that there was a small florist shop in Carmel Valley and the woman who owned it had suddenly died of a heart attack. Her husband was looking for someone to run it and eventually buy it. That's when I stepped in. Although I don't miss my flower shop, I do miss my little, rented, stone house in Carmel Valley. That house was the only reason to go to work every day. It was nestled safely on two hundred acres of lush countryside.

I need to get back to Hacienda, unload the wood, walk the dogs, and get ready for work. I get in the car, turn on the radio, and drive back to the loony bin.

With all my chores done, I prepare myself for work mentally and physically. The small mirror above the ten-inch green sink inside the fifth wheel is distorted, and the lighting is dim. I do my best to enhance my fifty-one year old features. I look okay to me. In fact, the only time I feel my age is when someone takes a picture of me, and then I am shocked! Who is that person? I put on my new apron. It's not armor, but feels comforting and protective anyway. I have several pockets to put things in. I turn on the air-conditioner to low, feed the dogs, and bag up my trash to drop in the trashcan outside. I take a deep breath and then head to work.

There are only a couple of cars parked in front. Inside, Helen is minding the counter and Betty is sweeping the floor. I clock in and have small talk with all-American Helen. There is a newspaper sitting on the first table in the restaurant. I glance at the headlines: The fires in Oregon are 50% contained. Over 500,000 acres have burned so far.

Betty approaches me. "Hi Denise! I'm your waitress today!" She seems pleased to be working with me.

"Hi Betty! Great! We'll make a great team! What's going on in the kitchen? Anything I need to know?"

"It's kind of quiet, but we always have stuff to do." Betty has a tray of salt and pepper shakers that she is quickly refilling as she speaks.

"Good, I'll have time to get my bearings on food prep."

I walk to the grill and see the regular mess that Bubba leaves for me. At least the oil drip pan is not overflowing today. I check it anyway, and see that it is only half full of grease at the moment. It irritates me that Bubba comes to work in the morning to a shiny grill, and leaves his mess for me. I suppose this is something I'll have to live with.

After twenty minutes of cleaning, I go inside the cold storage room to retrieve tomatoes, red onion, and to see if we need mashed potatoes or potato salad. I will need a vegetable and soup for the dinner guests. I see that Bubba has made some sort of sausage soup. I get a tummy ache as soon as I smell it. It looks like there is a fresh box of artichokes, which would be really nice with the dinners. Next to the box of artichokes I see the large bag of lawn seed. It makes me wonder if a product like that should be stored with food supplies. I also find an industrial size bag of semi-sweet chocolate chips and wonder if Billy would mind if I make cookies to sell?

I take some empty cardboard boxes out the back door to throw into the, once again, growing pile of boxes that will need to be burned. Bubba's large legs are sticking out from under the storage shed, directly below the full flytrap that hangs above the ramp. He is moving around trying to get at something and his feet are dangerously close to the dripping trash compactor goop. The flytrap is smelly and buzzing with dead and dying flies. Earlier I had seen a fresh flytrap inside the storage room. I will change that after Bubba leaves.

"What's going on under there, Bubba?" I say holding my nose.

He slides out gawkily from under the building. Once again I find the necessity to withhold a laugh seeing him on his belly. My impending laughter turns to horror when I see his fat hand clutching the tail of a dead cat. Unbelievable! Dead flies, rotten food, and a dead cat, all five feet from a restaurant kitchen!

"I HAD TO GET THIS SON A BITCH OUT FROM UNDER HERE. I SHOT HIM SOME TIME LAST WEEK. DIDN'T

KNOW WHERE HE WENT 'TIL TODAY." The horrible smell of death hits me like a brick!

"Why did you have to shoot him?" I say, still holding nose.

"CAUSE HE KEEPS KNOCKIN UP MY CAT! HE'S BEEN A DAMN NUISANCE!" Bubba waves the dead body at me like a wet rag.

"Oh." This obviously does not make me very happy. Stupid asshole wants to kill everything! He is putting the dead cat into a plastic bag. He's probably going to have that as his next special.

"So Bubba, did you get the mountain lion last night?" Huh, Bubba? Did ya get em? Did you shoot that beautiful creature too?

"NO, BUT DAMN NEAR! I'M GOIN TO NEXT TIME THO. HE'S BEEN HANGIN AROUND HERE TOO MUCH. THINKS HE OWNS THE PLACE!" Maybe someone should shoot Bubba for the same reason.

"Well, if you get him, I get dibs on a fang." I'm saying this in a cocky, sarcastic manner, because I have no control over the death of a beautiful creature, and if Bubba were to kill him, I would honor his spirit by keeping a fang. The mountain lion has always been my totem. My niece, and Lori's daughter, Tiki, has a book of totems that identifies which animal is your own through your time and date of birth. One day we all sat at Lori's house and claimed our totems.

Bubba gives me a weird look.

"I AIN'T GONNA GIVE YA NO DAMN FANG!"

"Just a joke Bubba." Now get the hell out of here!

"AND BY THE WAY, YA STILL AIN'T SCRUBBIN' THE GRILL RIGHT! I'LL COME IN AT CLOSIN' AND SHOW YA HOW ITS GOTTA BE DONE." This man has to be the nastiest human being I've ever met!

Bubba gets onto his scooter, throwing the bagged up dead cat into the pile of empty beer cans and drives away. I go into the storage room and retrieve the new flytrap and a gallon of bleach. I bag up the stinky old flytrap and throw it away and then hang up the new one, and then I pour straight bleach all over and around the ground below the trash compactor. Maybe it will smell a little better out here with all the death gone. What kind of a fog are Billy and Ray living in anyway? What they need is a manager. This could be a wonderful place, but all I see is dysfunction! Perhaps they are just plain old burned out after all these years, and I'm sure finding good help must be a nightmare!

Somewhere in the park I hear the mower start up.

I return to the kitchen and wash my hands. I see Betty taking an order from a lady sitting at a table. It is an older lady, at least older than me. She has wild bleached blonde hair, and is bejeweled with lots of glittery clothes.

"Lottie wants her regular." Betty hangs up the order on the crown of thorns.

"What's her regular?" I ask.

"Oh, I forgot. I guess you haven't cooked for Lottie yet. She comes in almost everyday. She always orders the same thing. New York steak raw, just thrown on the grill for a second or two on each side, enough to barely brown the edges, and burnt toast."

I'm appalled and still nauseated from the stench outside. "Really? Okay, if you say so. Does she want baked or mashed potatoes?"

"Neither. That's all she ever wants on her plate."

The slab of New York is in the cold storage room. I get it and cut off the one-inch thick slice that Billy had said to do for New York. I lay it on the grill for several seconds while the toast gets burnt. When I have finished I do not see Betty to deliver the order, but want to meet this lady anyway, and see if I have done this correct, so I take it out to her table.

"Hello. I'm Denise. I just started working here. Here's your order. I'm hoping I did this correct." I lay the unappetizing looking platter in front of her.

"Well, hi there Denise. I'm Lottie. I'm glad Billy got some help. Now let's see if you did this right. The toast could be burnt a little more, but this is fine." She cuts into her steak. Blood oozes out onto her plate. I instantly gag.

"Perfect! So what brings you to this part of the world?" Lottie says while holding a large piece of bright red dripping steak on her fork a few inches from her mouth.

"I'm wondering that myself. I guess you could call it a working vacation."

"Good Lord woman! Never heard of such a thing! Well, whatever brought you here; I'm glad for Billy and Ray. Good people those two. By the way, love the apron!" She stuffs the bite into her mouth. A droplet of blood drips onto her chin.

"Thank you. I found it at a thrift store." I happily look long and hard at my apron, giving her time to wipe her mouth with her napkin.

I chat with Lottie for a while longer. It seems she used to own a bar in Vegas for over twenty years, and has retired somewhere near Brandon. I like Lottie, even with her disgusting eating habits. She seems to like me too. It will be entertaining to get to know the local characters.

Betty has been in the background nervously watching me. When I return to the grill, she approaches me. "I'm sorry I wasn't here to take the order out. I had to use the restroom."

"Oh Betty, that's okay. I just wanted to meet her and find out if I cooked the steak as she wanted."

"Oh." I think Betty thought that I would be mad at her. She's such a nervous and hyper person. I'm sure working with Bubba could make anyone paranoid!

Billy walks in with a cup of coffee and sits down with Lottie. They talk for some time, often looking in my direction. They are both smiling, so I think that if they were talking about me, it would be good things they were saying. I hope!

Not too long after that, Billy enters the kitchen. She compliments me on my apron, and says that she is going to make her and Ray some lunch. She opens a can of tuna, and gets out a boiled egg.

"Billy?"

"Yes, Denise?"

"I noticed you have a big bag of chocolate chips in there. Would it be okay to make some cookies?" I sound like a little girl asking Mom if I can make cookies.

"I've had those chocolate chips for a few months now. I used to keep chocolate chip cookies in a basket by the register. People loved them. I haven't had the time or energy to fix them lately. So if you're up to it, and it's not busy, then go ahead."

Betty runs over and puts up an order for a Rueben sandwich and a hot beef sandwich. Since I had not made either one of those yet, Billy walks me through it. I'm catching on to being a fast-fry cook. It's when I'm overwhelmed that I lose control of my focus. At this pace I can ingest all the information.

After the order is completed, Billy walks over to a table and yells out to Ray to come join her. Ray comes out and walks over to the meat counter rolling his oxygen tank behind him. "Good day, pretty lady," he greets me sweetly.

"Good day, Ray. How are you doing?"

"Things could be better, but they ain't. Other than that I'm just fine. How ya doin in the kitchen?" Ray eyeballs the grill.

"I think okay. You be the judge of that."

"Why don't ya come on over to visit with Billy and me after work today?" he asks.

"If I'm not too tired, I just might do that."

"We'll see ya then. I'm gonna be turning the ground soon in front of your trailer, and beyond that about a hundred yards or so. Want to put in that lawn that we never got to last summer."

"Yeah, Bubba mentioned that to me. Sounds really nice. I'm getting all set up in the fifth wheel now. Thanks again for everything. Did you notice the fire pit?" I'm wondering if Ray might say it's too close to the propane tank.

"You bet cha. Gotta make it like home for ya if we expect ya to stay with us."

"You're very sweet, and I appreciate all that you are doing." I pat the top of his hand that is resting on the meat counter.

"Likewise, pretty lady." I detect some water building in his eyes. Ray is probably not used to a sincere thank-you. I feel my eyes water up and quickly go to retrieve the chocolate chips and all the ingredients to make the cookies. There are orders in-between my cookie preparation. But eventually the cookies are made. I have made them large, gooey in the middle, and crispy on the edges. I individually wrap each one up and put them into a basket up by the register. Helen opens one up and takes a big bite as soon as I lay them down.

"Very good!" She is holding the cookie like she is drinking English tea to protect her nails.

"Thanks. Let me know if they sell or not today." I say as I walk away.

Betty helps me get the special board down, and I write, 'Fresh homemade chocolate chip cookies at register.'

At around 3:30, Helen runs up to the kitchen in a panic.

"Good Lord! The bus is on its way!" She throws her hands in the air.

"What bus?" I am confused.

"The bus to Reno! We just got a call that they are stopping here for an early dinner break. This happens a couple of times a month."

"A bus full of people? To eat? Oh my God! Are you kidding me?"

"Would I kid you about something like this? Billy is on her way into the kitchen in a minute. We have to get busy slicing meats and tomatoes. I have to get lettuce ready for salads. Betty, you better get a few more pots of coffee going. Denise, it would probably be a good idea to make some hamburger patties ready for the grill, and thaw out another twenty pounds for later. Better warm up the soup too. These seniors love their soup! We have to get them out of here within an hour, so that they can keep to schedule."

This moment in time is like a blur to me. I know I was making sandwiches, hamburgers, and scooping up the rest of Bubba's horrid soup. The smoke from the flaming grill is making my eyes burn. We are bumping into each other. The line of seniors goes all the way out the door. The restroom is very busy. Our music from the stereo system is playing country, and all I hear is the hum of many people talking at once. I find Betty, at one point in the chaos, in the cold storage room slapping her own face and scolding herself out loud for something unknown to me. Whoa, now that is scary! Poor little creature is all screwed up.

When it was all said and done, Billy lights a cigarette and goes back to her home area. We have sold all of the cookies, and the kitchen looks like a tornado hit it. Betty is busy cleaning the dining area and the piles of dishes, she is still mumbling to herself. I begin my chore of cleaning the kitchen and grill for the dinner crowd. It is now 5:45, and a group of four come in for dinner.

After things are a little more in control, and I have cooked the four hamburgers with fries for the guests, I tell Betty that I need to let my dogs out for a minute. I know she will handle anything that comes up. I take them some leftover hamburger as a treat. After a quick break for all of us, I return to the grill, ignoring Bonita and Bandito's pleading eyes of abandonment.

At closing time, Bubba bangs through the back door. He is drunk, and I catch a glimpse of Terry sitting in the scooter outside. I am in the process of cleaning the grill.

"OKAY. THIS IS HOW YA DO IT!" Bubba grabs the large brick of pumice stone out of my hand, pressing and sliding it violently across the flat grill. He goes at it like a maniac! "YA GOTTA PRESS HARD. LIKE THIS! AND GET INTO EVERY CORNER!"

I say nothing. I am tired and he is just a jackass. I'll just stand here and let him clean it. I don't have the energy or strength to do it anyway.

"Looks good Bubba. Thanks."

He goes into the cold storage and gets a twelve pack. When he comes out he offers me a beer, which I take, and then he leaves.

I pop the beer and take a long gulp. I am hungry and thirsty. We are allowed a full meal of choice if we do an eight-hour shift, so I prepare myself a chilidog with cheese. I do not cook it on the flat grill, which is now clean and ready for Bubba to dirty in the morning. Instead I cook it over the grated grill, warming my chili on the stove in a small pan. I cut myself a piece of apple pie, wrapping everything up to take back to the fifth wheel to eat.

I bleach all the counters and mop the floor; Betty has finished all the dishes and cooking pans and counts up our tips. We have $80 each! I clock out. I have worked nine and a half hours.

The air is chilly inside my trailer. I turn off the air conditioner and open the windows. I had left a few of them cracked open for circulation during the day.

"Hi babies! Mom is sorry! I'm home now. Gotta work or we won't eat! You have to go outside? Let's go, and then I'll take you for a walk after I eat. Okay?"

"NOW! NOW! NOW! NOW!" Sometimes Bonita's bark can grind on my nerves.

After I walk the dogs, I sit at my picnic bench to eat my dinner. I use my camping lantern for light. The dogs are enjoying being in the fenced area and out of the trailer. I'm hoping it's too late for mosquitoes to bother me. I hear tons of frogs croaking on the lake's edge. Either I didn't notice them before, or they just arrived. I have no idea. I hope they eat mosquitoes. I see a few bats in the sky. There is a slice of moon to light them up as they swish around. Good! I know they like mosquitoes! The mud hens are honking out on the lake. Bubba must be coming down the road, because I hear him spitting. He walks past the back side of my trailer and heads over to Billy and Ray's house. As soon as he arrives there I hear his burly voice and laughter as Billy and Ray greet him at the sliding glass door.

I return to eating my dinner. My chilidog was wonderful! I needed a good dose of chemicals and mechanically separated chicken and pork parts to keep up with everyone else around this place. I save my apple pie for breakfast.

With the dogs leashed and pepper spray in hand, we go for a walk around the main building. I don't plan on going too far, since it's obvious that there is a mountain lion roaming around, and it is dark, so I stay tight within the lights of the building. When I walk by Billy's lawn area, her dog, Harley, starts barking at us. Billy comes out to see what he is barking at. She is smoking a cigarette, and I can see and hear Bubba and Ray having a jovial conversation at the bar area of their living room.

"Is that our little gypsy lady?" Billy shouts out.

"Hi Billy! Just walking the kids." Bonita and Bandito are barking at Harley. Harley has decided that my dogs aren't worth the trouble, and goes back inside the house.

"When you finish up that walk, get in here and have a drink with us!"

"Okay, that sounds nice. I'll be over in a while."

As I walk towards the front of the building, I see someone else walking their dog off in the distance. I feel safer knowing they are there.

Back at the trailer, I make myself a gin and limeade, change my clothes, close fenced area to keep the ducks out, and walk to Billy's. I am greeted with big tight hugs from Billy and Ray. Bubba is off to the side of the bar and has rosy cheeks and blood shot eyes. Tonight his demeanor is one of a shy, sweet, smiling, gentleman. He's not fooling me for one minute. Is he fooling Billy and Ray? Surely they've seen what I see. Or have they?

"What's that yur drinkin'?" asks Ray.

Sitting on top of the bar next to the questioning Ray, I see a half gallon bottle of Wild Turkey. It is nearly empty. That is what Billy and Ray appear to be drinking. Bubba has a beer in his hand. I wonder where Terry is.

"It's gin and limeade." I tell Ray.

"What kind of sissy drink is that?" I think Ray is drunk. Billy seems quite tipsy herself. Ray is scratching his arms.

"Ray! Quit your damn itching!"

"I can't help it, Billy. It drives me crazy!" Ray whines.

"I'll get out the witch hazel after a bit. So Denise, how'd yur day go? What do ya think about our bus load of seniors?"

"Now that was scary! How often does that happen?"

"Oh, a couple times a month. They always let us know an hour or so before hand."

There is a knock on the door. The heavy-set man with the mean dog that Ray was talking to on the other side of the lake, was standing at the slider.

"Jim! Get yur ass in here!" They all begin talking about people, places, and things I know nothing of at the moment. So I watch and listen for a while. Bubba is quite conversational when he is with Billy and Ray. I can see that the four of them are quite close.

Billy starts in about the door to the fifth wheel. "Damn thing's gonna cost $800!"

"Damn crooks! Denise, yur gonna have to work all summer to pay that off!" Ray adds. They all start laughing and I feel slightly nervous that this might be true.

"Ray's not serious, ya know that don't ya?" Billy does not wait for my response. "It's true though. They're gonna charge us $800 to build a new one. Won't get it for at least a month, maybe longer." I still have no time to respond. The conversation switches over to Little John. "Hey Bubba, we finally got rid of Little John, so you shouldn't be seeing him around next door any more. He agreed to let us have his motor home in back in trade for his bill. Don't need another druggie hanging around here. He was worthless! Jim and me are gonna take it into Willow Springs to get it registered sometime, maybe next week." Ray says proudly.

"DAMN STRAIGHT! IF I SEE THAT SON A BITCH AROUND THE PARK, I'LL SHOOT HIS ASS!" Bubba reacts with an anger flair-up, then calms down by changing the subject. "WHEN YA THINKIN ABOUT DOIN' THE LAWN?"

"Let's get goin' on that next Monday or Tuesday. We'll be having our annual fourth of July barbeque on Saturday, July the fifth the following weekend, so it'll help spruce the place up." Oh no! Another barbeque!

"Well everyone, it's been a pleasure, but I better get to bed. Thanks for the nice evening. I'll see you all tomorrow." I say as I pick up my empty glass.

"It's only 10:30. What's yur hurry?" Billy is starting to slur her words.

"I'm usually in bed by 10:00. I'll see you all later." I slide off the bar stool to leave. Bubba is smiling at me, not in a snide way at all, but more like a sexual way. Dream on, Bubba.

I am cautious walking alone back to my trailer. It is dark and I worry about the mountain lion. I get settled into bed with my dogs and my book. I can hear Bubba saying goodnight to Billy and Ray.

Sound sure does travel here. Soon after that I hear a tapping on the side of my trailer. Bubba wouldn't stop here to see me. Would he?

"It's me Bubba!" He is not yelling as usual. I think he's trying to be quiet so that Terry won't hear him from down at their trailer. I open the door enough to talk to him through a six-inch crack.

"Bubba, what in the world are you doing here?" I'm not sure if he heard a word I said.

"Yur a strange one. Can't figure out what a lady like you is doin here." He is supporting his body against the wall of the fifth wheel as he talks through the six-inch space.

"I'm just on a working vacation. I'll eventually head south at the end of summer. I don't know, Bubba. I guess I'm just crazy, and can we talk about this later. It's late. You should be getting on home, don't you think?"

"I think I'm gettin' crazy bout you! Hell, I'm practically in love!"

I'm speechless! If the mean, aggressive way he's been treating me is a love attraction, then he's a bigger hillbilly than I thought!

"Bubba, where's Terry?" I look for shadows lurking behind Bubba, but see no one.

"Oh, that bitch is passed out in the trailer. Anyway, I'm kicking her ass out. I've kicked it out before, but she always comes back, like diarrhea."

"Listen Bubba, it's not a good idea to be dropping by here like this. You're going to get me killed by a raging girlfriend. Okay?"

"Ain't gonna happen. She'll be outta here tomorrow. You'll see."

"Good night Bubba."

"Yur not gonna invite me in?" Bubba has a pouty look on his face right now that does not look right.

"Not a chance! Now go home. Good night." I close the door and hear his footsteps walking away. I turn off my light and try to hear his trailer door being shut. What I soon hear is Terry yelling. The trailer muffles it, but sure enough they are fighting. I pull the covers over my head. Suddenly there is silence, and I pop my head out and wonder if Bubba has killed her! Maybe it's Terry who killed Bubba. Oh my God! Now I have to worry about a murder! Perhaps my imagination is running away with me again. I've been known to do that on an occasion or two.

CHAPTER EIGHT

As soon as I wake up, I eat my apple pie with a cup of coffee. My stomach feels sour from all the stress and I needed to put something in it right away.

I can't believe it's only been eight days since I left Ashland! I wanted adventure, and adventure I have found! If I left here now, everyone in my family would know I've flipped out for sure. It would confirm their belief that I can't stick it out anywhere. I would have to tell them all the reasons for leaving, and then they would have to worry about me being in a tent again. I'm not ready to go home just yet, and I definitely don't want to sleep in a tent again as long as I live! It's all my fault really, the fact that they have a need to worry. I haven't always made the wisest decisions. First, I drop out of The California Institute of Arts after only three months to elope with Don, the father of my two sons. Then after going to work so he could complete his own college education, get his real estate and brokers license, I gave birth, raised my sons, enjoying every minute of motherhood. The wife part was lonely as hell. I was blind to the fact that a fortune was building. I was not invited to take part in this money growth. I did not even know our worth. I was at home cooking, cleaning, and playing with my sons. Bottom line, I left and waived away all my rights to financial security in exchange for freedom. The family's worry did not stop there. It must have appeared to them that I was bouncing all over the planet with wild schemes and spontaneous adventures during my single days, dragging the boys along. But guess what? We had the time of our lives being poor. The boys had all the friends, food, and fresh air they could want. They tell me so to this day. I think my gypsy spirit confuses my loved ones, yet at the same time, they are entertained when I share with them the many stories of my journeys and they always expect to hear more, and more I always have. Hacienda RV Park will be a wonderful addition to my life adventures portfolio.

I said I'd be here until the end of summer and that's exactly what I'm going to do, come hell or high water! What I need to do right now is make a closer bond between Billy, Ray, and myself. That way I have the safety of their friendship to fall back on. I do like both of them very much, so I need to keep my focus and energy on doing my job for them. It's obvious they need me desperately! I am beginning to see that I need them too.

From my table inside the fifth wheel, I hear the back door to the kitchen slam. When I look out, I see Bubba emptying the oil drip pan into the used oil barrel. I guess I forgot to empty that last night. Oops! He looks mad! So Bubba is still alive. Now all I need to see is Terry, to know if she is alive. I feel a little more powerful now that I am aware of Bubba's attraction to me. I now see him as more of a dangerous little boy than a rifle-toting killer. At the same time, I will keep my distance at all costs.

Bonita and Bandito distract me from my self-absorption. I have been staring into my coffee cup. They are sitting side-by-side looking up at me from the floor next to the table. If I hadn't adopted them a year apart, one would think they were related. Kindred spirits, that's what they are, always have been from the moment they saw each other. It's as if they could read my mind sometimes. They do not ever disturb me when I am in deep thought. They just stare at me in concern, and in hopes that I will notice that they exist. I know they need to get outside. They see that I have returned to earth, now they are happy. I leash them up to go outside. This is the way I've always wanted to take care of a pet. I've had so many pets through the years, mostly dogs.

My ex-husband and I had gotten a dog when we were first married. Her name was Trudy. I can't seem to remember the part Trudy played in our everyday lives. We were so wrapped up in starting a new life together. I was wrapped up in the fear that maybe I had made the wrong choice in a life partner, being pregnant, raising the boys, looking pretty, keeping up to the standards that my ex-husband wanted, and growing up myself. During and after the marriage, the boys were always bringing home dogs they had found, or a friend would give us a puppy. With all the chaos of my boys, their friends, cousins, school, soccer, baseball, my jobs, and lack of focus on dogs, most of them had no meaning to me. They came and went like passing strangers on the street. Some had gotten run over by escaping through a gate, carelessly left open by a group of laughing boys running out to play. One dog was mean and aggressive and had to be taken to the animal shelter. One could jump a six-foot wall and go anywhere it wanted. That one disappeared one day. I have always felt guilt for those creatures.

These two dogs are spoiled! They have had the best ten years of any dog on the planet! Sometimes I think they have become a substitute for my empty nest. I guess I need the ball and chain of dependence. I could imagine the simplicity of life without them, but I don't imagine that for very long, because all I see in being without them is a dark void. The same goes for my sons. Had I not married; I would not have had them to ground me to this earth.

We walk the perimeter of the park. I let the dogs dig by the fallen log for a while. It is Wednesday and more RVs are arriving. When I return to the trailer, I take a long hot shower, at least until the water turns cold. After getting dressed for the day, I go to the main building to look for insect repellent. Vi is on duty at the counter.

The list of chemicals on the insect repellent makes me quiver! I don't want this on my skin! I saw my arms and legs in the shower. My tea tree oil is not enough. It eases the pain, but does not help prevent the bite in the first place. I buy it against my will. I also buy an insect repellent candle for my picnic table. Bubba is busy in the kitchen cooking breakfast for the guests. Helen is waiting tables. When I am at the register I hear Bubba yell.

"HELEN IF YA DON'T GET GOIN' ON THEM DISHES NOW, YUR GONNA BE HERE ALL NIGHT! I'M NOT GOIN' TO GO THRU THIS AGAIN WITH YA!"

"Shut the hell up Bubba! I'll do them when I'm ready!"

Why do they argue in front of the guests? My mind drifts to Helen's prized possession: her fingernails. It's my guess that she does not want to hurt or chip them in any way. Why doesn't she wear gloves? I saw some there. I've used them myself before.

I decide to just hang out by the trailer, empty the holding tank, do dishes, clean windows, listen to music, and relax. The dogs are watching the world from the fenced area.

At 11:15 I walk to work. Terry is watering the flowers in front by the steps. Her head is down and her hair is covering her face. I have to walk past her.

"Hi Terry." Terry looks up at me. Her cheek has a large bruise. She tries to smile. I have learned through the years that you cannot help those who choose to live in a violent relationship. You also cannot help those who are alcoholics either.

"Hi Denise."

"Are you all right? Did you hurt yourself?" I ask.

"Yeah, I was drunk and I fell off the steps of the trailer. Looks ugly huh?" She is lying, but it is not my job to be a counselor.

"Ouch! That must have hurt! Be careful. I've almost fallen from my steps too. I have to get in there now, so I'll see you later."

"Okay, see ya later." Terry quietly replies.

I clock in and go straight to the grill. Bubba is making a chicken fried steak for someone. Helen is talking to a customer at a table.

"YA FORGOT TO EMPTY THE OIL DRIP PAN!" Bubba has something gooey stuck to his chin. The same goo is on the brim of his baseball cap.

"I know Bubba. I'm sorry about that."

"I GOTTA GET OUTSIDE AND WORK ON THE SEWAGE PUMP. IT KEEPS BACKIN' UP. LISTEN, DON'T LET THAT BITCH LEAVE WITHOUT DOIN' THEM DISHES! THE COOK DOES NOT DO DISHES! REMEMBER THAT. KAREN WILL BE IN AFTER A BIT AND IF SHE SEES THOSE DISHES SHE'S GONNA KILL HER!"

I'm not sure if Bubba even remembers last night, or knows that

I have seen Terry with the bruised face. At this moment, I don't really care. I take over the lunch he was making, and the two other tickets hanging on the crown of thorns. He goes over to the tip jar and counts out his share, then gets himself a beer, stuffs Copenhagen in his cheek, and leaves.

I am too busy cleaning up the mess on the grill and cooking, to notice if Helen is doing dishes or not. I find the source of the goo. It is gravy, and it is splattered everywhere. It looks as if Bubba threw the ladle with a tremendous amount of force back into the pan of gravy, splashing it in every direction.

Helen places an order for a hamburger for herself on the wheel and goes over to clean up a few tables. I am concentrating on my job. Karen comes in, rounding the meat counter. I catch a glimpse of her face as she suddenly sees all the dishes and starts to turn purple in the face. She storms back to the register area, where Billy and Vi are now registering a guest. I hear her yelling to Billy about Helen and the unwashed dishes. She's in a rage!

"As long as she is working here, I quit!" Karen says to Billy with her neck thrust forward and her chin raised.

"Now Karen, ya can't make me choose between the two of ya, now can ya?" Billy says matter-of-factly.

"Oh yes I can. I quit!" Karen rams out the front door. Billy walks over to the kitchen. Helen is fixing up the hamburger that I cooked for her. Billy begins talking to Helen in a calm manner.

"Now listen here Helen. Ya gotta start doin' them dishes. We've had this discussion before."

"Billy you know I can't! If I cut myself in the water, I'll get blood poisoning remember? I can't afford to go to the hospital again." Blood poisoning, my ass! She is making up some stupid excuse, even I can tell that.

"Okay, here's the deal. Karen just quit. Ya know how valuable she is 'round here. I might just have to keep you up front at the register from now on." Billy calmly explains.

"That's where I want to be anyway Billy. You know that! I hate being a waitress!" Helen sounds childish.

"Okay, we'll try that out for a while and see how it goes."

Helen wraps up her hamburger, gets her tips, and leaves.

Billy is leaning on the meat counter in deep thought. She turns to me and begins talking. I am working on a French dip for someone out there. "I sure do hate confrontation! Never have been able to do that correctly. I expect everyone to work out their differences on their own, like adults!" Billy obviously does not recognize that the people she has hired may be all grown up, but they are not adults! I thought that bosses were supposed to handle these matters? Maybe Billy just can't do that any more.

"Billy?"

"Yeah."

"Maybe you need a manager?" I suggest.

"Oh, I've tried that before. That guy was supposed to turn this place around. Well, everything got more screwed up than ever!" So much for my bright ideas.

Ray walks over to find out what all the commotion was about. He stands on the other side of the meat counter waiting to talk to Billy. She finishes up with my instructions for the day. "Well Denise, looks like yur gonna be on yur own today. Shouldn't be too busy, so I have faith in ya to handle it all. Ray has a doctor's appointment in Brandon. We'll be gone for most of the day. Vi can help ya with any problems ya might have. I need ya to cook up that one sealed package of tri-tip before I have to throw it out. Cost a fortune. I'm sure it's good. Think of a special for today. Make a soup for dinner if ya can. Sure am happy to have all yur help here. Ya know that, don't ya?" Billy places her hand on my shoulder. I feel like a soldier in combat.

"Yes, Billy I sure do. I'm glad I can help out. Don't worry about anything; I'll make it through the day. Get going now, I have to serve this French dip before it gets cold."

I pray that it stays fairly quiet in here today. After serving the French dip, I walk over to the dishes and fill the sinks with hot water. I keep my eye out for new customers and the ones that are finishing up their meal. Ruby walks in.

"Hi Denise. Where's Billy?" Ruby's hair needs to be washed.

"She and Ray went to the doctor today. I'm alone in the

kitchen and have a million things to do. What's ya need?"

"Well, I need some French rolls, some bacon, two tomatoes, and a twelve pack of beer." I get the items for her. I'm not sure how this is supposed to be handled.

"My tab is in the small file box under the counter here." Ruby points to the spot where we keep our tip jar. I pull it out and start to look.

"What name is it under?" I ask.

"John and Ruby."

I find her thick stack of tabs. According to the dates, this goes back for several months, and could be hundreds of dollars or more. In fact, the whole file is so stuffed with this that I wouldn't doubt that it is more like thousands of dollars! Some of the papers are even turning yellow from age.

"I know! Billy is too kind. Right?" Ruby says guiltily.

"You got that one right. I wrote it down. Nice to see you again. I have to get on with all I have to do. Take care."

When Ruby walks away I find Little John's tabs and Bubba's tabs and countless others who Billy has let slide. If I were in charge here, which I'm not, I'd add all this up and make everyone accountable for their debts! I'd have my new door paid for in no time. I wonder who John, of John and Ruby is? Boyfriend perhaps.

I work on the dishes for twenty minutes or so; at least I now have room to put more dirty platters. There is still a mountain left, but I think I can do it all eventually.

The tri-tip is dated: Sell or freeze by June 25th. That's today, perfect! I am going to make my Mom's famous Spanish steak! It's made with thin slices of tender steak, browned with onions and fresh garlic, then simmered in tomato soup, last but not least, you add lots of green olives stuffed with pimento. It's served over a mound of mashed potatoes.

While the Spanish steak is simmering, and potatoes are boiling, I look for ideas in the cold storage room to make a soup. I find a large box of broccoli and decide on a broccoli cheese soup. By 4:30 I have most of the details of dinner ready, including a pile of pre-made hamburger patties ready to throw on the grill. The dishes are slowly but surely getting done in-between cooking. I go up to the front to ask Vi if she would keep her eye out on things for ten minutes while I let the dogs out and bring them a treat.

Upon my return, I see that she is seating a family of four. While they are looking at the menu, I quickly write my specials on the board, erasing Bubba's mumbo jumbo about something dead. I decide to charge $7.95 for my special. The family is watching me do this and questions about the Spanish steak. The two adults would like to try it, and the kids want a grilled cheese sandwich and french fries.

I am excited about my special, and quite honestly, I am having fun being here by myself. I prepare the meals, adding to my special half an artichoke with a side of mayonnaise. A leaf of green lettuce with a slice of spiced apple laying pretty on top, and a sprig of parsley on top of the Spanish steak. I serve it to them. They seem pleased when they see it. Now, I hope they like it as well as my family always has. Another couple is seating themselves as I bring out the order. They are looking at what I am serving. They too would like to try it. This is fun!

It starts getting busy, and I feel like I am going in fifty directions at once. I take a deep breath and decide that I can only do what I can do, and to not get in a panic.

My family of four has gone and has eaten every bite of their dinners. When they left, they made a point to come and compliment the chef. I sell fifteen plates of my special, and almost all of the soup is gone. My pre-made hamburger patties paid off. It took no time at all to just throw them on the grill. Even old Henry came in and broke his habit of a New York steak and baked potato just to try my special. Henry is the man I first saw in here talking to Bubba. He comes in everyday. He is definitely flirting with me, but he is harmless and quite sweet.

As the place slowly empties of people, I am able to begin cleaning up the major mess on my hands. I dish up a large helping of Spanish steak for Vi and myself in to-go containers. The pan is now empty. I wrap up the last piece of banana cream pie for myself. I have been saving leftover meat for the dogs that goes with me too. Billy and Ray come back at 7:45 and look very tired. They go straight into their home area and shut the door. I hope everything is okay with them. Neither of them are very healthy, that's for sure, but Ray is definitely in trouble! I wonder what those rough patches are on his arms that itch so bad.

The store and restaurant are now closed and locked up. It takes me until 9:30 to finish all the work I have to do. I leave the special board up, just my way of telling Bubba that I am doing fine in here. I count my tips; $110! Wow! I love it! As I am clocking out, Billy comes out holding a drink, smoking a cigarette, and dressed in her nightgown. I am slightly put back by the sight of Billy in a knee length nightgown with her manly build. She would be better off wearing men's flannel pajamas. It would be more believable than that flowery pink nightgown.

"Vi tells me ya did real good today. And ya had a delicious special. Ya rang up $675 for lunch and dinner. Between the new RV guests, and the groceries, we did over $1500 in total. That's really good! Proud of ya Denise. Ray and I are beat, so we're heading to bed. See ya tomorrow." Billy gives me a gentle hug. A hug she obviously needs right now. My return hug confirms to her that I care, I know, and I'm trying my best.

Outside the wind has picked up. Bubba is burning cardboard boxes and tiny sparks are flying high into the sky and then dissipating.

"HOW'D IT GO TODAY?" He hollers out to me.

I walk closer to Bubba so as not to shout, but not too close, the smoke and sparks are bothersome.

"It was actually great! I had a fun time tonight. Made a special, and sold all of it."

"I WANNA TAKE YA TO A REAL PRETTY SPOT ON TOP OF THAT MOUNTAIN ONE DAY REAL SOON. IT'S MY SECRET SPOT. YA CAN SEE THE ENTIRE NATIONAL PARK FROM UP THERE." Bubba is pointing to the mountains far beyond the RV park. I can see these mountains from the window of the fifth wheel. Bubba is also once again drunk. It almost looks like the sparks are actually hitting him in the face when he stuffs more cardboard into the split oil drum barbeque. I then notice the shotgun lying on the picnic bench next to his beer.

"I see you're ready for the mountain lion." I walk over and touch the gun.

"COUGAR! IT'S A DAMN COUGAR! AND DON'T TOUCH MY GUN!" Cougar, scooter, pork and cheese, blah, blah, blah. I'm too tired for this! All I want is to let the dogs out, and go eat. It's so much later than I would ever eat dinner before. I've always had my dinner at around 5:00 for years, so that I could digest it before sleep. At least I can sleep in, maybe.

Bubba is all involved in the raging flames at the moment. I think he stuffed too many boxes in there. I walk away.

My poor puppies, I sure wouldn't want to be trapped inside like this for ten hours! I do my best to soothe my guilt by walking them around outside for a little longer than I want or feel like, and then I eat my Spanish steak, which made with tender tri-tip, is out of this world delicious!

While eating, I notice my fingernails. They are becoming stained with grease, probably from grinding the grill. I know that I wash my hands at least a hundred times during my shift, before and after anything I do. Gawd! Is this permanent? It looks horrible! My wrists are sore. They used to get really sore from cleaning the whirlpool tubs at the inn, and changing those California king beds! Talk about a back breaker!

I change into some cozy sweats. The dogs leap under the covers. I suppose they are too anxious to really rest or relax during the day. At least they can jump onto the bench by the table and look out the windows while I am working and see some of the passing world.

The wind is whipping the canopy against the side of the trailer. I see the half moon through the skylight above my head. Sparks fly by.

CHAPTER NINE

"QUACK! QUACK! QUACK! QUACK!"

The ruckus made by the ducks, alarms Bonita and Bandito and they jump up and stick their heads out from under the covers. Bonita bounces out, jumps on my tummy, and crawls over my head in a rush to get to the window. All she can see is the top of the canopy. Both of the dogs run down to bark at the door. I forgot to close the fenced area! It is later than usual, 8:45AM.

I climb out of bed and unhook the bungee cord to the door, I feel pain radiate in my sore wrists. The dogs yelping is loud and piercing. "Bonita! Bandito! Shut up! Please, shut up!"

I slip on my flip-flops and go down the steps. All the ducks are in a group by the bottom of the steps, looking up and quacking like mad at something, or me, like they are hungry. There is no evidence of them ever having been in the fenced area. In fact, I did not leave the fenced area open at all. Are ducks smart enough to know who buys the seed? Is this Bubba's way of some sort of revenge for buying the seed in the first place, by not feeding them anymore?

I walk sleepily over to the storage room. I'm sure my hair is all over the place and my eyes must surely be puffed up like balloons. The smoke coming out of the vent by the kitchen door smells like pancakes and burns my puffy eyes. The ducks are following me like in some children's fairy tale book. Bonita and Bandito are still barking from inside the trailer. I scoop out a large pan of seed, walk over to the lake's edge, and toss it on the ground. The quacking ceases as they eagerly eat.

Walking back to the trailer I notice the rumbling logging truck parked across the street. The highway is busy. I slept through most of the morning noise.

I put the dogs in the fenced area while I make coffee. They smell all around, marking their small confining territory. I'm too tired to care if they pee in there or not, maybe it will help to keep the ducks away.

After my shower and a bowl of oatmeal, I load the dogs into the car. We spend an hour walking by the creek. When I return, Terry is walking by my trailer at the same time I pull into my parking space. She looks like she wants to talk, because she is walking towards me. She has a cup of coffee in her hand. "Denise, can we talk for a minute?" Her coffee cup is printed with, "Shut the hell up. I'm not awake yet!"

"Sure Terry. Let me put these guys in the fenced area first. Come on in and sit here on the bench. Look out for duck poop. I'll get myself some coffee too." I close Terry and the dogs in the fenced area and go to make my coffee; I can see Terry from the kitchen window talking to my dogs. When I return to the bench, she starts in. "I'm scared Denise. Bubba's trying to make me leave. I have no place to go! We've been together for two years. He's gotten so mean!" Terry says distressingly. I'm not so stupid as to think that Terry is some sort of innocent victim here. I'll bet she could be as mean as a pit bull if she wanted to.

"Bubba did that to your face, didn't he?" I ask.

"Yes." Terry says touching her cheek.

"Terry, you can't live like that! Get the hell out of there!" I plea.

"Ya don't understand! I have no place to go! My Mom lives in Utah, and we don't get along. I don't even have a way of getting there. Bubba's gonna kill me. I just know he is. But I'll fight back. I'll kill him first. I'll fight until I'm dead. He won't be able to kill me easily. Listen Denise; if ya don't see me for a couple of days, I want ya to remember what I said. Do ya understand? I guarantee I'll be dead inside that trailer! Call the cops, cause I'll be dead for sure!"

Now this is going too far! "Terry, if you feel this way, then leave now! What in the hell are you trying to say, that you're so desperate that you're willing to stay and know he might eventually kill you? Is Bubba really that stupid? This is insane! Use common sense here. Get out now!"

Terry is now crying. "Never! I'll die first! He loves me. I know it. It's just that something is wrong with him right now. He used to have cancer, and I think he's worried about it again. I don't know. All I know is that he's changed."

I'm now wondering if he has changed because he is interested in me. Is this what a big bully does to get himself free—terrorize the living hell out of whatever is in his way? Terry is stupid! Flat out stupid! I hate this type of dysfunctional thinking. They are just addicted to violence and alcohol.

"Terry, I have to get ready for work. I'll remember. If I don't see you, I'll call the cops. I promise. You should think seriously about getting the hell out of here. Okay!"

"Ain't gonna happen, Denise."

"Whatever. I'll talk to you later." I resign my effort to advise. People don't really want advice, they just need a person to hear them vent. I have been guilty of having deaf ears once or twice myself.

I go back inside the fifth wheel and watch Terry walk over to Billy's lawn. She turns on the water hose and begins spraying the potted plants.

Drama. Drama. Drama. Oh, to be back at my little stone house by the river in Carmel Valley, feeding my wild birds, walking the river, my dogs running free, and that wonderful silence. I miss walking on the beach of Carmel on warm sunny days, Bandito biting at the foamy edge of the waves, Bonita barking at the sea gulls. Maybe I'm really a professional bum at heart, a recluse. How come my sons don't have any of my characteristics? They are into the man 'toy' thing and making lots of money, very much like their father. Maybe it's a good idea for them to be financially stable; I might need them to take care of me one day.

It's getting hotter everyday. I turn on the air conditioner, feed the dogs, and eat my banana cream pie. On the way to work, I walk past my fire pit. It looks as if I won't be spending much time enjoying that working as late as I do. I always have my two days off, I guess. The one twisted piece of wood that looks like a bird, still needs to be leaned against the pine tree, so I carry it over to display it properly before Bubba throws it into the fire pit.

Ray is watching me as he sits on the rear ledge of his truck parked by the propane tank. He waves, and I walk over to say hello.

"Hello pretty lady! I'm waitin' on a guest to fill his propane tank. How is my gal this fine day?"

"I'm just fine Ray. Thanks. And so how are you?" I ask.

"Besides not getting' enough oxygen, and this damn eczema, and being tired, I'm doin' fine myself." Ray scratches his arm.

"So that's eczema that's giving you all the itching problems huh?"

"What I need is a good nurse! Someone to make me relax and rub my tired bones." Ray is now scratching harder.

"Next time I come over, I'll make sure that you put some cream on that."

"Promise?" He looks hopeful.

"Promise. I've gotta get into your kitchen now before you fire me for being late."

"Never."

An RV is slowly moving in our direction. I walk away.

Inside, Billy is at the counter registering a guest. Helen is stocking the grocery shelves. I clock in as Billy explains: "Karen is still bein' stubborn. She doesn't seem to care that Helen won't be workin' the kitchen no more. She refuses to come to work until Helen is gone. She'll come around soon. She's done this before. She needs the money to help out with the grandchildren. Not many jobs round these parts. The fact of the matter is this; I'll be needing ya to waitress for Bubba for a few hours' till Betty gets here. That okay with ya?"

"Sure. I like to waitress." I answer, but leery of working with Bubba.

"Bubba's goin' a little crazy in there, so better get yurself over there and help out."

The special board is not even hanging up today. I wonder where it is. I put on my apron that I keep inside the kitchen now, and say hello to Bubba.

"Hey Bubba! I guess I'll be your waitress today." I announce.

"WHO TOLD YA YOU COULD USE THAT TRI-TIP? I WAS GONNA MAKE BEEF VEGETABLE SOUP TODAY!"

"Actually, Billy had requested for me to make a special out of it for the day. You should have told me, Bubba, and then I would have made other considerations to please both of you." I was being overly formal at the moment to keep my adrenalin at bay.

"WELL, OKAY, JUST REMEMBER THAT I'M IN CHARGE OF WHAT GOES ON IN THIS KITCHEN. SO YA BETTER LET ME KNOW NEXT TIME." Your kitchen my ass! He only cooks breakfast. It's me that cooks lunch and dinner. I think he's got it a little mixed up! Right! Like I'm supposed to go find him every time I make a move in the kitchen just to get his approval. I don't think so! I am feeling the adrenalin begin to pump through my veins anyway, disregarding my fruitless attempt to harness it.

"YA DID THE GRILL PERFECT LAST NIGHT! TODAY'S SOUP IS CHICKEN NOODLE." He was now giving me a smile. It's really weird how he goes from sinister to agreeable in two seconds or less, leaving me all drained, shaky, and fired up for battle.

Five men, who are obviously fishermen, sit down at a table. I put on my waitress personality, and go to take their order. I'm quite pleasant when I want to be, or should I say, when I'm not being threatened. All the men laugh hysterically at my Chihuahua bait story that I share with them. Each man orders a heavy meal.

While I am taking more orders from other guests, I hear Bubba yell to me. I walk back to the grill. He is holding the order for the five men in his hand, and shaking it at me. "YUR NOT WRITIN' THE ORDERS RIGHT! I CAN'T FIGUR OUT WHAT THIS IS! HERE, YA PUT, CHX SAL, LIKE THIS, TA LEAVE ROOM OVER HERE! DRINKS GO DOWN HERE, OUT OF MY WAY. JUST WRITE BBQBEEF SAN, HERE. NOT THE WHOLE

BLASTED THING! PRINT LARGE LETTERS. AND THIS ONE HERE, IS HE HAVIN' FRIES OR WHAT?"

"Good gawd, Bubba, I'm trying my best! Give me just a little more time to get your order language down the way you'd like. I'm new here remember?" I'm very close to losing it all together. I hope this is my last time to wait tables for him. No wonder Betty is such a tense, little, self-face-slapper-over-achiever!

"TAKE THESE PLATTERS OVER TO THOSE TWO GALS IN THE CORNER."

"Yes, Heir Commandant!" I salute.

"WHAT?"

"Nothing." I glare at Bubba and grab the full platters.

After several people have been served, Bubba decides to go over and talk to the group of fishermen, who are finishing up their meal. He starts joking loudly with them. He has just finished up with some macho, sexist type joke. I walk over with the pot of coffee to re-fill their cups. At that same moment, one of the men fart. They all laugh.

"DENISE! THAT'S NOT VERY POLITE! YA COULD AT LEAST SAY EXCUSE ME!" Bubba feels pretty good about saying that. I raised two boys, and know that burping and farting can be so fun to small boys and immature men. I laugh along with their silliness for the sake of peace. I raise my hand, and with my fingertips, I give Bubba a light push on his shoulder. "Oh Bubba, that's not nice to say." I am still laughing with the goofy men, trying to be a part of the fun when Bubba screams. "OOH! OUCH! DAMN IT TO HELL! THAT'S MY CANCER!" Bubba is holding his arm like I have just beat him with a baseball bat, and glaring at me as if I should have known that his shoulder hurt. I guess it was also funny to all the men, because, who would think a big, loud, brute like Bubba could be hurt by the touch of a finger? The fishermen start howling with laughter, thinking he is still joking around. I am not laughing anymore because I see the rage in Bubba's face.

"IT'S NOT FUNNY! I REALLY HAVE CANCER HERE IN MY ARM!" He looks and sounds like a bratty child as he holds his arm. The entire restaurant is silent and looking in our direction as the "C" word radiates fear in all the guests who are trying to enjoy their meal.

"Bubba, I had no idea! You've never said a word about this to me." I am so embarrassed standing here like this. I would never purposely hurt anyone! Everyone saw that I barely touched him. A couple of the men are still snickering. I don't think that they believe Bubba's big show of pain for one minute. I don't know what to think of this scene. Terry mentioned something about cancer.

Bubba storms back to the kitchen, counts out his tips, and leaves the kitchen slamming the door. I am left alone standing there with a pot of coffee, like an exhibit, everyone awaiting my next move. I'm sure they expect hysteria. Then I see Lottie sit down at a table. I walk stiff and awkwardly over to her, and am relieved to be free of my bewildering moment. The fishermen are getting up from the table now.

"Hello Lottie! Would you like your regular?" Lottie starts in. "Bubba is the biggest asshole I've ever met. What a rude son-of-a-bitch! I love Billy, and I love her food here, and if this wasn't the only place in town to eat, I'd stay away, just to not see him ever again! He did that show of pain to get to you! He's jealous! He's afraid you're gonna be a better cook than he is, which by the way, you are. He's workin' it good for sympathy of some sort. Don't let him get to you. He's gonna try, mark my words! And yes, I'll have my regular." I like Lottie. I guess owning and operating a bar in Vegas for twenty years has taught her a lot about alcoholic, temperamental, bullies. The fishermen have left me a twenty-five dollar tip. It appears it was me that was pitied.

I am getting the dishes all cleaned up when Betty comes on duty. She is raring to go! She gets me caught up on food prep faster than a bolt of lightening! I hear banging of dishes being cleaned. She zooms to the oven with a tray full of potatoes to bake. She chops the lettuce. With Betty's hyper-vigilance, I can concentrate on cleaning up Bubba's mess at the grill. When I cook, I clean as I go. Bubba only does his food orders and his neglected messes build up, one on top of the other.

It's not easy to make Betty slow down enough to chat. I'd like to get to know her better. What makes Betty tick? It's easy to see from her looks that it is not drugs. I start asking her questions that she answers while working. I find out that she is Amish, and was shunned by her family for an undisclosed reason six years ago. She has worked here ever since. She lives alone, and has no pets. This job is her life. She is apprehensive to admit to me that Bubba is difficult to work for, but is telling me in her own way, how happy she is to work with me in the kitchen. She greatly admires Billy and Ray, and has given her all to please them. Poor little thing! She says she's happy. She loves being free and on her own. I need to find out more about the Amish someday.

After my short break to check on my dogs, I return to the kitchen just in time for the dinner crowd to start arriving. We are extremely busy, and everything is running smoothly, thanks to Betty's efficiency. I am cooking two ham steak dinners and a Rueben. Betty has just picked up an empty, used, mixing bowl from my cooking area and zoomed around the corner to clean it. I hear the crash on the other side of the wall. It sounds like a jet airplane has just flown through the building and crashed through a pile of stainless steel pans. The wall vibrates. I see the restaurant guests stand up. Their mouths are open in shock, and they are looking towards the floor area by the sink. I walk around to the sink area, and find Betty on the floor. She has crashed into the tall drying rack full of dishes and pans! She is in a ball on the floor crying and holding her left arm.

Billy and Helen come running to the kitchen. We all hover over her. The left side of Betty's face, and her left shoulder and arm are beginning to swell. Bruises are developing that are the exact shape and size of the drying rack. She hit the rack with the force of a bullet! Betty looks pale, and is in agony. Billy and Helen walk her to Billy's car to drive her to the hospital. Helen does not go with them because she is needed at the register. The closest hospital is an hour away. Does the chaos never end? Karen has quit, and now Betty will be out for a long time. I know she has broken a bone, or bones, somewhere in that little body.

Henry comes in to eat. He has a severe limp from an old injury years ago. One leg is shorter than the other. He wants to know what my special is for the day. "I'm sorry Henry, I didn't have time to make one today."

"That's too bad. Sure did love yur Spanish steak, little lady. What's ya got goin' on with them angry looking bites on yur arms and ankles?"

"I guess the mosquitoes around here just love me." I am still in shock about Betty's horrible fall, so my conversation sounds monotone. It's hard to be conversational right now.

"Who wouldn't? I'll tell ya what ya need. Ya need some garlic tablets. That'll keep them buggers away!"

"Henry, Betty just took one heck of a fall. Billy just took her to the hospital." Henry does not seem too surprised about this news. "That little gal was headed for a fall for years! Runs around like she's all wound up tighter than a rubber band! That's too bad. I guess I'll have my regular, if I can't have one of yur specials. If ya ever feel like comin' out to my ranch some day, let me know. I'd sure love for ya to see my operation out there." Henry seems unconcerned for Betty.

"Thanks, Henry. Maybe I just might do that one day." Still monotone.

I return to the grill to finish the dinner hours. It does not take me long to clean up after everyone has left since Betty had done most of the work before she fell. The last customer leaves at 7:20. I clock out at 8:15. I have made $87 in tips. I leave Betty's share in an envelope under the counter. It is still light enough outside to walk around the park with the dogs. Guests are still barbecuing, fishing, playing cards at their outside tables, and kids are running around, so I feel safe. Bubba and Terry are collecting trash, and driving it in the scooter to the back forest storage area. God only knows where they are piling it! At least the trash is getting picked up before the weekend madness! The new guests will now have some place to put their trash.

The ducks see me, and run in my direction to be fed. I throw out a pan of seed before returning to my trailer. I hope they leave me alone in the morning. I decide to take a small bag of feed with me, just in case they are waiting by my trailer tomorrow. I guess I should have let them live off the dog food.

Before taking the dogs out I spray myself with the insect repellent and then walk the perimeter of the park. Ray is sitting with Jim having a cocktail at Jim's picnic table at the bend in the road. Once again the barking begins between all the dogs. I shout out. "Have you heard anything from Billy about Betty?"

Ray replies. "Yeah, she broke her shoulder real good! Billy wants ya to come on over later for a drink. She'll want to know about the day and how everything went. Billy should be home in about an hour. She had to take Betty home and put her ta bed."

"Okay, I'll be there."

Back at the fifth wheel, I eat the grilled ham and cheese I had made for myself, feed the dogs a mixture of dry dog food mixed with leftover New York steak, and take a shower. I see Billy's car lights entering the park. Ray's old truck squeaks by my trailer on the way back from Jim's, headed to his house. I'm anxious to hear about Betty, but do not rush over so that Billy and Ray have time to catch their breath and relax. I make myself a gin and limeade, and play with the dogs for twenty minutes or so by throwing their toys up onto the bed to fetch.

Bubba has his five-alarm fire going in his fire pit. Good, at least I can talk to Billy and Ray alone tonight! I have a few questions. When I get to their sliding glass door, I see Billy inside pouring a drink, and Ray is picking at his arms at the bar and is wearing his oxygen hose. They see me, and wave to come in. Ray greets my arrival by saying. "Well, there's our pretty gal! Ya got one of them sissy drinks again I see."

"Can't help it Ray, I just love these on warm summer nights." I look fondly at my icy green drink. "So Billy how is Betty?" I quickly add.

"She's busted her shoulder real good. Also has a concussion. I've told her a million times to slow down! Knew that'd a happen one day. She'll be out for several weeks, maybe the rest of the summer. Damn, is she bruised! Heard that racket in the kitchen, and thought the roof done come down on the place! Gotta real problem now with help. Karen quittin' like she did, and now Betty all banged up. Might have ta hire someone for the rest of the summer. Little local gal named Jamie asked the other day. Might give her a call. She needs work until she starts college in September."

"Boy, that fall of Betty's scared the heck out of me. She must have been going faster than the speed of light!" I say as the crashing once again flashes through my mind.

"How'd it go at the grill tonight? Any problems?" Billy asks.

"No, no problems to speak of. It's just that I was wondering about Bubba's cancer?"

"Bubba don't have no cancer! Never heard him mention anythin' about that before. Why?" Billy looks bewildered at me as smoke from her cigarette rolls into her eyes and makes her squint.

I tell Billy and Ray about the incident in the restaurant today, and question them about his aggressive behavior. "Well, if he has some problem with cancer, he's never talked to us about it. Has he ever said anythin' to you Ray?" Ray shakes his head no, and continues itching. "And as far as him being dangerous, that's also a big no. He ain't nothin' but a big teddy bear! It's all bark, and no bite, believe me, we should know!" I think they are in denial.

"Billy? Is Terry employed here with you?" I'm beginning to feel nosey, but my curiosity overpowers my ignorance. I want information!

"Naw, she's just hangin' around to be with Bubba. We've had a few problems with that gal, that's for sure! She gets herself drunk, and all hell breaks lose. That's why we won't give her a permanent job here. We've had to make her leave a time or two before, but she always comes back."

"Oh," like diarrhea as Bubba said.

"Quit yur damn itchin' Ray!" Billy slaps Ray's hand.

"I can't Billy. Ya know it drives me crazy at this time of the night!" Ray replies in frustration.

I make an offer to help out on that current problem. "Listen, where's that witch hazel? I can apply that to your arms while we chat."

"Would ya?" Billy was pleased with my offer. "I'd do it, but I'm too tired. Ray doesn't have the energy to do it for himself. We'd really appreciate that! I'll get the witch hazel." Billy gets up and begins looking under several piles of things in the disorderly house.

I clean up his arms with warm water first, then gently begin patting the tender skin with witch hazel. Ray's eyes are closed in the comfort of my nursing. He softly says, "Yur an angel! That feels so good. Can't thank ya enuf'. Ya know that this is yur job forever now, don't ya?"

"Why not? If I'm over here, I'd be more than happy to be your nurse." Nurturing is my specialty.

"I'm gonna start that lawn on Tuesday. Need to make a lawn for our pretty lady." Ray nurtures right back.

Billy is smiling and smoking as she watches me apply the Witch Hazel to Ray's arms. She says, "Ya know Denise, Ray's got that eczema problem all over his legs too." I gulp as I imagine the layers of clothes dropping. "Oh how horrible! Well, next time, you put some shorts on, instead of these tight, scratchy jeans, and I'll get the legs too!" They both seem trusting, pleased, and relieved.

"Billy? I hope you don't mind me asking, but what's with the trash situation? Isn't there an easier way to get rid of all that garbage?" I just can't help from asking.

"We think the dump truck has had it! I've gone online and found a used trash truck with a front loader for sale. It'll hold all we can give it. Anyway, I bought it. They'll be shipping it by diesel truck from Idaho soon." Billy says and then gulps down the last of her strong drink.

"Sounds good! That should make things a lot easier for everybody!" I say wondering to myself how reliable a used trash truck found online in Idaho could be.

After a short time, I say good night, and return to the fifth wheel. I listen to my Native American Indian music in the darkness of my druggy bed. Bonita and Bandito are curled up consolingly under the covers on opposite sides of my hips. The soft drumming and chanting helps to distract me from my small metal dungeon on wheels parked in the land of the lost and damaged. One more day of work, and then I have two days off! I take a deep breath and blow my anxiety up and out the skylight above my head.

CHAPTER TEN

I am wide-awake and there is the faintest deep blue glow hinting the beginning of sunrise. I slept like a log! It's very quiet outside, and nothing has stirred yet. Not the ducks, not Bubba walking by, not a logging truck—nothing! Even Bonita and Bandito are staying in bed late. I revel in the silence, drinking my coffee, and thinking about how I will spend the next five hours before going to work. A long drive sounds really nice. I need to get away from here for a while. I need to explore the national park. A drive is exactly what I will do!

By the time the sun peeks over the horizon, I have my camera, snacks, water, pepper spray, and my dogs, all ready to go. The ducks see me from their current spot across the lake, and run quacking like mad, in my direction. The feed I had brought back to the trailer comes in very handy right now. I sprinkle some in the dirt and drive away. Just as I pull out onto the highway, I see Bubba walking from his trailer on his way to work. He is looking at my car as I pass by, and no doubt, wondering where I am going at this early hour of the morning.

"Say bye-bye to Bubba kids. Bye-bye Bubba!" I wave. The dogs are cocking their heads at me, wondering what I am saying to them. They think I am acting very suspicious.

The morning is warm and glorious! I make a quick stop at a day use spot to let the dogs out, and walk around for a short time. I watch a lady catch a fish. The creek has slowed down a bit since I last saw it. I suppose it gets down to a trickle by the time summer ends. I ignore the trash I see scattered by the trashcan. Today, someone else can save the planet. Today, I will keep all thoughts positive and all concerns out of my mind, at least until 11:15.

I drive further down the highway and follow the signs that lead to points of interest. I explore a massive cave made by a lava flow, hike to a waterfall, and drive leisurely down a dirt road that carries me gently through a thick line of impenetrable redwoods where the craziness of the world is momentarily silenced. I stop my car and walk with Bonita and Bandito in reverence and veneration, feeling small and humbled below the whispering branches.

Later, down another dirt road where pines and junipers prevail, I study trees that have the shape of wild beasts, bent and twisted through time, trees telling me stories of seasons gone by. One tree particularly got my attention enough to get my camera out of the car. The tree was an old juniper that had a story to tell. A child, who is more than likely, old and gray by now, had left his or her bike in the split of two branches of this once young tree. The tree has grown into a giant, and swallowed the abandoned bike. All that remains are two halves of rusted spoke wheels sticking out from either side of the tree, and one tip of a handle bar, ten feet high in the air. How I would love to open up that tree, to slice it open like an onion, and discover how efficient the tree has been to compensate for the twisted metal, now compacted, within its body of rings and grain. The juniper has swallowed and preserved a child's day of play, a child who carelessly abandoned the bike in the unstoppable pathway of this tree's life journey.

My constant guilt over Bonita and Bandito being stuck inside a trailer all day is now alleviated. My hunger for the healing effects of nature is restored. I can now return to the chaos of Hacienda and make it through the day.

The temperature is rising on a daily basis, and the inside of a metal trailer is much hotter than the air outside. I turn on the air-conditioner for the dogs, and hope that it does not break until I am gone from this place in September. I leave for work a half hour early and go to the front phone booth to call Lori. I need a good dose of my sister's love as my final healing treatment. I update her on all my current trials and tribulations. She tells me that the Oregon fires are 80% contained. She will call mom and dad for me, and let them know that I am fine. Lori plans to come see me in mid-July, only a few weeks away.

It's Friday. As I walk through the doors of the restaurant, I can feel the momentum of commotion rising. Billy is busy at the register and Bubba is placing a platter of his famous basketball size pancakes on the table of a heavyset Indian with a long black braid down his back. The female companion of the Indian is having ham and eggs.

"NO ONE'S EVER ATE ALL THESE BEFORE. YA EAT ALL THESE AN YUR BREAKFAST'S ON ME!" Bubba is being loud and obnoxious. The Indian nods his head. I have found that Indian men can be men of little words, yet even without language, they say so very much!

Bubba and I walk into the kitchen at the same time. He walks over to his coffee cup sitting on the counter, and holds it out in front of my face. "DON'T WASH THIS COFFEE CUP EVER AGAIN! LEAVE IT RIGHT HERE! I HAD IT AGED TO PERFECTION! NOW I HAVE TO START ALL OVER AGAIN!" He gets a black marking pen, and writes BUBBA in big letters across the front of it, and bangs it on a corner shelf. That's the coffee cup I had seen him drinking out of on his way to work. It took so long to clean! I had to use a Brillo pad to get all the coffee stains out of it. Never heard of an aged coffee cup before. I thought I was being nice. Now that I've been served another dish of Bubba's bullshit, I can begin my day of work.

Bubba is staying longer than normal. We have no waitress at this point, so I get on with the waiting and serving of tables. At one point, when I am taking an order from a table of three, I look over at the Indian and his girlfriend and see them doing something odd. She is rolling up one of the pancakes as if it were a thick woven rug, while his large body shields her from Bubba's view. She then stuffs the rolled pancake into her large tote bag. Together, they slyly repeat this process with a second pancake. The Indian has eaten the third large pancake and she has finished her own meal. I'm elated from their deceit and can't wait to show Bubba the empty plates!

After taking the order for the table of three, I walk over to the

Indian.

"Hi! Are you all done here?" I ask with a big smile.

"Yes! Tell the big man cook to come see. Tell him I want more of his wee, tiny, pancakes!" The Indian is pointing proudly at his plate. His girlfriend clutches her tote bag.

"Hey, Bubba! This gentleman would like to show you something!" I yell for all to hear.

Bubba looks over the meat counter at the Indians empty plate. "NO WAY! NO ONE'S EVER EATEN ALL MY PANCAKES! YUR THE MAN! CAN'T BELIEVE IT! NEVER HAPPENED BEFORE!"

"Big man cook owes me breakfast." He demands without a hint of guilt.

"He sure does, doesn't he?" I take the ticket with a wide smile and a sassy gait, over for Bubba to sign. I can tell he is pissed, but I am overjoyed that the Indian got one over on him. The Indian leaves me a five dollar tip.

Helen comes on duty at 2:00. Bubba leaves as soon as he sees her. The lunch crowd has thinned out. I guess I'll have to put up with Helen, even though she's a worthless helper. She walks over to the grill, where I am dealing with Bubba's mess.

"Did ya get yur paycheck yet?" she asks while carefully peeling open an envelope using a knife instead of her precious fingernail.

"Oh yeah, today is payday! No, not yet."

"I'll get it for ya." Helen returns and hands me the envelope with my first paycheck. I rip it open. My gross pay for the week was $345. After all the deductions, I clear $266. With $352 in tips for the week, plus the $63 I had left from my original $400, I now have $681! Not bad! If I can survive the torment around here until September, I should have a small savings account!

I do my regular routine to prepare for the dinner crowd. I find a large can of clams in the storage room and make some creamy clam chowder. I also make spaghetti for my special of the day. I ask Helen, who is now filing her nails, to put all the info on the special board, which fills in her next half hour of time.

As the busy evening progresses, I become aware and eventually obsessed with the neglected and growing pile of dishes that Helen is avoiding. The good feeling from my wonderful morning has vanished. I start to become quiet and uncommunicative to Helen. She's a big phony and has some illusion that her fingernails give her some sort of attractiveness or youthfulness. As far as I'm concerned she's using her nails as an excuse to avoid hard work. Sure, I'd just love to baby my hands, but as I look at them I know that they have been used to the fullest extent. I've dug, glove-free, in the soil preparing and tending gardens, loving the feel and smell of wet earth. I have one small mark on my right hand from Bandito's habit of reaching over and pawing at my hand as I drive. He didn't mean to rip the thin skin with his claw. It's just that this is his way of telling me to extend my arm closer to him so that while he sits on his pile of blankets he can lay his tiny left front leg on my arm while I drive. It's hard to punish him for this, since he looks so proud and content resting his leg on my arm while he looks blissfully down the highway. I can't help but to be touched by this human-like show of affection.

Bandito has been this way since the day I rescued him from the animal shelter. When I brought him home he was nothing but bones and had been neutered just a few hours prior to my picking him up. I took him with me to my flower shop that very same day to keep an eye on him. When I walked out the screen door to display my sign on the side of Carmel Valley road, he bolted out and ran like he had an urgent destination in mind, which was not with me. I ran after him until I had no more breath and he was just a small black disappearing dot on the side of the busy road. Then I collapsed onto my knees on the shoulder of the road, crying. In one day, I had lost him. I could not believe that a malnourished Chihuahua with fresh stitches could run that fast. When I looked up again, I could see the tiny black dot returning as fast as he had disappeared. Bandito was running back and thankfully, staying on the dirt shoulder of the road. He ran right to me and jumped into my arms. He must have realized that he had no place to go. Bandito made me feel very special, and in that moment on the side of the road, we were bonded for life.

The rest of the evident premature aging on my hands is from working too damn hard for too many years and also from being a slightly clumsy left-hander all my life. I am nobody's princess that could warrant such panoply and luxury as acrylic nails. It's certainly a little late in life for Helen to be a pampered princess in a remote RV park located in the middle of hell, so she gets no admiration from me. I just want her to do the damn dishes!

Just when things begin to unwind and I prepare to shut down the kitchen for the night, a party of twenty walks in. They push three tables together. I have no time to fixate on Helen's laziness anymore. At least she is managing as best she can to help me through this nightmare! Everyone at the table orders something different. At 8:50 they have finished eating, and are starting to leave. I see Helen counting out her tips. She gingerly walks away.

"Get back here right now Helen!" I shout.

Helen responds. "I don't do dishes!"

"Oh yes you do! You are not leaving me with this mess! I'll be here all night!" I realize my fists are clinched and attempt to relax them.

"I don't do dishes." Helen says calmly.

"You don't do dishes because you're so worried about your fingernails!" She ignores me, and walks over to clock out. I storm over to the register and yell into Billy's house. The door is slightly ajar.

"Billy! Helen is leaving! She refuses to do the dishes. I'm not going to do those! I have yet to clean the grill, and mop the floor. Can you help me out here?" I sound like a tattle-tale, but screw it, I've reached my limit.

Billy walks out smoking her cigarette. "Now Denise, yur gonna have to figure this out on yur own. Ya know how I hate confrontations," she says with irritation in her voice.

"But Billy, you have to help me out here. I'm very tired, and I can't do this alone. You're our boss for heaven's sake! Just tell her to do the dishes! If she doesn't do them, then I'm sorry, but I will never work with her again. I'm not quitting you. I'm just telling you that I will never cook with her as my waitress again! That bullshit about being afraid of some sort of blood poisoning is a cop-out! She's just afraid of hurting her damn fingernails!" The anger explodes out of me like darts.

Billy guides Helen through her doorway, at which point she turns around to me and says, "Ya get started cleanin' up Denise, unless ya want to be here all night. I'll have a talk with Helen."

Is she serious?!...I am so pissed, that I can't even see straight! My adrenalin is flowing stronger than I have felt in years! I am also extremely mad at Billy for being such a coward. How dare her not stand up for the right thing!

I return to the kitchen to see the huge pile of dishes. My cheeks are hot and flushed with anger. I start throwing dishes into the sink, filling it with hot water. I bang pans around, making all the noise I can, mumbling under my breath venomous thoughts about every single one of these backwoods idiots! What in the hell is wrong with these stupid people?

By the time I finish cleaning the kitchen, it is 11:00. The $92 in tips does not make me feel any better. Helen never came out of Billy's house. If she did, then she left through the glass slider by their porch. My blood pressure must be really high, because my heart rate is beating through my chest! I'm not sure that I can make it through the summer. My $681 plus these tips, makes $773. I could leave now, but I'd be back to zero in no time.

What I need to do is get to bed and flush my mind of these malicious feelings for Helen and terrifying fears for my future financial security. I'm completely exhausted and have the feeling I have entered Dante's Inferno.

Once in bed, with Bonita and Bandito sweetly cuddled on either side of my hips, and my worn-out, aging hands resting gently on the backs of their curled up little bodies, my pounding heart gradually quiets and I drift off in the solace of the only unconditional companionship I retain.

Bandito turns his head under the covers and licks the top of my right hand two times, and then lays back down to sleep.

CHAPTER ELEVEN

"**NO!** NO! NO!" I scream.

"Now Denise, calm down, we had to cook 'em cause we ran outda meat. Now ya better get yurself in there, and get them dishes done." Billy is patting my back to comfort me.

Bandito wakes me from my nightmare by tapping my back with his paw. He sits by my face looking down at me in concern. My pillow is wet from tears. In my dream, someone had left the fenced area open and Bonita and Bandito had gotten out. We were having a tri-tip barbeque and hundreds of people were eating gluttonously at the picnic tables. An obese mountain lion was walking through the tables like a pet. People were hand feeding it their leftover scraps. I walked over to the oil drum barbeque where Bubba was drinking a beer and grilling up some meat. I looked closer at the grill, and to my horror, I saw my precious babies, Bonita and Bandito, sizzling on the grill! Ray, who had all sorts of strange tubes coming out of his head and chest, was sitting at the picnic bench laughing. Billy was standing behind me, patting my back with one hand and holding a cocktail in the other.

Bad dreams are not new to me. I have grown accustomed to the distorted reflection of my, often times, chaotic reality. I try very hard to understand what dreams are telling me. This bad dream is, flat out, easy to analyze. The only trouble is I can't leave here now, because of the uncertainty of what lies ahead. What would I be trading this job for further down the road? The embarrassing and humiliating acknowledgment of defeat, and the thought of yet, one more unknown, in yet, one more direction, would be an even greater nightmare to further haunt my subconscious mind. The good thing is I believe that I am a decent, healthy, human being, trying my best to survive, and be self-sufficient. I will survive this! There has to be some good that will come out of all this insanity. "I own my life, and only mine, and so I shall appreciate my person, and so I shall make proper use of myself." I chant out loud as I climb out of bed.

Bonita and Bandito think I am talking to them. "Sorry guys, I forgot, I own your lives too, don't I? You don't even know that last night Bubba had you all barbequed up, do you? Are you ready to go outside?"

I leash them up, and walk them out. I see Bubba feeding the ducks at the bottom of the ramp to the kitchen. Good! That's one problem out of my way this morning. Terry is in the scooter watching him. Surprisingly, she waves at me. I wave back. Maybe the sweethearts have made up. Bubba jumps into the scooter and they drive off. Gee, Billy must be cooking breakfast today. I only have one more day of work, until my two days off. Shit! I have to take Bubba and Terry shopping tomorrow. I can't even imagine what that will be like.

I'm not sure what time it is right now. According to where the sun is, it could possibly be around 9:00. I walk the dogs over to the front of the main building. Ray is standing over across the parking lot in one of my favorite, semi-private, safe areas to let the dogs walk around in. The area is about the size of two acres. There are scattered parts and pieces throughout the dirt area of the remains of an old miniature golf course that is now becoming part of the earth. Bandito loves to rummage through the crumbling remains. Ray is talking to a gentleman and pointing to a spot in the center of the empty lot.

I walk the dogs further down the road. On my way back, Ray is saying good-bye to the man, who is now in his truck and driving away. Ray sees me coming. He smiles and greets me.

"Good mornin', pretty lady!" he shouts. He is not wearing his oxygen hose this morning.

"Good morning, Ray! So what are you up to this morning?" I ask as I approach him.

"I was just meetin' with a general contractor 'bout them cabins

135

we got comin'.' ''

"You have cabins coming? What kind of cabins?" Is he joking? They can't handle any more responsibility. What they already have is falling to pieces. Who's going to clean them?

"Small rental cabins on wheels, like trailers. We've ordered four of them several months back. If, and when, they ever get here, we could make some pretty good money rentin' them out. The cabins come complete with a bed, toilet, kitchen area—perfect for fishermen. We're gettin' kind of nervous 'bout them cabins. They shoulda arrived 'bout three weeks ago. We got over $15,000 deposit all tied up in them cabins, not to mention the paid in full trash truck that Billy ordered over the internet that we haven't heard any news on yet either. "

Ray shows me where the four cabins will sit on the empty lot, but has failed to mention the amount they paid for the trash truck, disappointing my curious nature.

I have enough time left to shower, have some breakfast, and clean up the fifth wheel. My organic diet is going to pot! When I look in the small bathroom mirror, I suddenly realize that I have not thought about make-up the entire time I've been here. Make-up is not needed in this crazy place, so I will continue to be my natural self. I have no desire to impress a living soul right now, and I don't need Bubba thinking that I am looking good for his benefit, that's for sure! I'm enjoying the freedom of not wearing a mask.

Inside the main building I see Geneva's white hair moving about as she frantically cooks. Vi is behind the register and Billy is talking to a young girl, showing her where we clock in. They all look in my direction as I enter.

"Denise, I want you to meet Jamie. Jamie's gonna be our new waitress for the summer." Jamie is a little doll! Her straight, shoulder length blonde hair is shiny and she has a barrette on each side to keep it out of her face. She is free of make-up, but has pink lip gloss on that brightens her features. She is clean, dressed modestly, has a nice smile, and I get to train her! Best of all, Jamie is under fifty years of age, and that alone will be a huge improvement around here. This place needs some youthful inspiration.

"Hi Jamie, so nice to meet you." I shake her unblemished, nail polish free hand.

"Ya show Jamie the ropes and take over the grill for Geneva. She has ta get some trays ready for a group rollin' in around 3:00. I've got things ta do and oh, thaw out sum more hamburger."

"Billy, how is Betty doing?" I ask.

"Sore as hell! Got a sling on her arm. Said she's turnin' purple on the whole left side of her body and face. She's restin' a lot." Billy walks away.

"Lesson number one Jamie, don't be running too fast in here. Come on, I'll show you what goes on in the kitchen." I say with gentle authority.

I'm very happy about having Jamie in the kitchen. When I look at her, it's almost as if I am looking at my younger self. She is so sweet and innocent. Life has not jaded her enthusiasm, hopefully it never will. I'll ease her into the chaos. Poor thing, she has no idea what she's gotten herself into.

Geneva has a sweat going down her face as she stands cooking at the grill. Her gray hair is sticking to her cheeks, and her face is bright red!

"Denise, hurry and come take over these meals I got goin'! I've got to start them trays! Cookin's not my thing! With all these gals out broken and quittin', and lots of people arrivin', we better just keep our noses to the grindstone! Hand me that there platter!" I grab a platter. "NO! Not that one! That one there!" she yells. Geneva's platters of food look sloppy, some look over-cooked, some look under-cooked, there is no fruit on the plate. "Whoa! Geneva, slow down! Give me a chance to get up to your speed!" I plead. "Have you met Jamie yet?" I ask.

"No, hi Jamie, ya know how to cut tomatoes? See them tomatoes over there? Start cuttin' them up and clear off some of them tables out there too!" Geneva says anxiously not even looking at Jamie or wanting a reply.

I look at Jamie. She looks at me. Her smile is no longer there.

"Come over here, Jamie." I take her around the corner to the sink area to talk. "Listen Jamie, I know you're being overwhelmed at the moment. Please don't worry. As far as I know, you'll be working with me for lunch and dinner. We're going to make a great team, I promise you. It'll get crazy in here at times, but I won't be yelling at you. Just remember to ask me questions when you need to, okay?"

"Sure, thanks. Should that older woman be cooking? She seems really stressed out!" Jamie looks like a cornered puppy.

"Don't worry, Geneva doesn't usually cook. I guess she's just filling in for Bubba this morning. Okay Jamie, I'll do the tomatoes, and you go clear some of those tables and seat any new people. I'll help you moment to moment if necessary. Also, and this is very important, you need to keep all these dishes cleaned up as you go. Every time you have a lull in waiting on tables, get a few more done, that way it won't overwhelm you. I'll tend to the cooking and food prep, and when you start catching on, you can learn to help me out preparing platters for the meals. Don't worry; we're going to be a great team!" I had to express my point about the dishes.

"Thanks, Denise! I'll try my best. I'm really glad that I'll be working with you."

"Same goes for me. Now you better get going. I'll handle Geneva until she's out of here."

I take over the cooking for Geneva, who begins to take over eighty per cent of the counter space with large plastic trays, salami, turkey, vegetables, cheese, pickles, fruit, and crackers. The area that Geneva is making trays is the small space between the grill area and the sink area, but her supplies are scattered everywhere. It's very difficult to properly prepare my own cooking agenda.

Jamie is doing a great job. She has been keeping up with the dishes, and I can see her being sweet and pleasant to the guests in the restaurant. Geneva is in deep concentration arranging the trays and seems to be in a much more pleasant mood, so I converse with her. "So Geneva, I didn't know that we did catering here too. How's that work?" I'm beginning to believe that Billy and Ray are way over their heads. "Every once in a while we have a large group come in. This one's called Carefree Caravan. When they make their reservation online, they can order these trays for a get together after they arrive. I've been doin' these for Billy for five years now. I also fill in on cookin' when she needs me to." Geneva says as she plunges a knife into the top of a pineapple.

"Well, it looks very beautiful." I say to be kind. Geneva is spearing the spiky green top of the pineapple with chunks of cheese. Geneva finally smiles at me. "I've got an old black and white TV in the car. I was wondering if ya needed one." Geneva offers.

"A TV? Really? Sure, I could use a TV. How sweet. Thanks."

"It doesn't work that great, but maybe ya could at least have some TV to look at. Before I leave today, ya can follow me out to get it."

"Thanks, Geneva."

After Geneva has finished her trays, she puts them into the cold storage unit inconveniently in the way of my cooking supplies. The restaurant has reached that quiet time, in-between lunch and dinner. I'm pleased to see Jamie busy with the dishes. I arrange with Geneva to meet outside. She drives around to my trailer and hands me a tiny TV. It appears to be one of the first miniature black and white models ever made. It is very dusty and has certainly seen better days. I thank her for her kindness anyway. She meets my dogs, then leaves. I take advantage of the moment and get them out for a quick walk.

When I return to the back kitchen door, I see that the flytrap is full again, and change it. The fly problem is definitely getting bad around here! I just know that they are breeding profusely in the back forest area! The pile of empty cardboard boxes is halfway up the outside wall again.

Jamie and I have time to get to know each other. We work well together. This gives me encouragement. It turns out that she is the daughter of a local preacher in Brandon. She leaves for college in September, hopefully at the same time that I will be heading out of here. Suddenly Bubba bangs through the back door shocking me out of my thoughts. "WHERE'S THEM TRAYS?" he demands to know as he barges in my space making himself an immediate priority.

"In the cold storage room. How're you doing today Bubba? Have you met Jamie yet?" Bubba eyes our young, pretty, new, blonde waitress, and puts on the charm. Jamie reaches out to shake his hand.

"Hi Bubba, nice to meet you." Jamie says sweetly.

"YEAH, SAME HERE. I'M THE COOK ROUND HERE, SO IF YA HAVE ANY PROBLEMS, LET ME KNOW, AND I'LL TEACH YA ALL YA NEED TA KNOW." Oh brother! He has the biggest ego of anyone I've ever met!

Bubba grabs two trays and precariously carries them out to the open rear door of Billy's car. He returns and takes the final tray out along with a fresh twelve pack of beer.

"I thought you were the cook?" Jamie questions as we watch him drive away.

"I am Jamie, but Bubba is a control freak. He cooks breakfast. He thinks he runs this entire place, but take my word for it, he doesn't. If you have any problems, just go see Billy about it or ask me."

"He looks mean!"

"He can be, that's for sure, so just stay out of his way, and I think you'll be fine. Hopefully you never have to waitress for him." At this moment Ginger arrives with fresh pies and we help carry the pies to the case.

I am getting ready for the dinner crowd, when a tall man, dirty from head to foot with a black film of soot, walks up to the counter. I am not sure if he is a vagrant or what! He looks very tired and the black soot has settled in the creases of his facial lines and the outer edges of his lips.

"Can I help you?" I ask the man.

"Yes, I would like a chili burger with fries, to go please."

"Whatever your job is, I don't think I'd want to try it." I bravely say.

"Oh, sorry 'bout that. This is what happens when you're a

logger. My name is John. I'm Ruby's boyfriend. You must be Denise. Ruby's spoken highly of you." He knows better than to shake the hand of a food handler right now.

"Oh, John! Nice to meet you! How's Ruby? I haven't seen her in a while."

"I guess you haven't heard yet."

"Heard what?"

"Ruby got arrested a few nights ago."

"Arrested? For what?"

"All her warrants caught up with her. They came and handcuffed her and took her away. She might be in jail for a couple of years."

"That's horrible! Poor thing. I'm sorry to hear that." She was definitely the type to have warrants of some type or another. I can only think that she will have to dry out while she's in jail. Sobriety won't hurt her any.

I make his meal, and write the amount due on his and Ruby's tab. People are staring at him as he walks away; leaving black footprints on the floor.

My soup for the evening is cream of potato. I do not make a dinner special. Jamie is doing a great job, and this gives me a sense of normalcy. Finally, I can concentrate on my job. The tables are almost full of guests.

When Karen, Helen, or Betty were waiting tables, there was always a sense of drama, or urgency, but things are flowing along relatively smooth, thanks to Jamie's youthful and pleasant personality. She is willing to be a part of teamwork, something the others have no concept of. Betty tried, but the buzzing in her head, and her desire to be a willing slave, is, or should I say, was, disturbing to watch, to say the least.

I am cutting up more watermelon for the dinner platters when Bubba slams through the back door. The door bangs loudly on the outer wall and my body jerks in response. The knife slips in my hand, cutting my right index finger. Blood squirts all over the watermelon. I grab a paper towel to put pressure on the deep slice of tissue and turn around to see Bubba holding his shotgun. I am speechless! He is drunk and isn't aware that I am holding a bloody paper towel on my hand. His eyes are bloodshot and he doesn't seem to be focusing on anything in particular. He looks paranoid, so I wisely bite my tongue to keep from screaming at him in the manner he so deserves.

"HE'S OUT IN THE BACK FOREST! THIS TIME HE WON'T GET AWAY!" Bubba roars to no one in particular.

Jamie is now standing at the chopping counter with her mouth gaping in awe. She looks horrified! She sees my bleeding hand and Bubba with a shotgun. Some of the guests are now standing up to get a better look at the chaos going on in the kitchen.

"Bubba! What in the world are you doing in the kitchen with that shotgun? The cougar isn't in here for God's sake! Get the heck out of here! Look what you just made me do!" I hold up my hand with the waded bloody paper towel wrapped around it.

Bubba pushes Jamie to the side, and shuffles under the counter where we keep the tips. He pulls out paperwork and miscellaneous objects, and drops them on the floor and then pulls out a box of bullets. I do not have time to think of the pain in my finger at the moment. Why are bullets kept in the kitchen? He loads his gun, and storms out the back door. The two New York steaks on the grill are now on fire, the gravy I was heating up, is boiling like a volcano, french fries are ready, chicken fried steaks are burning on the flat grill, and three finished platters waiting for a slice of watermelon, are now cold.

Holding my bleeding finger I walk through the restaurant to find Billy. Vi is at the register. She acts like she did not hear any of this drama going on. Poor Jamie is watching me, and I'm sure she isn't quite sure how to handle the situation, this being her first day and all.

"Denise! Are you all right?" asks Vi who is looking at my bloody hand.

"Actually, Vi, I'm not! I cut my finger. Is Billy in there?"

"Yes, Billy and Ray are both in there."

I knock and enter at the same time. "Billy, you're going to have to get over to the grill. I've cut my finger. I need to get to my trailer and bandage it up. Two New York's are on fire."

"Damn it, girl! Ya otta be more careful!" Billy scolds.

"No Billy, Bubba should not bang through the kitchen with a shotgun while I'm slicing watermelon!" She can see I'm pissed! I quickly turn around and head out of the restaurant holding my throbbing finger.

I walk hastily to my trailer, trying to avoid Bubba, who is nowhere in sight. I retrieve the first aid kit that I keep in the bathroom. My cut is deep. It could probably use a stitch or two. After cleaning the cut and applying hydrogen peroxide, I find the butterfly Band-Aids, put two across the open flesh, dab antibiotic cream over the closed and leaking cut, and then bundle it safely in heavy gauze and tape.

There is no reason to return to the kitchen tonight. It's 6:45 and soon enough the dinner guests will be leaving. Billy can handle the rest of the cooking. She's had to do it for years; so a few hours won't hurt her any. Maybe she will appreciate me even more once she is tied to the grill again. It's a good thing I have two days off. Maybe my finger will have time to heal or at least close up a little.

I pour myself a glass of wine and sit at the table looking out the window. Smoke is pouring out of the vent from the kitchen. Bonita and Bandito smell my finger in concern. Off in the distance I hear the sound of gunfire. I shake my head in repulsion.

I turn off the air-conditioner and leash up the dogs to get them out of the trailer. It's a beautiful evening, regardless of the drama. I feel claustrophobic, and need some fresh air. I want to walk out of sight from everyone. I am in no mood to be around the busy, full park, and I don't feel like driving to find a quiet place.

As I look around, I decide to walk across the highway. There is the large dirt area where the trucks park, and beyond that, is acres of tall grass, where steer are grazing. A ranch is off in the distance beyond the barbwire fence that borders it. A dirt path runs along the fence line. I would be relatively safe walking next to the highway. If there is a mountain lion, I hope he is up in the mountains stalking Bubba. This is one of the areas that I hear coyotes at night, but it is still daylight, and I am keeping a watchful eye out for anything in sight. The dogs are enjoying their time of freedom outside. My finger throbs.

After about twenty minutes I see an animal approaching the highway from the park side of the road. I pull the dogs in closer to me, thinking it's the mountain lion, and stand behind a large bush for protection. I am a good hundred yards away from it, and hopefully out of sight. The more I stare at it, the less it looks like a mountain lion and more like a large pit bull. The mysterious beast crosses the road, walking fast, and in a straight line. A car barely misses him! He is the same golden tan color of a mountain lion and has blood dripping from his rear end. His body is covered with hairless patches from old wounds. He keeps a straight line from the park to my side of the road and goes through the barbwire fence disappearing into the tall grass. I can see the grass moving as he continues on in the direction of the ranch. I run the dogs and myself back across the highway, and go back into the trailer.

Could that be Bubba's famous cougar? Could that pit bull be the dark silhouette that killed a duck by the lake a few nights ago? Did Bubba shoot him? Is that the reason for the dog's bloody rear end? Maybe it's been that pit bull eating the pile of trash in the back storage area. I'm not sure which one I'd rather be more concerned about—a pit bull, a mountain lion, or Bubba. Bubba's eyesight must be bad. Perhaps he is mistaking that pit bull for a mountain lion, either that, or he is playing some macho, big hero of the day game with everyone. Our big protector!

I wonder if Bubba was in the Vietnam War. No, that's impossible, he's too young. I've met many Vietnam vets through the years. Those sad men are from my generation. I've even dated a few of them, years ago. It's like kissing a frog that stays a frog. The prince inside is missing in action. The goodness of life has been erased. The brain cells have been re-arranged. I hate war with every ounce of my being! My son's will never know how lucky they are to have been born in a time of peace. I would never have let them go to war, never!

My father was a Marine pilot of World War Two and the Korean War, so don't anyone ever try to convince me to think any different! It won't fly with my thinking. I love my dad with all my heart and soul, but he has always seemed so joyless, irritated, and stubborn, except in the presence of his male counterparts. I think Ray must have served in the same wars as my father, if not World War Two, then perhaps the Korean War. He too has that glazed look of one that has had to kill, coating and numbing the memories with alcohol. The only difference is that Ray has the temperament of a pussycat. Bubba truly believes he's out there fighting for the freedom and protection of the park, but instead he is a raging, dangerous, drunk, who disturbs the peace! Everyone internalizes their own life traumas in so many diverse ways. I guess mine has been to become a vagabond! I try not to be dangerous; but perhaps I am a danger to myself.

Bandito is up on the bed snapping at a fly. He snaps, and then runs and ducks in a corner, he is terrified of flies! My little hunter of fox, lizards, coyotes, deer, skunk, gophers, mice, rats, and even a bobcat once, is terrified of flies! He's had more than the nine lives of a cat. When Bonita and Bandito ran free on the two hundred acre ranch where my stone house was located in Carmel Valley, they had no fear of anything that moved. I always felt that they should have been killed a thousand times over, but it never happened much to my relief. But flies, they can bring Bandito to tremble. I've had to figure this out on my own, but I'm sure I know why he hates them so much. I adopted him when he was a year old from the Monterey Animal Shelter. The story told to me by the attendant at the shelter was that he had been abandoned in a house in Salinas. It was a small crumbling house that was home to several Mexican workers in the fields of lettuce grown in that area. His abandonment was not reported by anyone for several weeks. No one could catch him. He was an escape artist. He lived off of mice and whatever he could catch to survive. When I saw him inside the cage at the shelter, he was on his last day before being put down. He was extremely skinny and his eyes were glazed over from being wormy. His black coat was dull and full of fleas, but I fell in love anyway. So flies are his terror in life. They must remind him of his time of survival, when he had to fight the flies to eat a scrap or two. Bandito has the heart of a giant! He misses being free, of this I have no doubt, but I want to keep him safe now. We've had enough thrills and chills of the hunt to last a lifetime.

Bonita came a year later. The shelter had called to tell me that they had Bandito's soul mate in cage number three. Was I interested? So, after the two dogs met, it was love at first sight. Bonita is more of a bird and fish hunter. She is extremely emotional and very afraid of heights, slippery floors, and cell phones. Her fear over cell phones is the reason I don't own one. They don't have to be ringing. They don't even have to be visible or even turned on; Bonita can hear those wave currents from deep within someone's pocket or purse and go hide under a bed in the furthest place away from it. Sometimes it took me awhile to figure out where she was, or why she was acting weird, then I'd have ask whoever is visiting me, "Do you have a cell phone?" and sure enough, they did. They would have to take it back out of the house and leave it in the car, and then Bonita would re-appear out of her hiding place. This always makes my visits with my friends and family much nicer. It keeps them off the phone until they leave. Bonita was also abandoned in Salinas. She hates the sound of puppies crying. I think she was born in a puppy mill, a bad one, and kept in a cage until she was a year old. No one ever said to me that this was her story; I just have the feeling that her insecurity issues are related somehow.

I get my Bug Zapper and zap away Bandito's current frustration. Bonita hides when I do this. She can deal with the flies, but not the Bug Zapper. I can't please everyone.

It's getting dark outside. I hear Bubba clomping by my trailer. I see him enter the rear door of the kitchen to either get another twelve pack, or clean the grill for Billy.

I am eating a tuna sandwich with my bandaged finger pointing to the sky, and dabbing my mosquito bites with tea tree oil with my other hand, when I hear a knock on my door. It's Jamie. She hands me $74 in tips. Her first day was a little traumatic, to say the least! It gives me a sense of worth to have her confide in me.

It's also nice to have a welcomed visitor. She starts rambling on fast and nervously. "How's your finger? It looked like a deep cut with all that blood. Wow! What a weird place to work! Please tell me you're not thinking of leaving or anything like that, because I don't think I could work with any of the others around here. What's the deal with your door all duct taped up like that? Anyway, Billy was not very happy about having to finish the cooking. She wants you to come over to her house later. Is Bubba crazy? I don't think my parents would like me working around a guy like that! He came in to clean the grill for Billy. He was kind of flirting with me. Yuck! His girlfriend, Terry, came in too. She hung around while he cleaned the grill. You make the dinner platters so much nicer than Billy. One guy said his chicken was undercooked. Are you working tomorrow?"

"No, Jamie, I actually have two days off. Thank God! Are you?" It's the only question I could muster up, but I'm wondering about Terry coming in the kitchen. She's never done that since I've worked here.

"No, I guess we'll be on the same schedule. Anyway, I can't work on Sunday's, because of church and all. I teach Sunday school to the kids."

"Perfect! You have a nice couple of days, and I'll see you again on Tuesday. Thanks again Jamie. You did a great job today."

"Thanks, Denise. Bye."

"Bye."

I fiddle with the small television set for a few minutes. It's enough time to find out that the sound is scratchy, and the picture is fuzzy, flickers, and rolls upwards on the screen. It only gets three channels, even with the cable hooked up. Perhaps this cable is not connected to anything. I'll have to ask Ray about that.

I make a gin and limeade, and walk to Billy and Ray's house. Harley greets me at the sliding glass door.

"Hello! Anybody home?" I yell.

Billy comes around from her kitchen. She must be cooking their dinner, because I smell fish broiling. She greets me. "Well if it isn't our runaway cook!"

147

"Sorry about that Billy, but I couldn't bleed all over the platters and I don't particularly like getting shot either."

"Oh, Bubba don't mean no harm. He was practically born with a shotgun in his hand. Besides, we can't be havin' no cougar wanderin' round the park, we'd end up havin' a lawsuit on our hands. So, ya gonna run ever time ya cut yourself?" Billy asks with furrowed brow. She didn't seem to care about my well being.

"I don't intend on cutting myself ever again, and I don't think it's a cougar that Bubba is after. I saw a pit bull crossing the street with a wound on its rear end. He was a mess! He had scars all over his body!"

"Oh that was Jack! Jack lives cross the highway at the old cattle ranch. He's been shot and run over so many times, but he keeps on livin'. He's never bothered anyone or anything, just lookin' for scrapes of food. Bubba knows the difference 'tween a cougar and a pit bull." She is giving Bubba far too much credit for intelligence, almost as if he was her son.

Ray is now coming out of the back part of their house. He looks beat! His oxygen hose is trailing behind him. "Well, if it isn't our pretty lady! Ya gonna have some supper with us?"

"Sure smells good, that's for sure. I don't want to interfere with your dinnertime. I can come back in a little bit."

Billy responds. "Won't have that! Set these plates on the table and sit yurself down."

I do as I'm told and sit down at the table. The salmon is broiled beautifully. Billy has fresh green beans and a baked potato on the plates. I am suddenly starving! We chat about Jamie's first day. Billy also likes her and thinks she'll do just fine. I ask about Ruby, and Billy tells me more about her arrest. Billy plans on writing the court with an appeal to Ruby's good character. For some reason, Billy has in some way adopted Ruby, or perhaps she just really cares about Ruby's future. Billy has too soft of a heart for the undeserving.

Ray is falling asleep at the table with a fork full of salmon in his hand. They have been drinking bourbon, straight on the rocks. "Ray! Ray! Wake yurself up! Yur fallin' asleep again. Eat a little more of yur dinner then maybe Denise will rub ya with the witch hazel." Ray's eyes open, and he smiles dreamily at that idea.

Billy begins cleaning up the kitchen, and Ray settles himself on the couch facing the television set, which has been on all this time with the volume off. I get a bowl of warm water, a couple of washcloths, and the witch hazel. I begin gently wiping his arms with the warm water. Ray's eyes close.

"Ray? Do I have cable hooked up to my trailer?" I softly ask.

"Sure do. Only thing is wur havin' one hell of a time with the cable company. Half the outlets don't work, might be yur problem too. Wur dumpin' them, and havin' satellite put in real soon. Tired of hasslin' with those guys 'bout the problem. Why, ya got a TV?"

"Yeah, Geneva gave me a little black and white TV, and it doesn't really get anything, but that's okay, I don't really watch much TV anyway."

As I rub Ray's arms, I can see that the rough patches go toward his chest area too, and ask him to take off his T-shirt. He happily obliges, and I now see more red, raw, blotches. Poor guy.

"Ray? Have you known Jim a long time?"

He talks to me with his eyes shut. "Jim and me go way back. We wur in the Korean War together. He hangs out here in his trailer for the summer, and then he heads to Mexico for the winter." I was right. He was in the war.

"Were you in the Army?" I further question.

Billy, who is now smoking and drinking at the dinner table watching us, interjects. "Yeah, but we don't discuss them matters 'round here."

Ray is now asleep. My questioning ends and so does the massage.

I chat for a short time with Billy. We discuss our past lives and adventures. Billy has had an exciting life. She shows off some of the framed photos of her ranching days, and explains the history of the tarnished dusty spurs, and various bridles hanging on the walls. She was practically born on the back of a horse. I can tell that she is proud of her past, and misses the woman that she used to be.

I, too, owned horses in my other life. That's one of the few things I miss, riding the hills with my girlfriends who were also young mothers. If I concentrate on the memory, in spite of everything I've been through and all the passing years, I can still smell the sweat and hear the exhaling bursts of air from Maggie, my first and favorite horse, as she galloped along with me riding bareback through the hills and valleys of Big Bear. Despite the memories that can make me smile inside, I do not miss the woman I used to be. Billy and I both agree that it seems like we are talking about someone else in another lifetime.

Billy and Ray are currently the only connection I have right now to somewhat of a normal everyday relationship. This gives me the motivation I need to continue on at Hacienda, and God knows I need motivation. Ray is snoring, I am exhausted, and my finger is throbbing. Billy gives me a hug as we wish each other a good night's rest.

CHAPTER TWELVE

All I can hope is that Bubba and Terry have forgotten about our commitment to go shopping today. I do not see our day together as one of good conversation and laughter. It's Sunday, and I would prefer to be on my own. I like my aloneness, always have. Aloneness is far better than the loneliness of being with someone who makes you feel desperate to find refuge from their toxic poisons.

There is much to be said about routine. I am glad I have laundry to do, and a holding tank to empty. My finger needs hydrogen peroxide, and Bonita and Bandito need to be taken for a walk. The ducks outside my door have been fed. I can see them now, through my window, swimming along the edge of the lake. I also see and hear the high-pitched squawking of the Scrub Jays that seem to be in abundance in the forest. I wish I had a bag of peanuts in the shell. I'd try to see if I could get one of them to come to me and take it out of my hand, but I will never have another Scrub Jay like Ms. Blue, so why try. Ms. Blue made it her own choice to be my bird for eight years. It just happened naturally.

I was eating peanuts at my picnic table outside my flower shop when Ms. Blue landed on the table. I began by laying one or two peanuts close to her. She would grab them and fly away. After a week or two, I began to put them on the palm of my hand. She was apprehensive at first, but soon enough she began to trust me. After about a month of this, I started to stand outside and call her by name as soon as I got to the shop. I would have the peanut in my hand and see her flying towards me from way off in the distance, squawking loudly in return. She would not stop in flight, but come directly to my hand, pick up the peanut, and stand there for a few seconds with the peanut protruding from her beak, then fly off to some unknown destination. After approximately three years of daily hand feeding had passed, she appeared one day with two young Scrub Jays. She showed them how she retrieved peanuts from my hand and after a few days, I had three Scrub Jay's who ate from my hand. Her babies did not stick around for too long, but she was there everyday for five more years. I often wonder what happened to her. It was wonderful having a pet bird that lived outside. My clients were amazed every time I showed them how she would come on demand. Word spread to their friends about Ms. Blue, and the next thing I knew I had new clients.

Guests are packing up. I hear the squeaking axles of the heavy trailers passing a few feet away from my window on the way out of the park. I love it when they leave. If only they would stop coming back.

I find it hard to think about what I will be doing after I finish my summer here at Hacienda. It seems like my life has always been on hold. I could get a nine-to-five job somewhere in Lancaster, near my parents. The thought of that makes my skin crawl, not the thought of being near my parents, but the thought of being a hostage to airless, skyless, uncompassionate environments. I would prefer a one-on-one job, making proper use of myself, with time left over for my dogs, my sanity, my adventurous spirit, and visits to see my sons more than once or twice a year. If only life were that simple.

I load my laundry and my dogs into the car. We drive through the back forest area first. Perhaps I am being obsessive over the disgusting problem back here, but I can't help myself, it's just too weird! Anyway, it might make the dogs feel like they went on a small road trip.

I creep the car slowly down the dirt road until I arrive at the dump truck. It's parked near the center of the messy junkyard overflowing with trash and sitting with the hood open. Wires are draping out from the engine, and greasy parts are on the ground. It also has a flat tire. You can hear the buzz of flies coming from the bloated green trash bags piled high in the rear of the truck. I'd love to have the power to clean up these uninhabitable acres and return the forest to its natural state. The conflict between human waste and nature is so palpable I cannot even begin to comprehend how a chore like this could be undertaken. It would take an army to haul all this crap away. I roll my windows up and leave. I have seen enough, it stinks, and I don't want to get myself all worked up about something I have absolutely no control over.

At the laundry room a lady is reading a book while her washing machine spins. It is banging against the machine next to it. There is a fly swatter laying on the empty chair next to her. She strikes up a conversation.

"Aren't you the cook here?" the lady asks.

"Yes, I am," I say apprehensively.

"Well, could you tell me if there really is a mountain lion running around here? That scene in the kitchen last night was quite disturbing, and is this a bad year for flies? They're driving us nuts!" She swats at a fly and misses.

"Well...it's kind of hard to explain. I think the mountain lion was really just a loose dog, and yes, the flies are horrible this year." What can I say? Normally I'm far more honest than this. I'd love to sit down and tell her the truth of everything, and possibly cry on her shoulder about my current nightmarish working vacation! She looks like a really nice, understanding person that could knock some sense into me. But I'm not ready to pack up and leave, my purpose has not been fulfilled and I'm not quitting.

She continues, "That big guy with the shotgun cooked breakfast this morning. He had a special on the board, Cougar Cakes. He must have a sick sense of humor, wouldn't you say?"

"Indeed, I would! Don't know what to tell you, I'm only temporary help here. There is a lot I would change if I were in charge, that's for sure." Like calling the real trash company to haul away the garbage for starters.

She puts her load into the dryer, while I load mine in the washer.

"I'm going to go walk my dogs. It's been nice talking to you."

We walk around the perimeter of the slowly emptying park. Jim and his mean dog are not outside, so I don't have to anticipate any outbursts of barking, but Terry is. She is watering her wilting flowers in front of her trailer. I do not see the kittens. When she sees us, she turns off the hose and approaches me. "What time are we goin' to the market?" she asks.

"Oh, I don't know, Terry. Maybe around noon, or sometime thereafter."

"Yeah, Bubba will be off duty then. I hope ya have lots of trunk space. We really need to stock up, with the Jeep broken down and all. By the way, Bubba is being really sweet to me lately. In fact, we might get married soon!"

I am extremely suspicious of Bubba's sweetness and any hope of a future marriage. I also think about my camping supplies in the trunk of my car that I will need to unload before we go. "Lots of room in there. No problem. I'll see you then Terry." I have to get back to the laundry room before I say stuff I'll regret. "Just come on over to my trailer when you're ready. I'm glad things are working out for you and Bubba." The bruise on Terry's face is now faded to a yellowish green. She does not seem to notice or question my wounded finger.

After finishing my laundry, I return to the trailer. Immediately upon entering, I smell something stinky through the screen door. At first, I think it is the holding tank again, but I empty it so often, that it never has a chance to get an odor. Then I understand, with the door left open, and only the screen door shut, a breeze must have blown the pilot light out on the stove, located right next to the door. Propane sure smells like sewage! Most of the windows were open anyway, so I relight the pilot, and wonder if this is something else I need to worry about, especially with Bonita and Bandito in here a good portion of my working days.

I make myself an early lunch and feed my dogs. I hear someone outside the trailer doing something at my utility post. I look out to see Bubba hooking up a hose with a large, industrial size sprinkler attached to the end.

"Hi Bubba, what's going on?"

"NEED TO GET THIS GROUND WET. RAY AND I ARE GONNA START TURNIN' THE DIRT TOMORROW. NEED TA KEEP THE DUST DOWN. WE'LL NEED TA MOVE THE SPRINKLER FURTHER DOWN THAT WAY LATER. WE INTEND TA WORK THE GROUND ALL THE WAY OVER TO PAST THAT SECOND EMPTY SPACE OVER THERE."

"Great! How exciting! A lawn! I'll be glad to move the sprinkler for you when I can. Are you about ready to go shopping?"

"YEAH, AS SOON AS I GET THIS SET UP AND CHANGE MY CLOTHES, WE'LL BE DOWN."

"I'll see you then."

I hate to leave Bonita and Bandito alone today! It messes up my time driving around with them. I shut the trailer. Pilot is lit. Air-conditioner is on. Windows are cracked.

"I'll be back real soon kids. Sorry." They stare at me with such sad abandonment.

I empty the trunk, and put all the camping equipment on the picnic bench. Terry and Bubba are walking down the road towards my car.

Bubba sits in the front with me. The bulk of his body makes him seem uncomfortable. He will not use his seatbelt. Terry is all dolled up today, at least as dolled up as she can get. She is wearing a skirt and has make-up on. They both seem in good moods.

We actually have a fairly normal conversation on the way to Brandon. Bubba talks about his relationship with Billy and Ray, which is along the parent—son line. He idolizes Ray. Bubba has a daughter named Cynthia. She will be visiting soon. I never pictured him as a father. Terry was married once, but never had children. Bubba talked about the cancer in his shoulder. He said it was cleared up a few years ago, but it has been hurting lately. He wanted to have it checked out by a doctor soon. They want to know more about my past. I probably tell them too much. I can't help but mention that I used to be rich, and have chosen a more humble life instead. I tell them about my sons, the flower shop I had in Carmel, and my old stone house.

Once at Brandon, they tell me that they will be at least an hour or more in Safeway, so I drop them off. I want to go to the thrift store, drug store, and feed store. When I return, I can get the few groceries that I need, in less than ten minutes.

At the drug store, I buy a package of rubber finger protectors, and some garlic tablets suggested by Henry to help prevent mosquito bites. I run into the feed store, and buy another bag of duck feed. My final stop is to the thrift store. I leave there with a plastic tablecloth for my picnic table, a large bolt of pale yellow netting that I think would work to make a mosquito netting barrier around my canopy and a coffee cup that has a goose on it, wearing an apron, and waving a large mixing spoon in the air. The caption reads; 'Goose the cook, and she'll cook yours!' I'll put it on the counter next to Bubba's cup. All three of these items only cost me seven dollars.

Back at Safeway, I see Bubba and Terry, who are both pushing a full shopping cart, rummaging through the frozen food section. It makes me wonder how big the refrigerator inside their trailer is. It looks like I have time to grab the few items I will need to get by for the week.

Outside, I open up the trunk for them to load their groceries. Bubba sees the bag of duck feed. I explain to him my intentions, since I'm not really sure if he understands why I am doing this. "Bubba, I bought this feed for you to keep at your trailer for the ducks. You see, the ducks have been hanging out at my place in the morning. I was thinking, that if you fed them at your place, they would stay there, or at the back of the kitchen."

"YA CAN HAVE THE DUCKS!"

"Bubba, I don't want your ducks. I probably never should have bought them feed, but it just seemed better than dog food."

"THEY'RE YUR DUCKS NOW!" Bubba and Terry are smirking at each other over this debate. I think they are just yanking my chain.

"I don't want your ducks, Bubba! Come on. Give me a break here. I just felt that they should eat proper food. I'm sorry if I started something, but I'm hoping we can work it out." I'm trying to be more assertive, and show I can take a little teasing now and then, even though I'm not very good at that. I'm quite sure that they aren't really going to try to piss me off, when I have just spent half my day taking them shopping.

Terry interjects at this point. "Bubba is just teasing ya Denise. I think it's very nice of ya to buy the ducks feed. Ya might have to do that all summer though. We'd be glad to keep the feed down at our place."

They treat me to lunch at a small Mexican restaurant. I worry about their frozen food in the trunk of my car. Oh well, that's not my problem. I have a habit of making too many things my problem. Like what Bubba is eating right now. I'm appalled! He's going to have a heart attack! He's ordered enough food for himself to feed five people! He doesn't chew it properly, and most of it is deep-fried! He also finishes what Terry does not eat. His gut is stretched to the max! They both have two beers apiece.

Back at Hacienda, we unload the trunk. Bubba takes out the duck feed without a word said. I assume he will feed it to the ducks. I drive back to my space. The sprinkler has turned everything to mud, and needs to be moved to a new position. I can hear Bonita and Bandito barking at me from inside. They want out now!

By early evening, we have walked, and I have moved the sprinkler several times. I have tacked my new tablecloth to the redwood picnic bench and sprayed myself with poisonous insect repellent. Bubba is mowing the grass and Terry is watering. I am drinking a gin and limeade, watching the sunset, and trying not to worry about this summer from hell.

At nightfall, I do mundane things inside the trailer. I retrieve my small sewing kit, and sew together the four small rips in the window screens, where flies and mosquitoes sneak in. This will help to keep Bandito's torment down to a minimum, not to mention my own. I shower and shave my legs that look like they are scarred from some horrible disease. I go through my clothes and throw away several tops that have permanent grease stains from the grill, and pants spotted white with bleach from mopping the floors. I doctor my finger that is trying to heal.

I do very well keeping up with this façade of normal daily routine, until late at night while I am in bed reading. A loud banging on my door breaks the silence of the night. I jump, and Bandito and Bonita fly out from under the covers. I had heard Ray's truck start up a few minutes prior to the banging. Could it be Ray outside? The pounding continues and the dogs let loose with wild yelps.

I unhook the door connected to the stove. "I'm coming! I'm coming! Hush up Bandito! Hush Bonita!"

Bubba is standing next to my steps. There is enough moonlight to see his drunken, glazed eyes. "COME ON, WUR GOIN' FOR A DRIVE."

"I don't think so Bubba!" Is he out of his ever-lovin' mind?

"LET'S GO! I'M TAKIN' YA UP TO MY SPOT."

"Bubba, are you nuts? I'm not going anywhere with you. It's late. You've been drinking. Terry's down there. I'm in bed. The answer is NO!"

"COME ON, YUR DRIVIN' ME CRAZY!"

"No, you got that way all on your own. Does Ray know you have his truck?" I look in the direction of Billy and Ray's home.

"YEAH, IT'S PRACTICULLY MY TRUCK ANYWAY. I KEEP A KEY. COME ON, LET'S GO CHECK IT OUT UP THERE. WE'LL HAVE FUN."

Fun? I wonder what Bubba's definition of fun is. I briefly imagine myself sitting next to him in the truck, drinking a beer, and popping one open for him, both of us laughing and hollering at the near misses of the truck slipping off the mountain's edge. I can see us now, sitting embraced, side-by-side on the mountaintop, drunk. Me, a fifty-one year old, drunk, and in love with a big bully named Bubba, sharing our stupidity together, forever, planning tomorrow's special board, getting another twelve pack to go.

"Good night Bubba. I think you should go back to your trailer to tell you the truth. You've been drinking, and it's not a good idea to be mountain driving at night like that."

"HELL! I DRIVE MY BEST LIKE THIS. COME ON LET'S

GO!"

"Good night Bubba." I close the door and hear him get into the truck. He speeds away with the spinning wheels throwing gravel against the trailer. I look out the window to see him speeding through the park, heading towards the back forest area. Back in bed, I hear the grinding gears and spinning wheels as Bubba begins to climb the mountain behind Hacienda.

I just know that Terry had to have heard Bubba start the truck and come to my trailer. Is he trying to get me killed? I turn out my lights and look out the window toward the mountain. I can see the bouncing lights of the truck halfway up the mountain. I can also still hear the over-worked engine that is hostage to Bubba's drunken demands. I find it hard to believe that Billy and Ray would approve of their truck being used in this way. They are hard of hearing, so I don't think they hear much outside the walls of their home.

Almost asleep, I suddenly hear the distant and almost inaudible sound that Tarzan makes, coming from the top of the mountain. The coyotes join in. It is an eerie sound that haunts me to my very soul and arouses many concerns about my safety.

CHAPTER THIRTEEN

Tomorrow will be the first day of July. It's hard to believe that I've only been here for thirteen days. It seems more like thirteen weeks!

Ray's truck is parked over by the large propane tank. A fine dust coats every inch of it. I guess I must have been in a deep sleep, because I never heard Bubba return from the mountaintop. I vaguely remember a dream from last night. It seems that trees were telling me stories. Mythological creatures lived deep inside the core of the trees and their stories were written symbolically in the grain after they were destroyed by mankind. I was the translator of these symbols and was held in a position of great importance for mankind and the lost language of the trees. It was a very strange dream and I actually woke feeling special, like I had a secret to share. Maybe that dream was inspired by the sight of the child's bike that was swallowed by the tree. More than likely it was inspired by my affinity and empathy for trees.

Once again, as it was last Monday, the park is nearly empty. Bandito and Bonita are enjoying our walk through the park. I see the ducks floating lazily in the lake. They did not bother me this morning, so I guess Bubba fed them down at his place. There is a strong sewage smell emanating from the area between the restrooms and lake. The ground suddenly turns muddy beneath my feet. I look down to see sewage and bits of toilet paper bubbling up from a gaping hole in the ground and it is slowly flowing into the lake. I quickly pull the dogs away from the area. I can't believe it! Is everything broken here! Children play here on the shore! Dogs and ducks swim in here! People fish here, and then eat the fish! Why in the world would there even be a chance of such a thing happening? Why would a sewage pipe even be near this lake? Perhaps too many holding tanks were emptied from all the trailers this past weekend. They have a pump house, but where does it pump it? Do all RV parks have this many problems?!

We walk back over to the main entrance and I tie the dogs to the porch railing. I go inside to the counter where Billy is ringing up a customer. After the customer leaves, I tell her about the sewage going into the lake. She yells for Bubba, as she walks over to the kitchen. I leave.

I take Bonita and Bandito back to the trailer, and give them both a good bath in the tiny shower area. While they dry in the sunshine in the fenced area, I play with my netting from the thrift store. There is more than enough to cover the entire canopy. It is definitely getting hotter as the days go by. I'll bet it gets into the upper nineties today.

Bubba is over by the pump house. I have kept the sprinkler going all morning, and have moved it several times. My confidence on this lawn project has diminished since I have come to the conclusion that nothing goes as planned here.

I cut the netting in lengths that are the height of the canopy. I decide to use the bag of clothespins that I conveniently had packed in my car (I suppose to hang my laundry on trees while I lived out of a tent) to hold the netting together at the seams and rocks to hold the netting to the ground. This will make it nice for when Lori, Tiki, and the kids come to visit in a few weeks. We can enjoy our dinners out here, and the kids can draw or play at the table without getting bit by mosquitoes. I am almost done with my mosquito barrier, when I hear the tractor coming out of the forest area.

Ray drives the tractor over to my space, and Bubba drives the scooter over to talk to Ray. I can hear them discussing the pump problem. It looks like there are large bags of lawn seed sitting in the back of the scooter. Bubba walks over to turn the sprinkler off at my utility post.

"WHAT THE HELL KIND OF GIRLIE, GIRLIE THING IS THAT?" I suppose he is referring to my mosquito netting.

"I don't know Bubba. What does it look like?"

"IT LOOKS LIKE BARBIE'S PLAY CAMP SET-UP." I laugh, because he is laughing, not because he is clever or his comment is funny.

"You got it! That's exactly what it is!" I say sarcastically.

"WUR GONNA START TURNIN' THE SOIL NOW. I'LL BE SPREADIN' THE SEED AFTER THAT. WE HAFTA KEEP IT WET FOR A FEW WEEKS TILL IT COMES UP. YA SHOULDA COME UP WITH ME LAST NIGHT. IT WAS FUN. YA MISSED OUT."

"I'm sure I did. I'm glad you had a good time." I quickly change the subject. "Bubba, could you dig a hole somewhere in this area? I'd like to plant a tree. I saw a nursery in Brandon, and I'd like to donate a maple or something like that to this lawn project. I notice there are not many other trees in the park besides pine and cottonwood. It would be nice for Billy and Ray to have a tree that changes color in autumn."

Bubba is staring at me in a funny way and says, "TREES AIN'T CHEAP! BUT IF YA WANT TA PLANT A TREE, I'M SURE NO ONE WILL COMPLAIN."

"Great! I'll get one today!" I wave at Ray, who is sitting atop his rumbling tractor. He looks proud to be productive and useful, and waves back. Good, I have some place to go today. I don't want to hear or watch the tractor going back and forth all day. My Suzuki has a wonderful trunk that opens up larger when the back seats are down. A five to six foot tree will lay in there just fine.

With Bonita and Bandito in the car, we leave the park. Ray has begun turning the soil. Bubba is working the dirt with a rake behind the tractor. The soil looks moist and rich. I doubt that I will be here when the lawn is green and the maple I'm about to buy changes colors, but I will leave behind an improvement and a memento of my presence here.

I return to Hacienda late in the afternoon. I had spent a couple of hours walking the creek and had the car washed in Brandon. The maple tree I found at the nursery is healthy, and stands about five feet in height. I can see as I drive to the fifth wheel that the lawn project has been completed. The tractor is nowhere in sight. Bubba has dug a large hole for me to plant the tree in. A tree that I will never see to maturity, but one day, it will shade this trailer from the burning sun.

The sprinkler is on, and I move it to a new position and then plant the tree. Mud hens are gathered nearby. I think they have discovered the fresh lawn seed to eat. I throw a few rocks in their direction to discourage them. They scatter, honking back into the lake disgruntled.

Vi is approaching me from the direction of the kitchen. "Denise! Denise! We need your help in the kitchen right away! A bus is about to arrive, and Billy would like you to help out for a couple of hours until we can get them fed, and out of here!"

Gosh darn it anyway! "I'll be right there!"

Once I get to the kitchen, there is a feeling of urgency and confusion. Bubba is slicing roast beef. Billy is cutting up tomatoes, lettuce, and onions. Helen is filling up ketchup bottles. Geneva is making soup. No one is talking. Only simple commands are spoken. "Make hamburger patties!" "Get some salad plates goin'!" "Make sure the restroom has toilet paper!" "I need a new can of chili from the storage unit!" "Shuck some corn!" The line of seniors from the bus are now gathering at the meat counter, ordering, and then finding a seat. Several of them head straight to the restroom. We are bumping into each other in the kitchen. I do not make eye contact with Helen. I guess I am still mad.

An hour and a half passes and the bus finally pulls out of the park. Billy, who seems to take everything in stride, is lighting a cigarette at the grill, as I am about to go back to the trailer through the back door. I'm sure they can't expect me to clean up this mess on my day off. She finally says something to me. "Ya know what they say 'bout plantin' a tree, don't ya?"

I smile at her because I'm not quite sure what she means. "No, what do they say?"

"It means yur here to stay. Ya plant a tree when ya found yur home."

"Oh, I've never heard that before. I just wanted you to have a tree to thank you for the lawn, and also, I thought it would be nice for you to have one that changes color in the fall." I could never consider Hacienda RV Park my home!

"Yur somethin' else Denise. Well, we thank ya for that. Have ya made up with Helen yet?" Billy should be asking if Helen's made up with me yet!

"Am I supposed to make up with Helen?"

"I'd sure appreciate it if ya would. I need ya gals to all get along in here."

Helen is looking over at me from the seating area. Billy must have given her the same talk. She starts walking towards me. I feel my heartbeat gaining momentum.

"Denise, can we go in back to talk?" Billy is watching us. I feel like a child in grade school.

"Sure." I need a cigarette and I don't even smoke.

"Listen, Denise, we need to work this out."

"Helen, there is nothing to work out. If I am cooking, you do the dishes.   Do you realize that I did not get out of the kitchen until around eleven o'clock at night?" I feel my adrenalin pumping again.

"I can't do dishes Denise. I have a rare blood disease, and if I get cut, I'll get an infection." Helen whines.

"Listen Helen, as long as we don't have to work together, we'll be fine. I have nothing against you personally, but if we are forced to work together, then you do the dishes. End of conversation." I am on the edge of saying things that I will regret later. I get up and walk away. It's my day off.

Ray is leaning against his dusty truck that is parked by the propane tank, smoking. I stop to chat with him. He wants me to come over this evening to join them for dinner, and to tend to his wound care. I find that being with him and Billy is like being with family, so this is not a problem.

We talk about the new lawn, and I tell him about the mud hens eating the seed. He opens the truck door, and folds down the seat to retrieve something from the floor of the truck. He hands me the solution—a slingshot. I've never used one before so we go to the lake's edge and he shows me how easy it is to use. It is amazingly accurate! Gosh, I only want to scare them, not kill them, but this is fun, so I'll give it a try.

I move the sprinkler several times and from my picnic table I intermittently play with the slingshot. I'm not aiming at the mud hens or ducks, but off to the side of them, just close enough to frighten them back into the water. This slingshot is powerful enough to take their heads off. I put the slingshot away for the night when a stray, ninety miles per hour, stone comes within inches of a newborn mud hen who is learning to swim behind its mamma. I did not see them behind the bush I was currently aiming at.

I make a gin and limeade, and sit with my dogs inside the netted canopy to watch the sunset. It works! I can see mosquitoes clinging to the outside of the yellow netting. I am proud of my ingenuity. My insect repellent candle is also lit, to even further deter any mosquitoes from entering my Barbie set-up. I realize how strange my campsite with a fenced-in frilly looking canopy, must look to others, but I don't care. It works just fine for me. I might even get a string of lights to go around the border to glam it up. I might as well go all the way on being eccentric. If there ever was a good time in my life to let go of any social concerns, it's here and now.

I can see Bubba's flaming fire pit as I prepare to head over to Billy and Ray's. I'll just hang out with them for an hour or so tonight. I'm in the mood to build a fire, and stare into it, until I'm ready to fall asleep.

Ray's raw patches of skin are improving from the treatment I have been giving to him. Billy is very appreciative to me for this willing act of kindness. Tomorrow Ray will be driving the motor home that they traded for Little John's debt to get it registered and also to have a few problems inside fixed. Ray's friend, Jim, will follow Ray in his car, so that they can leave the motor home at the mechanic for the week that is needed to fix the problems. I suppose they are doing this in hopes that they can sell it and get some of their money back. God forbid that they take a trip in it!

I return to the trailer and build myself a fire. Bonita and Bandito are leashed up sitting by my side. The dancing flames are so soothing. It is reminiscent of my years in the old stone house in Carmel Valley. A wood stove was my only source of heat, even though it never got too cold in that part of California. In fact, the temperature never seemed to get below sixty degrees or above eighty, year round. I lived in paradise and leaving that house was like the death of a lover. I am still mourning the magical setting with acres of freedom.

I look down at Bonita and Bandito, leashed up, and feel so guilty. They never had to be leashed at the stone house. There was no traffic or mean loose dogs to worry about. The only dogs on the property were my landlord's two dogs, and a neighbor's dog. The six of us were a pack. I was the leader. We walked the river together everyday. Snickers, Sadie, and Nicolas would hear my car coming home from work and run to greet me ready for our walk. I would drop my purse inside the house, get Bonita and Bandito and we would run like the happy pack we were through the field of grass and purple lupine below my stone house and into the tree-lined river's edge. The dogs would swim the river and explore and I would find stones, old Indian mortars, and lots of golf balls from around the world. The river flowed by one of the world's most beautiful golf courses. Across the river were acres of corn, grown by Earthbound Farms, an organic company that began there. If it were past five in the evening, we would climb up to the golf course. It would be completely ours. The dogs would run like crazy across the rolling acres of pristine, rich, green grass. Little Bandito was always in the lead. He could run like the wind! One evening, when all the golfers had gone for the day, I walked right past Clint Eastwood having private time after hours with two of his bodyguards. I was slightly embarrassed for trespassing with five dogs, especially when Bandito nipped at the wheels of Clint's moving golf cart, but he just smiled at the sight of all the dogs having fun and waved to me as he drove to the green. Such was the life I had known and adored.

My chest begins to tighten, and I sit by the fire and bittersweet tears of sadness and frustration drip softly to the dusty ground.

CHAPTER FOURTEEN

It's funny how the human spirit can adapt to extraneous circumstances. I am no longer compelled to look out the window when the trailer shakes from the passing logging trucks, loaded with the carcasses of downed trees. Nor am I curious to watch Bubba walk by, drinking his coffee, spitting his chew. Perhaps the ducks and mud hens have eaten all the lawn seed in the night.

I did not sleep last night. This happens every now and then. I don't let it stress me out. I simply accept it, get up, and do other things. It was probably due to my heavy heart last night. I needed a good cry. Sure, it's obvious that things have changed dramatically in my life, that I am getting older, that I am no longer in paradise, and that this place is just a temporary detour in my internal roadmap. Ever since I left my Carmel Valley paradise, I have been a lost wandering gypsy. I can be so silly. To think that I envisioned a wonderful working vacation, seeing the forests of California, and meeting interesting people. Hey God! Laugh all you want. I plan on enjoying my golden years being creative, caring, curious, and I plan on all of this in a peaceful, visually beautiful, environment. I plan on being surrounded by positive, conscientious people of reason. I did not plan on being a fast-fry cook at an RV park, so I must be on some sort of learning curve. Maybe it's okay to make God laugh. Maybe He likes to laugh. I like to laugh. I could use a good laugh. I take full responsibility for my current state of affairs. I will remain positive and optimistic, even in the landmine of human dysfunction I currently find myself caught in. I walked in here, and I will crawl my way out, unblemished, except for the several scars from mosquitoes and the one on my finger from a chopping knife.

Finishing up my third cup of coffee, I finally open the door in the hopes that I will wake Bonita and Bandito who have been taking advantage of having the bed to themselves. Outside I see Jim's car behind the shabby motor home with the engine running. Jim sits at the wheel of his car waiting for Ray who is climbing into the driver's side of the motor home. Billy stands next to him holding his oxygen tank. Once Ray is inside she hands it up to him. Bubba is stooped down talking to Jim through his open window. Bubba and Billy back away and wave as Ray and Jim slowly drive onto the highway. Billy watches until they are out of sight, and then she and Bubba go back into the kitchen. Blue smoke fumes from the motor home mixes with the gray pancake smelling smoke from the kitchen vent and fills the forest air.

I finish my morning routine and keep myself busy and preoccupied until it is time to go to work, at which time, I am feeling the effects from lack of sleep. Once dressed and double checking the nuances of the fifth wheel, I leave Bonita and Bandito to their world within. In my pocket I have my rubber finger protector, and in my hand I have my new coffee cup.

Bubba has left the kitchen in its normal chaotic mess. Karen, who has obviously changed her mind about leaving, is counting her morning tips. Helen is at the register where she belongs, and Jamie is clocking in.

My spirits lift when I see Betty walking in. The left side of her face is bruised and she is wearing a heavily padded sling on her left arm. She walks with a slight limp. Betty's zoom has been knocked out of her. Her movements are slow and calculated. We take turns lightly hugging her. It's nice to see united compassion as we share our love and concern.

After Betty leaves, we all go about our duties. I set my new coffee cup on the shelf next to Bubba's, and put my rubber finger protector over my bandaged wound. Jamie and I make a giant tub of potato salad to hopefully last the rest of the week. I make bean and ham soup, twice-baked potatoes, and meatloaf for today's special. Jamie cheerfully erases Bubba's road kill meals and writes our menu on the special board in her colorful, youthful way.

A little after lunch there is a commotion at the front register. Helen is hugging Billy who seems very upset and is crying. Billy has her purse in one hand and her keys in the other, ready to leave. Jamie and I walk over to see what is wrong. Helen explains as Billy runs out the front door heading for her car.

"God, this is horrible! Ray's in the hospital! The motor home burnt to the ground! The police said it had a gas leak that ignited while he was driving. Ray had just filled up both tanks at a gas station, Jim was following him when somehow the trail of gas caught on fire. Jim tried to signal to Ray about the fire by honking his horn and flashing his lights, but Ray did not respond. Then it exploded! Ray pulled over, barely in time. His oxygen tank exploded just as he climbed out and threw him to the asphalt! He's not burnt, but his lungs are in trouble from all the heat and smoke and he has some cuts and bruises from when he landed so hard. The motor home burnt to the ground and caught the mountain on fire. They are still trying to put the fire out."

My first thought was of Little John. Had he sabotaged the motor home out of anger or revenge of some sort? Motor homes do not explode! If it had a gas leak, wouldn't he have told Billy and Ray? I feel so bad for Ray. I can only hope that he will recover without further injury to his weak lungs.

During a pause in cooking, I take a break to take Bonita and Bandito outside, and feed them an early dinner. There are three large trucks parked in the three empty spaces next door to my trailer. The trucks have large white plastic tanks full of a clear fluid hitched onto the back. I cringe thinking of what it could be. Several young Mexican men are sitting on a picnic bench drinking beer. Mexican music is playing from an old radio on the table. I see the silhouettes of more men inside the trailer that has sat empty since I've been here, four spaces down, cooking what smells like tortillas and beans.

I move the sprinkler and turn it on to keep the new lawn seed wet. My thoughts are on Ray and his horrible accident. The men are watching me and one of them walks in my direction to talk. "This good! You make lawn?"

"No, no, Ray makes lawn."

"Good. Will be very nice."

"Could you move this sprinkler for me in an hour or so? If it's not too much trouble?" The young man does not understand what I am trying to say. I point to the sprinkler, and wave my hand around the lawn area like some ancient sign language.

"Si! I move for you," he says with a big smile brought on by my theatrical gesture.

"Thank you very much. Gracias," I smile back embarrassed for being presumptuous in asking for his assistance. I'll have to ask Helen if she knows who these guys are, how long they will be staying, and what kind of fluid is in those large tanks.

When I return to the kitchen, Bubba follows soon thereafter to get himself a twelve pack. He looks very upset. I'm sure he's heard about Ray.

"Bubba, you've heard about Ray's accident, haven't you?"

Bubba's lips are clinched, and his chest rises, as if he's holding his breath, fighting off tears. His sadness immediately turns to anger. "I BETTER NOT EVER FIND THAT PUNY SON OF A BITCH! IF I DO, I'LL KILL HIM FOR SURE!" I'm sure Bubba is referring to Little John. He obviously suspects Little John had something to do with this, as do I.

"Maybe we should just keep good thoughts for Ray's recovery right now."

"HE'S DEAD MEAT!" Bubba is obviously still referring to Little John.

A tear slips out from Bubba's red eyes. He turns around and leaves the kitchen.

I am grilling five hamburgers when Helen walks up to place an order for herself on the crown of thorns that is already full of orders. I guess when Helen is hungry, she has no consideration about my stress level. She answers my question about the Mexicans without me asking. "I see that the tree planters have arrived."

"Tree planters?" Of course! Who else would it be but tree planters? It's the Mexicans who have always been responsible for seeding and harvesting America. We'd be lost without them.

"Yeah, they stay here when they're plantin' the trees for the forest service. The contracted company owns that trailer. They keep it here for the workers to stay at during the plantin' season." I am slightly relieved that some trees are being replaced for all of the full grown, mature, trees that are being chopped down. I am more than relieved to presume that the clear fluid in those tanks is just water.

"Helen, is there any word about Ray yet?"

"I guess he'll be comin' home tonight. Billy said he was in shock, and seems despondent, more from mental pain than physical. Probably has something to do with Ray's post war trauma, being a flame thrower operator and all."

"A flame thrower operator? What's a flame thrower operator?" I ask in total disbelief.

"Oh, I guess you didn't know about that. Billy and Ray keep that kind of quiet, so don't say nothing. Ray was one of those guys in the Korean War that came into the villages with blowtorches strapped to their backs and burnt down the villages. He's never been able to get over that."

I now understand more than I want to. The grill is flaming up. Helen backs up from the grill area. I have lost my much-needed concentration on the cooking. I see villages, families, children, the motor home, the mountain, and a good portion of Oregon within these flames. I see Ray as a young man, forced into a wartime job of such horror! I see his desperate mind, forever trying to erase the memory. I see him now as the motor home's flames surround him. I see Little John, laughing somewhere, smoking crack, feeling proud of himself by getting one over on Billy and Ray.

Helen returns to the front counter, and I am forced to continue with this overload of human consumption, regardless of my own personal thoughts and concerns. I want to scream into the dining room through all the loud jabbering and clanging of forks on plates, break through the sound of the country music playing in the background.

"Everyone shut up! All of you eat too much! Do you realize

how clogged up your arteries are? Most of you are beyond overweight! How many of you line up your prescription drugs every morning? Those drugs are really a plot to kill you! Who wants my job? Look at my hands all stained with grease! It's hotter than hell by this flaming grill! Guess what? I used to be rich! I'd still chose this hellhole in place of over-consumption! There's sewage in this lake! A lake that is a breeding ground for every mosquito in the county! The flies are torturing you because we pile months of your garbage in the back forest! A forest that, because we are all so damned concerned about owning things, is slowly disappearing! You buy and own too much stuff! You eat too much! The owner of this place was almost killed today from a greedy, sick, addicted to drugs, asshole! Is there one single person in here that has a soul? Hey Helen! God bless America! You didn't have to blowtorch a village full of mothers and children! What the hell are you so proud of?"

I wish I could be crazy enough to explode those feelings into reality. It would do me a world of good, but it would do absolutely nothing to solve the issues at hand. I'm beginning to understand crazy, homeless people that shout out crazy talk on street corners a little more than I should. Perhaps they drop out of society because they have had it with all the bullshit, kind of like, (gulp) me.

Jamie is a wonderful extension of my cooking. She is doing such a great job. I thank my lucky stars that she came to work here. Our conversations are short, to the point, and pleasant. I know that she wishes she could be somewhere else right now, as do I, but she is doing her best under these circumstances. It blows me away every time I see my younger self in her eyes. She will probably get married to some charming young man in college, more than likely within her first year, like I did. Jamie is a nurturer, and will make a good mother. I hope her journey in life does not end up in an RV park, like mine.

It is 8:00 PM, and I don't remember the past few hours. I have been on auto-pilot and lost in my head with thoughts. Jamie and I made plenty of tips, no dinners came back, and we had no complaints, so whatever I cooked must have been just fine.

GRILL!

Billy and Ray come through the front entry. Ray's head is hanging low. He can barely walk. Billy is by his side, holding his arm, pulling his oxygen tank behind her. I can hear his strained breathing from across the room. Ray lifts his head and sees me. Our eyes meet. Mine fill with tears, his are distant and shielded. I do not approach their personal tragedy; there is nothing to say.

CHAPTER FIFTEEN

The ways that grief and stress can alter a mind is amazing. My first thoughts upon waking go something like this; Today—Wednesday. Hour—6:22 AM. Date—July 2nd. Location—Hacienda RV Park. Emotional evaluation—Low. Current concern—Ray. Needs—Coffee. Reality—Bonita and Bandito. I feel like I am on auto pilot, that a computer is taking over my personality and thoughts out of necessity.

I should call my sons, but I'm not in the mood to communicate with anyone just yet. I should take a shower, but will do that in a few hours. Right now I need a good long walk to put things in perspective and try to relax.

After loading the dogs in the car, I drive to the front of the main building to get a newspaper. I see through the clear plastic of the newspaper stand the headlines and photo. CLOSE TRAGEDY FOR LOCAL MAN! The photo is of the motor home completely ablaze. There are flames shooting from both sides like a torch. The mountain next to the motor home is burning. Firemen have just arrived, and I see an ambulance with Ray on the gurney being lifted into the back. I begin to cry. I can't help it. Seeing this in living color is so shocking. I want to see him, but I know they just want some peace and quiet right now. I may get a chance later. I need to give him a hug.

As I retrieve the newspaper, I hear yelling in the parking lot. I turn to see two large vans. One is the cable company, the other is a satellite dish company. The satellite dish man has unloaded a dish and several boxes of equipment. I am guessing that Billy and Ray have decided to switch over to satellite. I wonder why they are both here at the same time. Maybe the cable man came to fix the many cable problems today, and it is just a coincidence that they saw each other. The cable man is purple with rage! These guys must know each other. I'm sure they do in a small town like this. Hacienda is probably one of their major clients having hookups in every space as it is now.

The cable man is yelling that the satellite company cannot use the cable company cables. He's yelling that he will rip them out. They begin to push each other in the parking lot. Someone's going to get hit! The cable guy takes the first punch, landing the satellite guy on his ass. Bubba comes running out of the front entry. His fists are clinched, and his chest is puffed out. "JOE! WE TOLD YA LAST WEEK WE WUR DONE WITH YUR DAMN USELESS CABLE! NOW GET THE HELL OUT OF HERE BEFORE I RUIN YUR DAY FUR GOOD!"

The cable guy cowers back into his van and slams the door before Bubba reaches him. He peels out of the lot, throwing dust and rocks everywhere. I get into my car and leave. I see through my rearview mirror Bubba and the satellite guy laughing.

Once out on the highway, I realize I have no idea where I am going. If it wasn't for the fact that I had to be at work by 11:30, I'd drive west until I hit the ocean. There I would get myself a seaside bungalow, walk the beach, and revel in the sound of the waves.

I look over at Bonita and Bandito, and I can't help but smile. They are sitting proudly atop the piles of blankets in the passenger seat. Both of them have their noses pointed down the long stretch of highway ahead. Their large pointy ears are erect in anticipation of the destination that they must think I have in mind. They both look at me at the same time. They feel my glance, and see my eyes, even with my sunglasses on.

"What in heaven's name would I do without you two? Life would make no sense at all!" Their tails, THUMP, THUMP, THUMP, as they hit the pile of blankets. In unison they turn back to enjoy the view ahead. I do likewise and put a Tracy Chapman CD in the stereo and cruise down the highway. She sings to me…"The whole worlds broke. Ain't worth fixin'. It's reason to start all over, make a new beginning. Too much pain, too much suffering. It's reason to start all over. Start all over. Start all over..." You're telling me, Tracy.

The heat of summer is slowly creeping higher. The air is dry. I wonder how hot it will get in this part of California. I was very surprised to find out that Ashland could get into the triple digits a good part of the summer. Pushing those housekeeping carts around in the heat of summer was a real bitch indeed! At least I could close the door to the room, tune in to some easy listening music, and turn on the air-conditioner while I cleaned. At least I didn't have crazy people doing crazy things on a daily basis. It was only the owner of the inn that drove me to run. Other than him, I liked the job, the guests, and my fellow maids. What a beautiful environment it was! The gardens were extraordinary! The mineral tubs in each room were fed from the sulfur springs that flowed beneath the property. This gave the rooms a stinky smell that was not understood by all the guests, but once they bathed in their own private whirlpool in the room, they understood. People came from all over the world to stay there and go to the Shakespearian Festival in Ashland.

It was the vacuum incident that made me lose my mind. Seven maids worked there, but not all at the same time. Some days no one showed up. I was in charge of linen control, quality control, room refreshes, scheduling of time cards, and cleaning eight to ten rooms a day myself. We had only four vacuums. Two were broken. They were cheap vacuums. They could not get under beds, and had no hose for corners and edges.

I was constantly putting in a request for new vacuums. The owner was a millionaire! He had all sorts of property in Oregon, and several concepts going to expand the inn. He was about to add a large elegant spa, a gourmet restaurant, and a bar. He was obnoxious and demanding on setting time limits to clean the rooms. I had an excellent eye for detail. I would go above and beyond the call of duty to make the rooms perfect for the guests. I would even sew a rip in a curtain or bedspread on my own time to assure quality, after all, the rooms were priced at two to three hundred a night!

Now at this point we, the maids, were running back and forth to find a maid with a vacuum. Then a third one broke, and we were spending most of our precious time fighting over the one remaining vacuum. I started to get pushy with my constant requests for vacuums. He refused! I could not believe that he did not understand that the vacuums were causing chaos and making us completely lose our ability to keep up with the heavy demands of a full to capacity inn! A beautiful inn! Not a second rate piece of shit motel! A beautiful inn!

Gee, I'm getting all worked up about it again. Anyway, I quit. It didn't make any sense. I think he had a bit of dementia going on. He often did the weirdest things in front of guests, like having his cluttered desk, computer, and piles of magazines sitting right in the middle of the main dining room. People would be enjoying the unbelievable morning buffet, and he would be talking loud on his phone and messing around on the Internet right in front of them. He was a very heavy set little person, not quite a dwarf, but almost. When he ate at his desk, he snorted and moaned, really loud! It was enough to make anyone lose their appetite! He also treated me like crap! He never complimented my work, but only increased my workload, due to the fact he had never ever had an employee with my strong work ethics before. He was a user. As the saying goes, 'Do not cast your pearls to swine!' I hope he misses me. I think Hacienda RV Park will also find an empty hole when I am gone. Maybe I'm wrong, maybe everything just goes on and not a soul even thinks for one single second about what is missing. Perhaps I give myself far too much credit. Everyone and everything is replaceable. I don't really care about that. I know I'll never change. I'll never, ever let myself be abused by an ignorant egotistical idiot! I will never beg! I will never undervalue my integrity. 'I own my life, and only mine.'

I think this 'life' needs a good hot shower. I think, and I pray to the Great Spirit within and without, that I will be okay, that I have a sense of my own destiny, that ahead there is a future of contentment and love. Not in dependence on another human being, but a firm comprehension that I will find that life has more meaning than I have yet to know. Time seems to be running out, and I am afraid that if and when I finally get to a future of contentment and love, my mind and body will even give a hoot any more. It seems I have always had the faith of a little child. As I age, my innocence becomes so irritating to me. Damn my consciousness and values anyway!

Bud's Creek is slowing down. There are not as many fishermen now. The aqua green of the winter melt off has turned the water an emerald green. It is easy to see to the bottom of the many pools of flowing water. Bonita and Bandito do not care one way or another, they are about as happy as they can get. We walk for about an hour, and then head back.

As I enter Hacienda, I see several Highway Patrol cars leaving the parking lot. I'm hoping they have just had breakfast or something instead of a murder or arrest of some sort. Maybe the cable guy came back and killed the satellite guy. Impossible! When I think about it, there are several possible scenarios. Besides, it would be Sheriffs, not the Highway Patrol!

Once at the fifth wheel, I set the sprinkler. I do not see any sprouts of grass yet. I feed the dogs, and take a shower. When I finish, I make myself a peanut butter and jelly sandwich, then head to the phone booth to call my sons.

I finally reach my younger son Eric on his cell phone. He is at Lake Havasu. His big brother James is with him. They are sitting in Eric's cigarette boat (that can go up to 150 miles an hour) lined up with the hundreds of other boats in the canal by the London Bridge. I'm sure they have had their share of beer bongs. The boys took me with them once to the river. Never again! Everyone there seemed like they were on some sort of suicide mission! The loud engines of hundreds of boats going faster than the speed of light, drinking all day, lots of nudity, and all this fun in 110 degree weather! I absolutely hate going fast in anything! When Eric hit 100 miles an hour with me, I about died! I never want to go to the river again as long as I live. Not only that, but I ended up with a huge floater dead center in my left eye (those black spidery things that float around as you move your eye) because of the constant banging of the boat on the rough water. Such a pleasant reminder of my time spent there.

When I was married to their father we would go to the river all the time. There were several of us who would go as a group. The boys were just children then. We all had boats that went 35 miles an hour at the most. We would water ski, float around on inner tubes, barbeque, camp, and play with all the kids. There is not one single water skier on Lake Havasu anymore, no one floating around laughing and playing, and actually, no children anywhere. There is only the sight and sounds of very expensive, large, extremely fast boats showing off to each other. Anyone floating in the water must have a death wish.

"Momma! What's happenin' !" Eric says far too loud.

"Hello my little darlin'."

"I miss you Mom. How have you been?" I hear the low thumping bass from the stereo of a passing boat. These stereo systems are so powerful and so expensive, they can vibrate the water for miles, and they all have them. I also can hear the high-pitched yelps of some girls nearby. I can visualize it all, everyone is in the water next to their boats, pissing out the morning's six-pack together. The water has an oily film floating on the surface from all the parked boats. I'm sure all the fish in Lake Havasu are dead or mutated.

"I miss you guys too. Are you having fun?" I guess I want to pretend that they are still innocent little boys catching fish by a stream at summer camp, even though they never went to a summer camp.

"You know it Mom! It's beautiful here right now. How's your new job coming?" I will lie. I have to lie. If I told him the truth, my voice would fill with shame. Not because I am ashamed, but because we are from two different worlds, and I've never done a very good job at explaining my world to my sons. Maybe that's because they never asked.

"The job is great! All is well here. I just wanted to touch base with you sweetie. I have to head to work now. Tell James I love him. I love both of you very much. Please be safe."

"Oh Mom, you know me. I'm always safe. I love you Mom. Bye."

As I walk back to the fifth wheel, I see the satellite guy up on a ladder at the rear of the kitchen. It looks as if he is finishing up his installation. I'll have to try that tiny black and white TV again later and see if the picture is better now. I go back inside the fifth wheel to prepare for my day.

Upon leaving and shutting the duct-taped door, I notice a young woman with her two small children playing in and on the water's edge of the lake. A shiver runs up my spine when I remember the sewage spill. I walk briskly over to her and tell her the truth. I cannot let these children catch a disease from this water. She is horrified! They are not camping here, and have just stopped at the restaurant for a bite to eat. She was letting the children run off some car-bound energy. I offer my hose by the fifth wheel to wash the children off.

Billy is at the front counter when I enter. She looks very tired. She sees me and asks, "Did ya see this mornins' paper?"

Before answering her, I give her a hug. "Yes, Billy, I did. How horrible it all must have been for Ray. How is he? Can I say hi?"

"Sure, why not? He's in his easy chair. He's very depressed, and awfully quiet. Maybe he'd feel better seeing one of his favorite ladies."

I walk through the doorway into their house. I hear his heavy breathing. He is facing the TV set, which is not on. I walk around to face him. His blue eyes fill with painful tears when he sees me. I can tell he isn't up to speaking, so I do the talking.

"Hi sweetie, you'll never know how sad I feel for you right now. I know you don't feel like talking, so don't, okay? It's not that important. Would you like it if I came by tonight and gave you a massage?"

Ray smiles.

"I take that to mean yes!"

His smile becomes wider.

"Okay, get some rest. I'll be by later. I gotta go do some cooking for you and keep that cash flow going."

I walk next to his chair and get on my knees to be at his level. I hug him. His head rests on my shoulder. He takes a labored deep breath. I whisper to him that everything will be all right. It does not matter if either one of us believes that or not. I leave him to go to work. Billy thanks me as I pass. I can't answer; I have a knot in my throat.

Karen, who is finishing up her shift, has an ugly sinister look on her face. She is obviously very pissed at someone. I'm so glad it could not possibly be me! I walk into the kitchen just at the same time Bubba makes his escape. I wonder what he did. Karen approaches me with her face thrust forward on her neck like a bull charging.

"Ya didn't fill up the sour cream cups last night!" A piece of spit flies from her mouth as she yells at me and lands on my shoulder.

"Karen, what sour cream cups? What are you talking about?" I say as I get a paper towel.

"Ya know damn well what sour cream cups I'm talking about! The ones I needed for the Highway Patrol annual breakfast this morning!"

"What annual breakfast? No one said anything about an annual breakfast, and what is a sour cream cup?"

Karen grabs a dirty breakfast plate from the pile next to the sink, and removes a small paper cup that is squished and has sour cream running from the edges. "These! Ya wur supposed to have these ready for this morning!"

"Karen! How could I have known to do this without anyone informing me of an annual breakfast that needs sour cream cups? Besides, isn't the waitress supposed to be doing those things?"

Karen's volume rises. "That's what I'm telling ya! Yur the cook! Yur in charge of Jamie! Yur supposed to get her to do this! The cook controls the kitchen! It's yur duty!"

"Karen you're going to have to back off right now. I'm getting very pissed. I repeat; I knew nothing about an annual breakfast! I knew nothing about sour cream cups! I never knew I had so much control as the cook here. This is all new to me. Show me where the list of duties is, and the calendar of upcoming events. I'd like to read it and get all this insanity straight." My adrenalin is pulsing through my veins. Karen is purple with rage. She tosses the dirty platter that she was holding dangerously during all this time, onto the floor, and heavy, thick pieces of it fly several feet in several directions. She gets really close to my face and screams. "I Quit!"

As she storms out of the kitchen, I calmly reply. "Silly girl, you can't quit. You already did that last week."

She starts to spin around to charge at me, but changes her mind, and out the door she goes!

I walk over to the grill. Grease is dripping onto the floor from the grease overflow pan. A heavily coated and crusted pot sits with less than a half an inch of gravy cemented in the bottom. Gravy is dried and dripping all over the stove. Hash browns are everywhere, as if there was a food fight. Dirty pots and pans are all over the place.

Jamie walks in and stops short of the overflowing dirty dishwater, and piles of platters full of half eaten food. Almost every table has been left dirty.

"Oh my gawd!" Jamie shrieks.

"Oh my gawd is an understatement. Good morning Jamie!" I say playfully. "We can do this Jamie. Just don't stress out. Pretend we work someplace normal. Go to a happy place." I smile at her, and surprisingly, she smiles back. Gee, what's wrong with me? I'm not having a nervous breakdown! Am I adjusting to this screwed up lifestyle?

My eye catches the color of bright yellow on the shelf that displays Bubba and my coffee cups. I see a third cup sitting next to mine. It has a large yellow 'CAUTION' diamond on it. On closer inspection I read the caption.

'CAUTION! Angel to bitch in three seconds or less!' Karen didn't need a coffee cup to say that.

At the end of my shift, I take two thick slices of grilled New York steak, an artichoke, baked potato, and slice of berry pie, back to the fifth wheel. One steak is for dinner tonight for my little friends, and myself, and one will be for breakfast. All this stress is making me need more protein. By morning this hunger I have deep inside, will hopefully be gone.

I pour myself a gin and limeade, and take my dinner, along with the dogs, out to sit under the netted canopy. I have moved the sprinkler. The ducks seem to be spending much of their time down at Bubba and Terry's trailer. The mud hens have been spending more time near mine, probably due to the muddy ground of the new lawn area. I think about getting the slingshot, but let go of that idea as soon as I remember almost killing that little newborn chick.

After I have finished eating, I walk the dogs around the loop of the park. It's 8:30 and a few RVs are setting up their chosen spots for the Fourth of July weekend. We will be a madhouse!

The lake seems to be getting a layer of thick green algae. I can see the mosquitoes buzzing above several floating algae islands. The water source is down to a slow trickle through the pipe. I am really bothered by the floating trash that I cannot reach. As I walk by Bubba's trailer, I see the small, beat-up boat on a trailer that was parked in the back storage area. The boat is positioned to be unhitched in the lake. Bubba and Terry are drinking a beer by the fire pit. We wave at each other. I wonder suddenly, shouldn't the sour cream cups have been Bubba's job, especially since he is the breakfast cook? Shouldn't he have made Karen get them ready? Geez! Why don't I think of these little important details at the time I need too? It doesn't matter; it's all just craziness. How will we handle the big barbeque without Betty and Karen? Not to mention a worn out Billy?

I put the dogs in the fifth wheel and refill my drink. I walk over to massage Ray.

They have just finished up their late dinner. I noticed that they always eat very late, too late in the night to digest properly. Ray's plate looks barely touched. Billy is pretty tipsy and states that she needs to take a shower. I prepare the warm wash clothes, and find the witch hazel. I have brought over my organic, unscented, body cream for the massage. Ray is reclined in his chair with his eyes shut. I touch his arm to let him know I am there.

"Well hello pretty lady," he says groggily.

"Hello sweetie. Just relax. You don't need to talk. I'm here to massage you."

"Yur an angel. Ya know that?"

I smile and help him remove his long-sleeved pajama top.

He stares at me while I am doing this. I realize this is kind of an intimate thing to do, but continue as if I am a professional masseuse, which I am not, even though I spent ten years massaging my husband after he ran his twenty miles a day. I did not do this out of choice; I did it because he made me do it.

I clean up Ray's rough patches of skin first, and then I ask him to lay face down on the couch so that I can massage his back. He does so, very slowly. I am glad I no longer have to look him in the eye. He lies there very quietly while I begin and I now notice several bruises and scrapes. I hear him moaning. I barely hear him when he speaks. "Ya aren't thinkin' of leavin' us are ya?"

"No! Now what would make you think such a thing?"

"We wouldn't blame ya if ya did."

"You hush now. I have no intention of leaving you."

"Can't thank ya nuf for all yur help 'round here."

"My pleasure Ray. Now you hush."

"I guess we aren't very good managers."

"You're both doing the best you can. Listen Ray, I promise you that I'll stay until you and Billy get your much-needed vacation. The only thing that would make me leave, would be if my parents became ill and needed me to help out. I'd certainly have to leave for that, and also if I am no longer happy. I mean if it gets so crazy that I am jeopardizing my own health." I wanted to add, "or my life", but refrain.

"That's understandable. Ohh this feels soo good!"

"Well hush then, and just enjoy."

Billy walks out in her nighty. She walks over to us and puts her hand on my shoulder while I massage.

"Thank you Denise." Billy is a little wobbly and uses my shoulder to balance herself.

"I need to head to bed. Ya just cover Ray up with this here blanket when yur finished." She bends down to kiss my cheek in the same manner that my own mother has done many times in my life.

"Goodnight, Billy."

"Nite."

I can tell that Ray has also fallen asleep. I go into the kitchen and spend the next hour cleaning up their kitchen from dinner, lunch, and breakfast.

CHAPTER SIXTEEN

Around 9AM, I wake to a new sound in the morning. I haven't slept this late since I've been here. Bonita and Bandito are cocking their heads from left to right in the direction of the new sound, the peeping sounds of ducklings. We jump down to peer out the window by the dining table. The dogs have their paws up on the window ledge on either side of me. Their excitement escalates when they see the source of the new sound, and they start bouncing all over the place in an effort to get me to let them out. Billy is standing by the edge of the lake, nearest me, chatting with a woman who is holding a large empty cage in her hand. A dozen or so frightened ducklings are clustered together on the ground by the women and are making a frantic raucous fuss. The group of resident ducks are quacking at the intruders from a position in the lake about twenty yards away. Billy walks back to the kitchen, and the woman gets into a car and drives away, leaving the newborns to fend for themselves. They all press together in a united pale-yellow ball of feathers for security, one or two popping their little heads up to spy for danger. The resident ducks paddle away as a group to the other side of the lake in complete rejection for the needy ducklings.

If there is one thing that can get these two crazy dogs all jacked up, its baby birds, baby kitties, baby anything, and right now I need to leash them up to take them out to pee.

To avoid embarrassment, I manage to steer Bonita and Bandito away from their deep desire to charge toward the ducklings, and walk them across the highway for a while.

When I return, I set the sprinkler on the dry patches of soil and seed, sit at the picnic table sipping my coffee, and watch the ducklings who are slowly detaching from their cluster. I've allowed Bonita and Bandito to be with me as long as they behave. They are side by side, and both of them have their noses to the fence sniffing the air in the direction of the ducklings. They are as alert as they can be without barking, but are making a throaty whine together, waiting to see who will be the bravest to start reacting so that the other can do the same. I am quietly doing my part to keep control with subtle re-enforcing commands. "Better be quiet. I mean it. Keep still. I'll put you both back in the trailer."

One of the ducklings has a problem holding its head up, like its neck is broken or something, and is shunned by the rest of the group, either that, or it cannot see where the group is from its awkward upside-down broken neck position.

The ducklings slowly increase their united peeping noise when they see the mature ducks climbing through the cattail grass further up on the shoreline. The ducklings begin running towards the mature resident ducks, causing an angry outburst of wing flapping and charging, frightening the ducklings who back off and huddle together again, quivering. The one with the broken neck is a few feet away from the rest of its siblings, on its side, with its yellow feet running in the air. It is at this point that I decide to take the dogs back inside, since Bonita and Bandito could no longer withhold their pent up emotion. The quacking and barking was way too much to bear. Anyway, it was time to get ready for work.

Henry, who was anxiously awaiting my arrival, overwhelms me with sentimental, shy, and obvious attraction. His sweet invitation for dinner has to be immediately halted with made-up excuses. It's hard to be nice to someone who is lonely and mistakes friendliness for interest.

Jamie is a little off tonight, and is not too happy working here. I don't blame her. Even with her lack of enthusiasm, she is twenty steps above any other fellow employee.

For my special, I make beef stroganoff. The smell of onion and garlic sautéing in sherry is making everyone hungry. Some of the guests tell me that they will return for dinner. I set aside two heaping servings of the special for Jamie and I. The rest of the stroganoff was gone in the first forty-five minutes. I could have made three times the amount I did and it would have sold.

We make it through our long shift, and we each take the large portions of beef stroganoff that I had stored safely away, our ninety dollars each in tips, and I head to the fifth wheel.

On my walk back to the fifth wheel, I notice the first few sprouts of grass, and set the sprinkler on the dry area right away. The hot days and virgin soil, have speeded up the germination time; not to mention my perseverance on keeping the ground moist.

Bubba is near the lake working on the beat up old boat I had seen in the forest with all the rusty equipment and garbage. The boat is balanced precariously on the trailer and Bubba is bent over pounding on something inside the bow of the boat. Never in a million years would I have thought it was water worthy, nor would I believe that the lake is deep enough for even a rubber raft. Come to think of it, what in the heck is he doing? Terry comes from the direction of their trailer jabbering about something and hands Bubba a beer.

The ducklings are trying to get into the lake, but the resident ducks attack them as soon as they touch the water. They follow the ducks around the perimeter of the lake and hide in the nearest bush. I think they are hungry, and do not understand the hostility they are receiving. Welcome to Hacienda, tiny, innocent ducklings.

The duckling with the broken neck looks weaker than it did this morning. It probably won't last the night.

After eating, walking the dogs, and making myself a drink, I sit and re-count my mosquito bites. At this point I have thirty-one. I apply my dwindling supply of tea tree oil, that I'm sure is nowhere to be found in Brandon, and head over to Billy and Ray's house.

Ray is still depressed. My only comfort is to soothe his raw patches, and rub his weary bones. Billy's had a few drinks and seems to be in her own world tonight, so I just listen and take it all in. She rambles on about several subjects that I have been inquisitive about, one of them being the ducklings.

It seems that the lady who brought the ducklings has too many on her ranch, and needed to find homes for some of them. Billy has known her since high school, when they rode their horses together, and fell in love with the same man—A man who went off to college and disappeared.

Billy discusses her frustration over all the legal forms she has been filling out on Ruby's behalf. She is working on a statement for Ruby's trial date coming up. A statement of Ruby's good character, and guarantee of employment upon release.

The cabins are still a mystery for Billy, and she feels foolish for ordering something that appears to be a con job. Likewise, the dump truck may have been another huge mistake.

The final subject that Billy confides in me about is a bill from the fire department. She walks over to where I am rubbing Ray, who was asleep, and flails it over her head, on the verge of tears. It's a bill for the fire caused by Ray's exploding mobile home. She doesn't share the amount due, but I'm sure it is substantial. I don't believe the mobile home was insured yet since Ray was going to get it registered when he had the accident.

Billy never mentions my eight-hundred dollar RV door; and I am thankful for that.

When it's time to leave, Billy embraces me for a long time, longer than comfortable. Not that I feel it is a sexual come-on, but more of expressing her frustration in life. She needs reassurance and proof that the place her life is at right now is worth the battle. She just wants love in any form possible. I have plenty of love, so I try to squeeze some into her aging bones. Fortunately, she imparts to me much needed tenderness in return.

I return to the fifth wheel, walk the kids one more time, and build a fire. It is definitely a night for contemplation. Instead of sitting on the hard bench, I decide to bring a thick blanket and pillow to be low to the ground and closer to the fire. With the dogs leashed up and curled by my side, I watch Bubba burn cardboard boxes. Terry is sipping her beer, and handing Bubba more fuel for the fire. Billy is leaning on the railing of her porch, smoking, and looking up at the sky. Together, we all gaze silently into our isolated infernos, like prisoners of war.

CHAPTER SEVENTEEN

Today is Friday the fourth of July, my least favorite holiday. New Year's Eve follows close behind. How could I enjoy a holiday where someone always losses a limb? A holiday where people begin the snapping and popping of dynamite a month before the actual day, and for days that follow. A day when the piercing sound of fire engines constantly interrupts the BBQ's and social gatherings, and hundreds of dogs are lost, terrified, and end up in an animal shelter or run over by a car. I understand and appreciate the base concept of the day, but do those who take advantage of a free-for-all blasting rampage know? The same goes for hearing Christmas songs when it's Halloween; two months of hype. It's all about the money.

Being in the middle of a national forest for the fourth of July will be a relief. Fireworks are not allowed, but I did notice we had a few sparklers for sale at the register for the guests and their children. Our barbeque is tomorrow, and I wonder what Helen, our patriotic queen, will be wearing. She must have the ultimate patriotic outfit to show off.

With today's paycheck, plus tips, I should end up with around $1,800 in the bank. That's more than I've seen in an account for years! I think I'll pick up my check and drive to Brandon this morning to deposit it and splurge on a string of lights for my Barbie canopy. Lori will be here Sunday the 13th and I want to make it special for her and the kids.

The resident ducks see me open my door, and run in my direction. The ducklings waddle at a safe distance behind, obviously still trying to be adopted. I don't see the duckling with the broken neck. I walk over to the storage shed, retrieve a pan of seed, and throw it across the bare dirt. While the resident ducks are eagerly eating, I get another pan of seed, walk a good distance from them, and throw it out for the ducklings. They eat ravenously, but do not get a chance to finish before the fat mature ducks charge over and take over their much-needed meal. I repeat the process until everyone is full.

Walking back to the fifth wheel, I see Billy and Ray leave the park. They need to get supplies for the barbeque and Ray has a doctor's appointment. It feels as if it will be a very hot day and several new sprouts of grass are bursting through the surface, so I move the sprinkler and turn it on.

With Bonita and Bandito proudly on their pile of blankets, we head to the creek, to Brandon for groceries, the bank, and to search for my special string of lights. When I return, I head to work and have a pleasantly uncomplicated, drama-free, busy day. I am turning into one hell of a fast-fry cook!

The park is full to capacity. There isn't much time for drama. Of course, there is the expected lack of toilet paper in the restrooms, the trash problem, flies, and Bubba being loud and obnoxious, but hey, that's nothing new, at least nothing blew up, and no human or animal got killed, or eaten, except maybe a duckling with a broken neck.

After my morning routine the next day, I begin hanging the lights on the canopy. Occasionally, I get a whiff of the revolting stench from the thick film of algae growing on the lake. The mosquitoes and trash congregate on the sludge and make for an eye and nose sore. On top of that, Bubba is down by the dilapidated boat holding a paint bucket and he seems to be brushing the source of an additional toxic resin smell from the bucket and slapping it on the interior walls of the boat.

He seems as determined to get that boat afloat, as my father is to keep driving his 1960's Ford Falcon with the three speed gear shift at the steering wheel. The Ford is dented, faded blue, and the clear coat is peeling off. Last time I visited mom and dad, I noticed that it had 375,000 miles on the odometer. Dad duct taped over a deep rip on the outside passenger door, and painted the duct tape a clashing shade of blue in an effort to match the car. He's proud of his ninety-nine cent repair job. Dad has done all the engine repairs and oil changes on that car since the day he bought it—forty years ago. There is as much wire and tape in the engine, as there is on the exterior, but what's amazing is this; it runs like a jet plane! Dad becomes angry and defensive when we mention to him that he has more money than one person could ever need in their lifetime hoarded away in several bank accounts. He could easily buy a new car. This type of thinking does not fly with his personal agenda and miserly ways. Dad will drive that car until it disintegrates into the road.

I'm almost done stringing the lights when I catch a glimpse of the ducklings slowly and cautiously test the lake water. They are peeping softly, and are apprehensive to experiment with swimming. One duckling gets brave and begins to float a foot or so from the edge. Like a secret raid on the enemy, the resident ducks storm out of their hiding spot and attack the ducklings, who scatter into the dirt terrified. The ducks quack together with their heads arched in pride, claiming the edge of the lake as their own and then float freely away. One of the ducks separates itself from the pack and slowly returns to the ducklings. The ducklings once again huddle in fear. The duck approaches them slowly. I look for my sling shot, just in case it tries to kill one of them. It swims to the shore, gets out, and stands a few feet away from the ducklings, making a gentle quacking sound. The timid group begins to peep softly in reply, but do not move a feather. The duck steps back into the lake and swims in a tight circle, quacking. The perplexed ducklings stretch their heads up to get a better glimpse of the swimming duck. The duck once again walks to the edge of the lake, even nearer to the ducklings, returns to the lake, and repeats the process of swimming in a circle. If I'm not mistaken, it's trying to teach the ducklings to swim. Sure enough, the ducklings guardedly advance to the water, entering one at a time. The duck quietly circles around the joyful ducklings and leads them away to the far end of the lake, claiming them as her own. I am overwhelmed to have witnessed this event. That duck has some heart! A painful tear creeps from my eye as the happy peeping fades slowly away.

With the chaos of the barbeque at hand, I apprehensively go to work feeling much more confident in what is expected of me. Bubba talks jubilantly about his boat and his intention of ridding the lake of the surface scum by cruising back and forth in the boat, chopping the stringy algae with the motor blade. Of course, he is not chatting idly away with me, but with his good buddy, Karen. I happen to be within earshot and listen intently to his ridiculous scheme. He intends to launch the boat tomorrow when most of the guests have left the park. I will be peering out from the fifth wheel to watch that—a big man in a shitty boat in three feet of muck.

When the insane barbeque finally winds down, a nice warm summer wind comes up to blow away all the flies. I take Bonita and Bandito for a walk. A musical trio, who have obviously been together for decades, is playing old country tunes on Billy and Ray's patio for the few remaining guests. I walk around the kitchen to the outer side of the dirt road, hugging the unlit tree line, so as to not be seen by the scattered few individuals left enjoying the music. Terry is harassing some lady and accusing her of flirting with Bubba, who is currently doing a jig with a beer in his hand next to the trio.

Safely inside the fifth wheel, I pour myself a drink and listen to the people outside. Car lights flash by my curtained windows as people slowly leave. The trio has finished playing, but have turned on some cassettes through their sound system.

Exhausted, I put on comfortable sleepwear, and crawl up to bed. Suddenly, I hear the microphone making a high-pitched squeal, that horrible noise they make when a connection is bad or when someone handles the microphone in the wrong way. An unfamiliar song vibrates loudly through the speakers, and a familiar voice sings along. "DON'T GIVE ME NO CHAMPAGNE, NO FANCY LITTLE DRINK. DON'T GIVE ME SWEET COCKTAILS THE COLOR OF PINK, CAUSE I LIKE BEER!!..........I LIKE BEER!!!!!........I LIKE BEEEEEER!!!!!

"Shut the hell up Bubba!" Billy shouts.

Just like that, the music stops, and I fall asleep with a smile on my face.

CHAPTER EIGHTEEN

It is Sunday, and I cannot thank the Great Spirit adequately for the reprieve in grief, even if its just for one morning. Being raised stanch Catholic, I have retreated from the guilt of going to church many years ago. As I sip my morning coffee, I ponder how comfortable it is for me to use the term Great Spirit, instead of the over-used word 'God'. None of them being the contradictory, white-haired, old man who is invisible.

From my birth, until I eloped with the father of my children, I don't believe I ever missed any of my weekly confessions, mass, or any holy days of obligation, nor do I recall ever having a choice. I went to a Catholic elementary school, so there was catechism and many hours of memorizing the laws of the church taught by the nuns. Dad was one of eighteen children raised on a farm in Kansas. Dad's mother went to church every day of her life and pretty much raised the eighteen children on her own, since grandpa was hitting the bottle or something. I'm not sure about all that. One brother, who is almost ninety years old now, has been a priest since his early twenties. Six of his sisters were nuns, but slowly left the order for a normal life and marriage.

Mom and her family were members of a Christian church, but she became Catholic in order to marry dad. My parents still follow all the rules. Mom would probably prefer to let go of some of dad's strict demands and church schedules, but has remained loyal, even at the cost of losing her right of freedom of choice.

Dad would give mom a much needed break after mass by taking the five of us kids for a Sunday drive. Our destination was to The Longhorn Bar and Grill in the outskirts of the desert. Dad would leave us in the car while he went in to have a beer and bring us out a greasy paper bag of salty french fries as a treat. Believe it or not, we always looked forward to the french fries.

Since I have withdrawn my membership to Catholicism through avoidance, I have discovered many Gods and Goddesses. Due to my curiosity and appreciation for discovery, I have had many breakthroughs. The greatest breakthrough of all is that the Absolute does not care one way or another what title it is given, nor does it expect you to become a member. The misconceptions came from the visionaries who walk the earth portraying to mankind the meaning of truth. Misguidedly, we give this truth a name, such as, Allah, Buddha, and God. There were, and still are, many of these separate names, too many to count. These visionaries are listening to their internal voice where the Great One lives, the Great Spirit of them all, living inside our hearts. That's one of the reasons I am drawn to the spirituality of the Native American Indians, they knew this, and called it by its proper description, the Great Spirit.

It's time to walk Bonita and Bandito, so I meander down the road towards Bubba's trailer. I'm sure he is cooking breakfast in the restaurant, so I feel a little more comfortable to not have to run into him. I make the turn by Jim's trailer and see my hero, the wonderful compassionate duck that adopted the ducklings. She, it must be a she, is pecking in the mud. The ducklings imitate her behavior. This touching union is the highlight of my entire summer experience—witnessing a duck separate herself from her social order to follow her own truth to save the lives of frightened and abandoned newborns by giving her care and skill. To me she is as one of the messengers who have found truth. She can be put in the ranks of all the other Gods and Goddesses.

I am still hanging around the fifth wheel doing odd jobs, writing letters, and journalizing for the first time since my arrival here, when noon rolls around. Bubba retreats quickly from the kitchen clutching a twelve pack and walks towards my trailer. I have the sprinkler set on the sprouting lawn. He seems in a good mood and begins talking.

"LOOKS LIKE MY LAWN'S COMIN' UP. I NEED TO PUT

197

UP SOME BARRIERS TO KEEP EVERYBODY OFF 'TIL IT HAS A CHANCE TO GROW."

I use my coffee cup to weight down my paperwork and exit the fenced area. I walk over to him and look down at the sprouts and say, "Well I'll be darned! Would ya look at that! By the way Bubba, I didn't know you could sing. I'm impressed."

Bubba's eyes roll upward in an effort to find the memory. "OH YEH, I ALWAYS SING THAT ONE AT OUR BARBEQUES. IT'S EVERYONE'S FAVORITE."

"I can see why," I reply in all honesty. It made me smile, especially when Billy told him to shut the hell up.

"I'M 'BOUT TA PUT THE BOAT IN THE LAKE. WANNA COME? TERRY AND ME GOT IT ALL READY TA GO."

"Not this time, but thanks Bubba. Maybe next time. I'll be watching from the shore here."

Bubba walks briskly over to the dilapidated boat. Terry walks over to him from their trailer carrying two folding aluminum lawn chairs. I suppose it will be more comfortable than the splintery boat bottom, since I saw no built-in benches in the boat on one of my snoopy journeys around the lake, casually spying the fragile rotted interior of the boat.

Terry climbs in the boat, unfolds the lawn chairs and then Bubba hands her the twelve pack. Bubba grunts as he lifts the trailer hitch and rolls the boat into the murky water. The boat, which is not attached to the trailer, begins to float away.

"Hurry Bubba, get in!" Terry shouts.

Bubba wades waist deep in the muck and grabs a hold of the edge of the boat. As he attempts to boost his heavy body up and over the side, his jeans fall down, showing his white hairy ass. His jeans are coated with a thick layer of algae. The lawn chairs fall over and bump him on the head. Terry is clinging to the opposite side of the boat trying to counter-balance it. The tipped edge is dangerously close to taking on water.

"GOD DAMN IT TO HELL TERRY! CAN YA HELP ME OUT HERE?" Bubba says, still unable to get a leg up and over into the boat.

"I can't Bubba! If I come over to help you the boat will tip over!" Terry says exasperated.

A small crowd of giggling guests are gathering on the shore.

Bubba makes one giant roar, like a wild beast, and finally gets his muddy, green body over the edge and into the boat. The audience watching claps and I smile from ear to ear.

The confusion and reorganizing inside the boat lasts for another ten minutes. Bubba then struggles with the engine in an attempt to start the motor. The motor coughs and dies, coughs and dies. Finally it starts and smoke fills the air. Bubba yells out, "YAHOOOOOO!" Terry joins in.

They begin to slowly cruise towards the center of the lake. I hear the beer cans pop open as they settle into their lawn chairs. Bubba sits near the rear steering the boat and a layer of blue gray smoke surrounds them.

Suddenly Terry screams out, "Bubba! Water's comin' in! Hurry! It's comin' in fast!"

"DAMN IT TO HELL!" Bubba says, as he starts frantically scooping the murky water with his hands.

The rear of the boat begins to sink and the engine starts to flood, making a bubbling, putting sound, and then stalls completely as it disappears below the surface along with Bubba and Terry. They flail around before they realize that the lake is only waist deep. Both are cussing up a storm and blaming the other for causing the capsized boat. They strenuously waddle their way slowly to the shore, still clutching their opened beers, and retreat to their trailer.

I am beyond myself with hysterical laughter and must run safely inside so as not to be seen or heard. I look out my window to confirm that I hadn't been dreaming and I see the nose of the boat sticking out from the center of the lake and fall over in laughter. I hear Ray's truck start up and speed past my trailer heading in the direction of Bubba's trailer. Ray must have seen this spectacle and found the energy to go kick Bubba's ass, because he looks pissed! I can hear him yelling at Bubba from his idling truck that is in front of Bubba's trailer.

I remain a homebody most of the day and by early evening I am still sticking it out at the fifth wheel. I've made a weeks supply of healthier meals for Bonita and Bandito—I added boiled brown rice, olive oil, and carrots to the hodge-podge of finely chopped leftover restaurant meats.

Periodically, I see the mother duck and her happy group of ducklings brave the open water. Just awhile ago, she led them to the sunken boat and as the ducklings swam and quacked, she stood atop the tip of the bow like a queen securing her kingdom. The rebel group of resident ducks are becoming curious, or perhaps jealous, of the joyful new family and periodically advance cautiously towards them in an effort to unite with their runaway duck and her adopted ducklings. The runaway duck, on the other hand, does not give any indication that this will happen—she turns tail, and leads the fluffy yellow group to a private spot.

I turn my attention to my private spot and decide to enhance the mood. I plug in my string of lights around the canopy and walk a distance away to witness the effect. The eccentric lit canopy gives my space a party atmosphere. If Barbie had a camp set-up, she would certainly have pretty lights hanging on her canopy, and I will too! I decide against my usual evening nursing job at Billy and Ray's and choose instead to stay put, build a fire, and make this Sunday completely mine.

CHAPTER NINETEEN

Lori, Tiki, and the kids should be arriving any time now. They decided to come a day early since the kids have school on Monday and all. So I am busy at the grill and keep looking out the kitchen window for their car. I am nervous because I feel like I won't be able to show them a good time and I'm ashamed of the chaos and dysfunction of my new job and living quarters, but we always have a good time, even under the pressure of outside negative energy. When I finish work tonight we'll build a bonfire and I'll light up my canopy lights. I'll have all day tomorrow to spend with them. We'll get out and see the national park. It'll be hard staying here at the grill when they finally arrive, I want to absorb every ounce of love and positive energy that I can while they are here.

Henry is having an early dinner and I spend a few anxious minutes jabbering to him about my sister, her precious, beautiful daughter, and grandchildren coming. He offers his miles of acreage and hidden trout farm as an option to visit. He said to be sure to bring fishing poles, since he has a small lake thriving with trout that is private and not available to the public. He promises that we are sure to catch a fish. He jots down his phone number for me. I am elated! What a thrill for Kiowa, who fantasizes about fishing, but has never had the opportunity, since Tiki is so busy teaching psychology at the University of Southern Oregon, and Kiowa's dad is not available, being all wrapped up in some unfortunate addictions. Jacy, who is four years older than Kiowa and has a different and slightly more involved father, just loves nature and is a free spirit. She's happy with everything that comes her way. She will probably sing to us by the fire with her new guitar. She has a voice like an angel. Lori and Tiki are single, like myself. We come

201

from a long line of strong minded, independent, can't put up with bullshit from the male species, type of women.

As the dinner crowd gets into full swing and I am frantically cooking, I hear Kiowa screaming out my name as his running feet enter the kitchen area. "Aunt Denise! Aunt Denise!" He jumps into my greasy arms and firmly hugs my neck with his legs wrapped around my waist. I embrace him and walk him out to the other side of the meat counter where Lori, Tiki, and Jacy are now standing with big happy smiles on their faces.

"You're here! I'm so happy! I have to get back before I burn a bunch of orders. Hold on! Let me turn some burgers and then I'll point out my fifth wheel to you. You can get settled in. I'll be done in a few hours. I love you. I can't wait to visit." I'm happier than I imagined I'd be. I hope I make it quickly through these final hours.

While Lori and the kids look around the restaurant area and buy some candy, I finalize the cooking orders I had going on the grill. Jamie is placing three more orders on the crown of thorns, so I run outside with them to point out the fifth wheel while Jamie delivers the completed orders. "Could you get Bonita and Bandito out on their leashes for a few minutes for me? You can hang out by the picnic area and the dogs can stay in the fenced area with you. Do whatever you'd like. I can't wait to get off work! I'll be there as soon as I can."

At dusk, I peek out the window by the grill and see Tiki and Kiowa by the lake. He has a fishing pole in his hand and Tiki is tying a bobber to the line. My heart races as I look around to see if Bubba is near. I run out the door and race over to Tiki and Kiowa. "Oh darn it sweetie. They don't allow bobbers in this lake. You don't want to fish here anyway, it's yucky! I have a surprise! Tomorrow we're going to a real trout farm and you can catch all the fish you want."

Kiowa's bottom lip protrudes and he begins to pout. Tiki manages to distract him with another idea and I run back to start my evening clean-up detail. There are only a couple of guests left drinking coffee and having pie.

I finally finish and run out to join them. They are all sitting at the picnic table with several munchies laid about. Bonita and Bandito are happily begging. Bubba is walking away from them and is headed towards his trailer. Lori, Tiki, Kiowa and Jacy are all staring in his direction with concerned looks on their faces. As soon as I get to the table we all embrace and greet each other properly.

"Who's that guy?" Kiowa asks.

"Yeah, who's that guy?" Jacy echoes.

"You mean that guy?" I ask pointing in Bubba's direction.

"Yeah, that guy," Kiowa says.

Lori and Tiki are waiting for my answer as much as Kiowa and Jacy are. Lori speaks before I do. "He's that good ole boy you spoke of, isn't he?"

"Yes, that's Bubba." I am looking at Bubba tromping towards his trailer.

"I thought you said that you were the cook," Jacy questions.

"That I am darling. There's no doubt about it."

Lori begins to explain how they were all just sitting there having fun, when Bubba walked up and asked them who they were. They replied who they were in their joyful way and that they were here to visit me, the cook. At which point Bubba had laughed loudly and said, "SHE AIN'T THE COOK. I AM!" He then spit his chew and stomped away.

"Well Kiowa, let me tell you this. Bubba's a big nobody and I want you to help me build a fire in the fire pit, like right now. Let the party begin!" I let out with a huge "Yahoo!" along with everyone else.

Lori and Tiki set up a small tent for Tiki and the kids. Lori will sleep at the dining table that makes into a bed. After they prepare everything for the evening, we sit by the fire and talk and laugh and sing songs, until the kids finally crawl into the tent exhausted from the long day. I revel in the comfort of my sister and niece. We chat softly about everything under the sun, often belting out uncontrollable, stress relieving laughter as I relate my Hacienda farce until 2:00AM, when we reluctantly give up and go to bed.

They loved my joyful canopy! I fall asleep feeling halfway

normal again.

In the morning the kids join Bonita, Bandito, and myself in a walk around the perimeter of the lake. They see the ducklings following their new mother and I share with them her valiant and heroic story. Kiowa especially enjoyed the story of why there was a boat sticking out of the middle of the lake. We feed the resident ducks and prepare to go to Henry's to fish for trout. While we were walking, Lori and Tiki have packed up the tent and gathered all their supplies so that they could take off after we spend the day playing.

Jacy and Kiowa each catch three fish, which Lori puts on ice to cook for Kiowa tomorrow night in Ashland. Henry had met us there and showed Kiowa the proper way to clean fish. Kiowa was in heaven! Tiki and Lori tease me about how obvious it is that Henry is madly in love with me. I hope he did this out of the kindness of his heart and doesn't expect a favor in return. The best I can do for him is to buy his next dinner.

We then explore the national park for the rest of the day, which ends much too abruptly. I sadly say goodbye and drive back to Hacienda alone. Bonita and Bandito were surprisingly asleep on their blanket pile beside me.

As soon as I get to the fifth wheel, I set the sprinkler up on the thriving lawn and go to make myself an evening gin and limeade. I am content to sit within the canopy and rewind every precious moment of our time together. I've not seen hide nor hair of Bubba and Terry, which is a bonus for my day.

It's the middle of the night and I'm sound asleep when I hear the grinding gears of a diesel truck pulling into the parking lot of Hacienda. After several concerning minutes of listening to the engine rumbling, I crawl down out of bed and look out the window facing towards Billy and Ray's house and the parking lot area. It is a diesel pulling a long trailer that seems to have a dump truck on it. Billy and Ray are definitely sound asleep and it looks like the driver is trying to figure out who or where he should go to finalize this midnight delivery. I walk out in my sweats to see if I can be of any assistance. As I do this, he is unhooking the chains that hold the dump truck to the trailer. I watch while he rolls it slowly down the ramp. There is a large puddle of dark liquid covered over the trailer floor where the dump truck had sat for however long it had taken to get from Idaho to here. It continues to drip as he slowly brings it to the asphalt. Even in the dark I can tell that this dump truck has been deceivingly dumped on Billy and Ray. It's a mess!

"Hey lady, if ya don't mind, I'd appreciate it if ya tell the folks here that I brought their delivery. Here's the paperwork."

He leaves me standing there like a ghost in the night and drives off. I walk slowly around the dump truck and bend down to see the continuing bleeding of dark fluid hitting the asphalt. I don't know a lot about the mechanics of dump trucks, but I think it's coming from the hydraulic lifts, which tells me it probably can't lift a feather right now.

Suddenly, I come out of my middle of the night delivery daze, and realize I am standing in the dark parking lot of an RV park where pit bulls and mountain lions roam. I run clutching the paperwork back to the fifth wheel and feel like the wonderful day I had is already disappearing. Once again, my current reality begins to consume me.

CHAPTER TWENTY

By the end of July the ducklings, who's feathers are now a soft, light, fluffy brown, have grown considerably and have matured with the confidence they so deserved. They are now brave enough to venture off together and explore on their own, but re-join their foster mother at times of rest within the cattail grass.

Tiki had brought along a grocery bag of books for me when she came to visit. She knows how much I love to read. One small book was called 'The Names Of Gods And Goddesses', which is so like Tiki to have found an obscure book like that and pass it on to me. Inside, I found the Goddess of orphans, Orbona, which is the name I have given to the foster mother duck who has now taken to following me around. Bonita and Bandito have resigned their aggression and accepted her presence as a tolerable pest behind us on our daily walks around the park.

My lawn, which is really Bubba's lawn, has grown tall enough to have finally been mowed once. The maple tree I planted has several new tender branches. Not much else around here has brought forth any hint of life in its natural progression besides the ducklings, the lawn, and the maple tree.

The dump truck is now parked in the back forest area. Several mechanics have come and gone in unsuccessful attempts to repair the hydraulic lift. Its large steel belly is now being used as storage for the accumulating piles of garbage and the womb for future generations of billions of flies.

Bubba has just come into the kitchen to get his daily twelve pack. I am currently cooking and Jamie is on duty as waitress. He is becoming more sour every day. He has a constant scowl on his face. This might be due to the fact that I completely ignore him and Karen and just do my job. Karen and Bubba have become the enemy in a very cold war. In fact, they secretly conspire to defeat my daily tasks with hidden landmines. These traps they set are difficult to see, but become an urgent issue once I uncover them. Such as the one I came across this morning. Bubba, upon leaving his breakfast shift, turned all six burners on the flat grill to the highest setting, which in turn, burnt my first three orders to a crisp, and since it takes at least a half hour to cool down the thick plate of solid steel to proper cooking temperature, I am unable to cook in the manner required of me. Also, as I stand at this counter slicing pickles, I notice the calendar tacked to the wall. Since this is the last day of July, I decide to go ahead and lift July to expose August. The last day of August is circled in a red Sharpie pen. Next to it several things are written—PARTY, CELEBRATE, and AT LAST! It takes me a few minutes to understand, but it does finally sink in. Bubba, because I recognize his handwriting, knows I am leaving in September, has made his joy for that day loud and clear. It's little things like that that make the atmosphere seem warlike.

Jamie, who has also caught on to this subtle grenade, walks over to where we keep the Sharpie marking pens, gets Bubba's coffee cup and writes 'Skowler' in permanent black letters across the front of it.

"I'm not sure if that's spelled right Jamie," I say casually, but inside I'm freaking. Oh my God! Bubba will think that I did that! He's going to blow his top for sure. Why did she do that?

"I don't care," Jamie says. "Bubba needs to learn how to smile once in a while," she adds as she puts the coffee cup grenade back on the shelf.

Jamie, who is slowly losing her beatific world vision, has also lost her youthful, bouncy step. She knows her time in this crazy pokey is nearly over. I too, count my money and my days.

I warily rewind my thoughts. I hear myself thinking and gruesomely understand what I hear. It is not Jamie who has lost her beatific vision and youthful, bouncy step, it is me. She just wanted to make money for college, I expected a glorious traveling vacation and salvation from a corrupt planet. It is me who is withered and drained. I am pained from my own startling realization and I am suddenly frozen in place.

"Jamie," I whisper.

"What's wrong Denise?" Jamie says with her glowing, sparkling face cocked to see me better.

We are currently making what feels like our hundredth barrel of potato salad. We have learned to giggle and conspire while doing our chores, it keeps us sane. She notices that I am no longer giggling.

I turn to look her in the eye. "Jamie, sweetie, run for your life. I'm serious. This place is a skewer for souls." Now I am out of control crying. "Do you know that you have the power to refuse anything but the best? Is this the best? No, it isn't! You have a whole lifetime to absorb life's mysteries. This place is no mystery Jamie. It's hell! Accept only the best Jamie. Promise me." I can't bear that I am witnessing the reflection of my own lost hopes and dreams in Jamie's hopeful eyes. "I'm sorry Jamie, I must really be stressed out." Right now I want to bolt out of here. I want to run as far as my middle aged body can take me. I feel small and compressed like a tiny microscopic cell. My face is flaming and my mind is racing with frightening realizations that I have lost my life somewhere on this distorted dirt road in the forest where I have made too many wrong turns and have no idea where I am.

Jamie is about to speak when Billy walks in. "Your new door is bein' delivered today. Gonna have Bubba put it on. Damn! $800 dollars! It better be made of gold!" Billy notices my lack of enthusiasm.

"Denise, did ya hear what I said?"

"Sure Billy, I heard you. Sounds good." The pickle I was chopping is now mush. Billy came in to retrieve some tomatoes and onion from the cold storage unit. She gets them and leaves, unaware that I am drowning in despair. Jamie is waiting on some new guests, but eyes me from afar.

So, if the door is being delivered today, then I need to shake this growing depression and figure out what I will do with Bonita and Bandito while Bubba installs it. I wouldn't put it past him to let them escape. In wartime one must think ahead of the enemy. What's really weird about all this is that I've always hated war, but here I am in the trenches, a fast-fry warrior protecting my happiness.

The dinner rush absorbs my focus on my dying spirit. I look out from the kitchen window and see some activity at the fifth wheel, so I ask Jamie to keep an eye on things long enough for me to secure Bonita and Bandito. My timing was perfect since Bubba was removing the bungee cord from the tattered door. The new door leaning against the trailer wall looked nice and solid.

"Thanks Bubba. I need to get the dogs locked up in the bedroom area before you begin," I say as I squeeze past him on the steps feeling the painful pin pricks of alert nerves on the surface of my body where our butts slide against each other.

"CAN YA MAKE EM SHUT UP?" Bubba asks me without looking in my direction.

I am doubtful that will happen and don't even bother to answer him.

Bonita and Bandito are nervous inside with all the commotion, but I give them a dog biscuit and get them up on the bed. I reassure them and plead for silence, leaving them behind the folding canvas door that snaps to the wall. I am completely uncomfortable about this situation, but need to run back to the grill.

Finally I complete my long shift and return to the fifth wheel. The new door fits perfectly and is a welcome improvement. There is also an attached new screen door that is much more solid and fly proof. It clicks open and shuts like butter.

As I enter, the dogs are high-pitched squealing behind the claustrophobic canvas door. The small air-conditioner was not able to circulate cool air in that part of the trailer with the barrier shut. I had the skylight open all the way, but still, it's hot!

Bonita and Bandito fly off the bed as soon as I open the door. They are fine, but ready to be in the open air.

As I leave with the dogs for a late night walk I notice the small key sitting on the stove next to the door. I'm pleased that I will finally be able to lock the trailer when I am sleeping.

Not many nights pass without my evening care for Ray, so tonight is no exception. The consistency of my daily cleansing, along with the new cream prescribed by his doctor, has much improved his skin condition. I think he must also be on some sort of anti-depressants, since after a few drinks his eyes are almost completely dilated, which can't be a good thing for anyone. He doesn't leave their house much these days and has his oxygen on at all times.

Billy talks about Ruby's court hearing that was a few days ago. All of the efforts made by Billy to redeem her were a waste of time and energy. Ruby was sentenced to two years in jail.

Billy is so wrapped up in her own suppressive thoughts that she fails to see my obvious drained mental and physical condition, but I wouldn't have the strength to talk about it anyway, even if she did notice.

I thank her repeatedly for the wonderful new door and leave. At the fifth wheel I shut the new door against all the dark elements that scurry in the night at Hacienda. The key feels good in my hand and I am anxious to try it out. It slides easily into the keyhole, but will not move the deadbolt. I open the door to look closer at the mechanics of the locking system. What I see is another hidden grenade. Bubba has purposely rigged the door so it will never lock.

CHAPTER TWENTY-ONE

It's a Saturday in the middle of August and Hacienda is exploding with guests. It's dinner time and it hasn't let up since I began my shift. I have absolutely no clue as to why this is so. We have no tri-tip barbeque lined up. We have not made any crowd pleasing improvements on the premises. The sunken boat is protruding more than halfway out of the progressively receding, scummy lake. Flies are everywhere. The parking lot is full to capacity with assorted vehicles and the occupants of these vehicles are all inside this restaurant making me insane with immediate food demands. There is the possibility that this bedlam could kill me. Jamie looks like she is ready to walk out at any moment and I have no idea where Billy is. She could be helping me out right now. We are quickly running out of food and clean platters.

I have every pot and pan bubbling with heavens, I have no idea! The smoke from the grill is overwhelming, even with the back door wide open.

"MOVE ASIDE! LET ME HELP! Bubba yells as the screen door slams behind him. He can barely stand up he's so drunk.

I have several platters set up for something that is cooking amongst all the sizzling and frying items laid out on the grills. Bubba's violent entrance completely obliterates any remaining menu memory right out of me. Fear of his drunkenness and covert motives superseded any of my cooking demands.

Bubba grabs the spatula out of my hand and blindly takes over. The crown of thorns is full and doubled up. I mercifully back up and go into a strange trance leaning against the microwave. All sound stops and I am watching Bubba as if he were a hallucination. Now I've really done it I think to myself, I've finally lost my mind.

Everything is now in slow motion. I see from my peripheral vision a silhouette of what appears to be a demon behind the screen door. The demons arms are spread up high and pressed against each side of the door frame. The dark unidentifiable face pushes against the greasy screen. It speaks, moving and wetting the screen with its large mouth. This voice echoes like an inbound train to the core of my being.

"Bitch...Can't handle cookin?... Huh?... Ya fuckin' wimp!... Used to be rich?...Too bad!...So sad!...Now yur a fast-fry cook!... Fuckin' bitch!... Bubba!... Ya fuckin' asshole!... Get yur ass back out here!... Let the bitch do it on her own since she's the cook!... Ya are the cook, ain't ya bitch?"

I am now in a cold sweat. Bubba throws all the utensils against the splash guard behind the grill and thrusts open the screen door. Everything is burning. I am still standing in the same spot in my wide awake hallucination, so I do not worry about the food at the moment.

Bubba is yelling at the demon in slow speed.

"G..E..T....T..H..E...H..E..L..L...O..U..T....O..F...H..E..R..E ....Y..A.....S..T..U..P..I..D....B..I..T..C..H...!!!!!!!

I see the audience now. They are all gathered against the meat counter. Their mouths are moving, but I hear no sound again. I think they are hungry. Jamie is trying to get through the crowd. I wave as if I have been expecting her at a party.

Bubba slams the main wooden door on the demon's face. I watch the little window for any evidence that the demon will return. Then it appears again pressed against the glass. I can see now that the demon looks a lot like Terry, only deformed in a grotesque, vile way, like a female Satan. She focuses in on me and moves her mouth in wide phonation.

"I'm..going..to..kill..you..ya..fuckin'..bitch!"

I wonder what I did to provoke this demon to want to kill me, so I momentarily distract myself from this scary hallucination by searching my remaining memory banks for an answer. I find nothing inside—no memories of any kind! All I notice inside my head is a continual electrical squeal coming from my inner ear like some circuits have snapped and the wires are exposed and buzzing. I now comprehend that the only thing working is my vision, which now sees Bubba fling open the door crashing it against the deep fryer. Hot grease and over-cooked french fries spray into the air like brown elongated snowflakes in a winter storm. He leaps like Superman taking off in flight. I am impressed that such a bulky man can fly so effortlessly. He lands, rather ungracefully, on top of the demon's body in the pile of cardboard boxes. My ears are working now and I hear fists hitting flesh and horrible screaming sounds, male and female.

I see Billy run by my paralyzed body. "Oh no, not again!" I hear her say as she runs through the screen door.

"Again?" I ask out loud and am glad I have finally spoken.

I turn my head towards the audience and see that they are dispersing towards the front exit. Bright yellow flickering, which I now see is a fire, is overtaking the entire grill area. I stare at it lovingly.

Then Jamie begins spraying white Christmas tree flocking all over the beautiful flames.

"Good night Jamie. I'm beat. How about you? I think I'll go to bed now." I say in a monotone, stupor-like voice.

Jamie embraces me and says, "We got to get out of this place if it's the last thing we ever do!"

Gratefully, I find I am laughing and finish the song for her, "Girl there's a better place for me and you…..Gee Jamie, I thought you were too young to remember that song!" Jamie looks bewildered and extremely tired, so she does not laugh.

The ringing in my ears has subsided to a dull buzz. Jamie and I stand there looking at the smoking kitchen mess. The silence is eerie. The restaurant area is empty and we can see commotion out in the front parking lot. Car lights are streaming by heading for the highway. There is still a crowd of people gathered around Bubba and Terry who are going at it again on the asphalt.

Once I understand what I need to do, Jamie thinks the same thing. We don't even have to voice it. We know we are finished with Hacienda. Without a word spoken we begin cleaning the kitchen and restaurant. We do this for nearly four hours until any evidence of this nightmare has been wiped off the planet earth. I turn fifty-two years old in three days. I'll be gone from here by then.

We do not see Billy until we have polished every inch of the area. It is very late, perhaps midnight. Billy walks over to where Jamie and I are standing, admiring our triumphant victory in the battlefield. Billy looks deadly tired. I can not carry her dysfunctional problem any longer.

"Billy," I begin. "I am no longer happy. I have to leave now."

"Yeah, that's what ya told us when we hired ya. Don't blame ya one bit." Billy takes a long drag on her cigarette.

"Billy," says Jamie. "Me too. I'll be by for my check in a couple of days."

"You gals go get some sleep. We had Terry hauled away by the police. Don't ever want to see her again. Thanks for cleanin' up everything."

Billy walks dejectedly back to her house.

Jamie will hopefully have a good life and I resolve to spend the rest of the night packing.

CHAPTER TWENTY-TWO

Bonita is coughing inside the fifth wheel. It is a violent incessant cough that sounds more like honking. I smell propane and quickly open all the windows. Bandito is slightly lethargic. I leash them up and get them quickly outside. Bonita's cough does not let up any and echoes loudly through the dark park, but Bandito starts to perk up. I walk over to the propane tank holding area and open it up to shut the valve off. I keep a flashlight in there for emergencies. I examine the hose that leads into the trailer and see a small hole poked in the line. A small sharp stick lays near the fresh hole, the last and final hidden grenade in this futile war.

Packing was easy. All food supplies are bagged up and taken to the trash can outside. My clothes and books are also put into trash bags and thrown in the trunk of the car. I clean everything inside, make the bed, and vacuum. I will leave the fifth wheel fully prepared for the next unfortunate cooking victim. They will have dishes, pots and pans, silverware, microwave, vacuum, comfortable bed and pillows, boom box, canopy, clean windows and curtains, a small black and white TV, lawn, fire pit, and a maple tree.

My car is lightly packed and ready for morning. I make my last cup of coffee from the single cup Melitta filter and write a note warning the next tenant about the propane leak. I want to warn them about their life being in danger, but know that the note would be gone before any new cook saw it.

Bless Bonita's heart, she is still coughing. I cannot do anything about this until morning. I saw an animal hospital in Brandon. I will take her there as soon as morning comes.

With everything ready for my escape, I sit holding Bonita in my arms. I find that keeping her chest straight up in a sitting position and rubbing it lightly eases the cough somewhat.

The sun begins to rise and I load the dogs in the car and head to Brandon. I don't even feel tired. I have no idea what is keeping me going except for my survival.

I sit in the parking lot of the animal hospital for one hour until I remember that today is Sunday and I am almost ready to panic when I see someone finally arrive. Thank you Great Spirit! I say out loud.

I suddenly realize that I have no idea what I look like. I have not looked in the mirror since early yesterday morning. The motel I stayed at when I first arrived here is across the street and down the road a bit. I will get a room after I get Bonita taken care of, return to Hacienda for my last and final pay check, and come back to shower. I will sleep all day if that's what I need to do.

Bonita's cough is starting to drive me nuts. It is so repetitive and loud. The doctor takes x-rays of her chest. It reveals a slightly enlarged heart, a lung infection, and possibly pneumonia. He sets her up with antibiotics, a mild tranquilizer, and wants to keep her for a few hours for intravenous fluids, which will be perfect, since I can no longer stand to hear that painful cough any longer. He will prescribe a strong cough syrup for my long road trip. She will sleep most of the time. I explain to the doctor about a possible propane leak and he thinks that could explain Bonita's current problem. He says they are lucky to be alive. He checks Bandito over and gives him a clean bill of health. My bill is $585.

With Bandito alone on the pile of blankets, I drive to White Fences motel and get a room for the rest of today and tonight. I leave with the key and drive back to Hacienda.

I park the car in front and take only the small key to the fifth wheel over to the sliding glass door of Billy and Ray's house. Ray is sitting alone at the couch watching TV. He hears me knock and motions me to come in. I suddenly realize that this will be the hard part. I am crying before I even get to the couch.

"I'm losin' my little angel aren't I," Ray says as tears fill up in his eyes.

"God Ray, I tried so hard." I drop down on the couch and encircle my arms around his neck, my head lays tightly beneath his chin.

"I'll never forget you Ray. As long as I live you will be in my heart. I'm sorry I can't stay so you can have a vacation. I tried Ray. I really tried." My heart is breaking.

"Now you listen here. I don't think I can go anywhere anyway. I'm pretty sure that this here couch and this here oxygen hose is going to be my two best friends from now on, so don't ya be concernin' yurself 'bout some vacation that can't ever happen. Understand?" Ray says as he gently lifts me from his shoulder to look into my eyes.

"I'm not sure if I will ever really understand anything anymore Ray."

"Sure ya will baby girl. All this will just be a bad memory one day."

How tender and loving it was to hear him call me baby girl. I don't think I've ever been a baby girl to anyone.

"I love you Ray," says the tow-haired child that lives deep in my heart.

"Ya know darn well I luv ya too. Wish ya were my own. Oh, and thank ya for all yur tender lovin' care. Never looked forward to anything so much in my life. And just so ya know, I'll tell ya what I think was gettin' Bubba all worked up 'bout you. Billy and I never had any kids, and we aren't gettin' any younger. Bubba has always believed that if he worked hard 'nuf, he'd end up with Hacienda some day. He probably figured that ya were trying to nose in on his inheritance, comin' over and takin' care of us a good part of the summer like ya did. Denise yur one hell of a hard workin' woman, but ya got better things to do than be out here in this God forsaken hellhole, so get in that funny car of yurs and drive on outta here, and don't look back!"

Billy walks into our painful and tearful farewell.

"Here's yur check right here Denise." Billy is walking towards me, holding the check out. "We're gonna miss ya more en you'll ever know."

We embrace and Billy begins crying softly in my arms.

"I'm going to miss you too Billy. I'll e-mail you as soon as I get myself a computer. You're a wonderful lady, and I've enjoyed all our long talks. I'm so sorry that I am abandoning you. I hope you'll be all right."

"Oh hell, we'll be just fine. Wur used to all this crazy stuff that happens 'round here. Yur too fragile anyway, so get yur butt outta here and drive safely." She slaps my butt.

"Oh Billy, I forgot, here's the key to the fifth wheel. It never worked." I hand her the key.

"What do ya mean it never worked?"

"I don't know what to tell you Billy, you'll have to ask Bubba about that. I love you both. Bye!"

Once I'm in the car I fall apart. The tears keep dripping down my face. I am so relieved to be leaving, but at the same time, I am so sad. I'm sad about everything. Is my outlook on life so simple and childlike that I trust that all things will turn out hopeful and positive? I'm too old to be so naive. Ray telling me what he did about Bubba helps to clear some questions from my mind. I always forget that many people have ulterior motives and are not to be trusted. Maybe I need therapy on this, having the faith of a child like I do. Still, maybe not, I like who I am. I don't want anybody messing around with my mind or spirit ever again.

I proceed slowly taking one last look at Hacienda. I see Orbona and her growing family walking the road by the fifth wheel. They are coming for feed. This does not help stop the flow of tears any. Good bye Goddess Orbona! I say softly. Bandito is staring at me and then turns to look in the direction of my eyes. He follows the view of the fifth wheel as it slowly disappears. He has seen me pack and leave before. He knows we are never returning. He turns back to me and almost smiles, puts his tiny paw on my arm, and then focuses down the highway.

"You're such a good boy Bandito. Have I told you how much I love you lately?" His thin arm tightens on mine.

When I reach the first day use area I pull in. It isn't very often I walk Bandito without Bonita. I am putting Bandito's leash on when I see it. It is very still and watching me from the edge of the creek. Bandito begins to growl, but does not bark. My heart is racing. It's the mountain lion. My God, it is so beautiful! It slowly begins walking along the edge of the creek coming in our direction. Its eyes, the color of a wheat field in the sun, pierce into my own weary blue eyes. There is an invisible thread that connects our solitary and private worlds as we momentarily bond through the windows of our separate existences. We have both escaped the terror of an angry ignorant man.

The mountain lion releases me from its probing trance and turns its head downward to lap water from the creek. I watch proudly as my totem gazes at me one last time before disappearing into the darkness of the forest. I suddenly feel limp as if a long time affliction has left my body and calmed the panic I had felt inside. How blessed I am to have seen this majestic creature at this last moment. I will be okay.

I head to the animal hospital to retrieve Bonita. The queen size bed and color TV will be a wonderful recompense for my lost days and nights as a fast-fry cook at Hacienda. We will have many miles and much to see before we reach Lancaster. I will worry about my future later. I do not plan on planning anything. God probably needs a good rest from laughing so much. I'm glad I can entertain the invisible man.

GRILL!

ABOUT THE AUTHOR

Diane Stegman has been an artist throughout most of her life and spends her free time painting or writing. She owned and operated a custom picture framing shop in Carmel Valley for thirteen years and currently resides in the high desert of southern California with her parents, tending to their daily needs and health concerns. Diane is the proud mother of two grown sons and grandmother of four grandchildren. This is her first published book.